DEFENDING THE FUTURE

BEST LAID PLANS

SERIES EDITOR
MIKE McPHAIL

Special thanks to "DAN•E"
...Fix it!

PUBLISHED BY

eSpec Books LLC
Danielle McPhail, Publisher
PO Box 242,
Pennsville, New Jersey 08070
www.especbooks.com

ISBN: 978-1-956463-01-9
ISBN (ebook): 978-1-956463-00-2

Series Website:
http://www.especbooks.com/DefendingTheFuture/index.html

Design: Mike and Danielle McPhail
Cover Art: "Shit!" Mike McPhail, McP Digital Graphics
www.milscifi.com

Copyeditors: Danielle McPhail

Contents

This book is dedicated to the memory of:

Anne McCaffrey
April 1, 1926 – November 21, 2011

Award-winning science-fiction author
of the Dragonriders of Pern, and
The Ship That Sang series.

TRADE WAR
James Chambers

A FAINT SHIFT IN WEIGHT SIGNALED THE RELEASE OF THE CARRIER POD. IT VIBRATED for a time as it slid down Nydro's gravity well, and when it broke the mesosphere, it began to buck and shake. Captain Moss tried to imagine the external violence of atmospheric entry, but he and the ninety-nine other soldiers locked down in the carrier were well shielded from the friction and heat. The drop had only begun, and so far it had been as smooth as the brass had predicted. Moss's first hint the brass were wrong came when the front quarter of the carrier vanished in a flash of light—and when the brightness faded Moss found himself staring out a gaping hole at open sky.

"Nuts," he said, but his voice was lost to the same roaring wind that sucked away the screams and shouts of the other soldiers.

The front quarter of the carrier was gone, twenty or thirty soldiers and their pilot and nav equipment along with it. A few of those left activated the manual release of their lock-harnesses, only to be sucked from the pod into open sky and almost certain death. Moss was relieved to see most of the unit followed their training and stayed in place. He didn't much blame the ones trying to escape, though. He shared the same icy urge to ditch what seemed to have become a massive target in the sky. Instead, he cleared his mind and tried to figure out what had happened. It was hard to fix their position. The airstream buffeting the carrier set it spinning like a wild carnival ride. Through the massive breach in the pod's hull, Moss flash-glimpsed other pods plunging past scattered clouds. More than a thousand carriers were falling to put down enough boots to secure Nydro from the Rise, and it seemed they had only thrown themselves into a matrix of death.

Almost every carrier pod he saw was on fire.

Or whirling uncontrollably.

Or damaged and disintegrating from friction.

Or burning a trail of smoke.

Two disappeared into fireballs.

Shafts of glittering light lanced the air. Particle beam blasts. Rising from Nydro's surface, Moss thought, but he was too disoriented to be sure.

Metal rain peppered the sky.

Worse were the soldiers and the parts of soldiers blown free from their carriers and orphaned to gravity. Some might survive if their parachutes activated and they dodged the debris and energy blasts. But Moss wondered what awaited them on the ground.

His stomach kicked with nausea. He closed his eyes to short circuit his vertigo.

He wanted to be ready when they completed planetfall. Then it would be his job to keep the troops focused—and keep them alive. He counted down from ten, steadied his breathing despite his racing pulse, and swept fear from his mind. Death could take him at any time; until the moment came, all he could do was his job.

The carrier jolted, and Moss opened his eyes. A burst of amber light suffused the air.

Taking it for a particle beam, Moss expected his life to end as his body disintegrated into a cloud of loose atoms—but the electric sensation that tingled through him didn't kill him, and it was gone before he could tell what it was. Then a flashing chunk of debris struck the carrier's broken end and sent it gyrating even faster.

Moss spied flashes of red and brown through the broken hull. The ground was close, their drop almost done. When the damaged pod came within range of the surface, automated sensors fired the landing rockets, but the spinning carrier was at a bad angle. The thrusters didn't slow the craft's descent but instead shot it along a horizontal line.

The sight of a mountainside spotted with red trees quickly filled the hole in the hull as the carrier accelerated. Red light doused the cabin, and proximity alarms wailed only to be drowned out by rushing air. It looked like a cyclone was barreling through the carrier, but Moss felt almost none of the wild energy whirling around him. His war suit had kicked into impact/defense mode at the same moment as everyone else's.

They sped closer to the mountainside.

Shadows filled the carrier...

...a bone-shaking crash...

...everything dark....

Moss shuddered down to his bones despite his suit's protection.

What took maybe four or five seconds seemed to grind on forever before the carrier scraped to a stop.

Moss's lock-harness released, dropping him to all fours.

Glimmers of daylight leaked through cracks in the hull and spaces in the dirt and debris that filled the carrier's ruined front end. The pod had been driven halfway into the mountainside, like a pipe slammed into the earth. Anyone fore of the craft's middle was crushed or buried, and many farther back had been impaled or sliced apart by debris.

Moss found himself uninjured.

The soldier to his right looked fine and was slipping from his harness. A soccer-ball-sized boulder had crushed the head of the soldier to his left.

"Nuts," Moss said, his voice silenced this time by the alarm sirens.

He crawled to the aft hatches and triggered the emergency releases. Two above popped outward on explosive charges, letting daylight stream through clear openings. The lower pair popped into packed earth and bounced in place, jarring the carrier. Moss leapt to one of the upper hatches and clambered out onto the hull. The carrier had indeed been partly embedded in the mountainside. The only thing that had saved it from annihilation against a sheer rock wall was that it had grooved along a valley and found its way to soil at the edge of a forest.

Maybe that was good fortune, maybe not.

A glance at the sky told Moss it might have been better if they'd all died before they hit the ground. Although Nydro orbited only one sun, now it appeared as if it had four. The *Argentina*, the *Great Wall*, and the *Mariana*—three of the six interplanetary cruisers that had spawned the thousand carrier pods—were burning with nuclear fire in the exosphere and tracing a slow arc downward. Shafts of lethal light lanced the sky, which was riddled with fireballs and smoke and the dark specks of wreckage and falling soldiers. Few carrier pods would complete planetfall even partly intact. The plan had called for the cruisers to pop into realspace, disgorge the army and its support satellites, and then fall back into slipmode before the pods touched down. That they were burning in the heavens meant the

Rise had expected them—and there were a lot more of them on Nydro than anyone had known.

"Fucknuts," Moss said.

This time someone heard him.

"Damn, but you can say that again." Sergeant Devane joined Moss on the hull, her gaze fixed on the aerial carnage. "An' the news don't get no better neither. Klavachev says off-planet and intra-unit comm's jammed tighter 'n Uncle Sam's fist on Rebate Day. All sorts of staticky garbage in the air. We've got maybe half a klick effective range. We're on our own."

"Well, then, fucknuts again," Moss said.

He clicked open a keypad embedded in his sleeve and tapped in a string of commands.

The world dropped behind a haze as his visor command display resolved before his eyes. He ran bio stats and turned up thirty-two live personnel within a half-klick radius and forty-one dead. They had lost twenty-seven plus their pilot in the airstrike. On the edge of his sensors' range were other life forms: the Nydron. Enough to indicate a nearby village that wasn't on the map. It was downslope to the east. If Moss had pegged their position correctly, they were at least 500 klicks from the nearest major population center. The Nydro sticks. He doubted the Rise were nearby, but he couldn't make any assumptions. They weren't supposed to be dug in on Nydro with particle cannons in the first place. They were spread so thin in this quadrant of space that command hadn't anticipated they'd mount such a defense— but Rise technology had been known to more than make up for their lack of manpower. Moss didn't know if the Nydron had allied with the Rise, if they'd been taken over, or if they even knew why their planet had become a battleground. Xeno branch pegged the Nydron as "most likely neutral" but refused to certify their status due to "difficulties in cultural translation."

Regardless, the Nydron village was their lifeline. They would take position there.

He watched his soldiers emerge from the carrier. Some helped the wounded; some carried the dead. All moved in a daze, gaping when they saw the deadly lightshow above them. A few flipped up their visors as if they trusted only what they saw with their naked eyes. Moss found Lieutenant Colonel Pravhit and Major Obatu listed among the dead on the roster, leaving him the highest-ranking survivor.

So be it.

He opened the comm channel. "This is Captain Moss. As the ranking officer who survived the crash, I'm taking command of our unit, and I need all of your undivided attention RIGHT THE FUCK NOW!"

Everyone faced Moss and froze.

"Get and *keep* your visors in place. Lock your suits in melee/survival mode. We have no idea what we'll face out here. You can see by the sky that our intel on Nydro was well and truly fucked. Either that or some dumbass in a Martian bunker rewrote the dictionary on 'low-level enemy presence' and 'minimal resistance' and neglected to send us the damn memo. Until we hear different, consider yourself officially in the thick of it, permission to fire first if you see the Rise. But play nice with the Nydron. Our immediate objective is to establish a secure location in a Nydron village half a klick east." Moss identified two medics on the live roster. "Galves, Leibowitz—triage the wounded. The ambulatory will come with us. Squatters will camp here; we'll leave them extra rations and supplies. The dead, I'm sorry to say, will have to stay where they lie. We are effectively behind enemy lines under unknown circumstances. All personnel are ordered to activate Personal Advisor and Motivator Models—in three, two, one, *initiate*."

On Moss's order each soldier keyed a command into his or her suit.

The group dispersed slightly making room for the ghosts who now walked among them.

Moss kicked his gear over to command mode, allowing him to see each soldier's PAMM on his visor display. The life-sized holographic figures possessed a wispy transparency. Moss noted the usual array of drill sergeants, combat-hardened vets, gods, demons, pin-up girls, VR avatars, and vid stars. Of course, every group came with its oddball; his was a soldier whose PAMM was a tottering purple blob with spongy white hands, bulbous eyes, and a pie-slice smile. The Purple Pal. Moss knew it from a children's cartoon his nieces watched.

"Well acquitted, Captain," Moss's PAMM said. The holographic Ares, God of War, stood three feet from him holding a massive, double-bladed ax marred by chips and notches. He wore battle-scarred, classical Greek armor, but from his belt dangled a short sword, a holstered .45, and an ionic saber. Ares slung the ax across his back then removed his helmet and tucked it beneath his arm. A wreath of laurels adorned his head, an oddly elegant adornment above his scarred and weathered face. "You've acted bravely and decisively. Those who command—who sit in safety as if they were the companions of mighty Zeus himself watching from Olympus—they have sent you and your troops to the slaughter. Only true warriors can pluck this day from the grasp of defeat. You must confront the treacherous Nydron. Take their village. Destroy all who dwell there. Do not hesitate. There is *war* to be fought and *victory to be gained—and the enemy must be destroyed!*"

"All right, I'm on it, chief. Don't get your panties in a wad."

Moss wondered if he would ever live down the one-night stand with his psych evaluator that had inspired her to assign Ares as his PAMM. Of all the options, Ares had been at the bottom of his list, but the brass refused his every request to upgrade to another PAMM. They liked how Ares balanced his personality, but Moss found Ares irritating. He suspected his old flame was still pulling strings.

He jumped down from the hull and surveyed the troops. Ares followed him, invisible to everyone but Moss because no soldier except a commander could see another's PAMM.

"Worry not for the dead, Captain Moss," Ares said. "A soldier who perishes in combat is secure in glory while the living must yet walk the warrior's noble path and honor their memory. Take the battle to the enemy and make them pay!"

"Uh-huh, got it. Kill the enemy, win the war, but let's not get ahead of ourselves." Moss was accustomed to Ares' infinite fervor for combat, but this was bloodthirsty even for the god of war. "Tell me something useful, why don't you?"

Ares paused then nodded and said: "Nydro, oxygen/nitrogen atmosphere, planetary mass 87 percent the size of Earth. The Nydron, are a young, quadripedal, mammalian race, thought to be peaceful and rated three on the Zither tech scale. They possess no interplanetary travel. They are an uncommonly unified race, which practices a form of collective capitalist anarchy. Once a single Nydron strikes the terms of a deal with an offworlder, all other Nydron assume the agreement applies to them as well. Those who make the best deals become their leaders. They are neutral with regards to our war with the Rise, but Nydro's deep reserves of rare earth minerals, a depleted resource on Earth, give this planet strategic value. Sources report the Rise lack sufficient forces in this quadrant to occupy Nydro, so they have sent a delegation to obtain exclusive rights to the rare earths. Up to three dozen Rise are believed to be on Nydro. Our job is to drive them out and secure a trade agreement with minimal damage to the Nydron—except now we must kill them all and seize their world because they have become the enemy."

"Three dozen Rise," Moss said under his breath. "Update intel."

Ares stood at attention. "Yes. Go ahead."

"What you actually know about the Nydron and the Rise on Nydro wouldn't outweigh my pinky toe," Moss said.

"Input acknowledged," Ares said.

"Get me clarification of our orders." Moss said. "No way can we kill all the Nydron while doing minimal damage. Which is it?"

Ares hesitated, shook his head, and then donned his helmet. "The Oracles are deaf to my pleas for prophecy."

"In other words, off-planet comm is still down," Moss said.

He scanned the troops. All of them were obtaining similar intel about the Rise and the Nydron from their PAMMs along with inspiration on whatever terms best fit their psych profiles. Moss thought that after fifty years of the PAMM program, someone would've devised a better way to keep the troops on their toes. If they hadn't lost the off-planet comm, at least their intel would've been updated in real time, and maybe he could make sense of this mess.

Moss didn't expect that to happen anytime soon.

He checked the triage report. His live roster had dropped to twenty-nine and six would be staying with the carrier. When the wounded were tended to, he ordered the troops to fall in and put Sergeant Devane on point. Her PAMM was the hardest, most grizzled combat vet Moss had ever seen. It stalked beside her as she led them into the woods. On Nydro, the trees grew tall and cast deep shade. Their bark had a reptilian texture, and most of their leaves were deep red and the size of truck tires, their color amplified by the sunlight. Snug to the ground was sparse, fiery ivy that clung to their legs.

The Nydron were waiting for them on the village outskirts.

"Captain," Devane reported over the comm. "I have met the welcoming committee, and they are furry. My PAMM says I should blast 'em to molecules. What does my Captain say?"

"Are they armed?" Moss asked.

"With cattle prods, sir."

"Spineless beasts!" Ares said. "They insult us as warriors. It must be a ruse. Destroy them for their arrogance."

"Cool it, Ares," Moss said. "The Nydron are mammalian. They've got spines."

Ares looked grim. "Spines we should rip from their flesh."

Moss ignored his PAMM and made his way to the front of the line.

Half a dozen Nydron sat spread across the trail, their tails curled in front of them. Their narrow, humanoid faces were hard to read even by xenoform standards. They wore light, colorful clothing: sleeves and cloth strips wrapped around their limbs and something like a doll-sized opera cape that fastened to a metallic collar. Their fur was deep reddish brown, like a fox's pelt, and streaked with orange. Four of the Nydron held low-yield energy dispersal rods. Devane was right; they were tools not weapons. Moss assumed the two at the center of the group were the village leaders.

He approached them but stopped a respectful distance.

"If you *must* parlay," Ares said, "the Nydron expect a short bow to open formal dialogue. But be prepared to attack them—*before they attack you.*"

Hands at his sides, Moss bowed. The taller Nydron leader stretched out his forelimbs and lowered his head. Then he straightened and spoke in a string of barks, screeches, whistles, and growls. Moss waited for his suit's computer to translate the speech.

"Translations of Nydron may be considered up to 78 percent accurate," Ares told him. "Do not let them trick you with their lies."

"Enough with you already," Moss said.

The translator blipped his display and read back the Nydron's words via his earpiece.

"I am Kaal, governor of [untranslatable name of village]. We saw your ship fall from the sky. So many of your ships have fallen. So many of your people are dead or hurt. All over our world this is so. We are sorry for your losses. Are you injured?" Kaal said.

"A little beat up, but I'm all right. Thanks for asking."

Moss waited for his suit to translate his words and then to render Kaal's response.

"Why have you come to Nydro?" Kaal asked.

"We came to protect Nydro from the Rise," Moss said.

"The Rise came here like you did," Kaal said. "As if our world is theirs. This is not their world. It is not yours."

"We hoped to give you aid and resources to keep the Rise from establishing a base here," Moss said.

Waiting for the translation, he jumped to command mode and surveyed the soldiers. A shimmering phantom stood beside each one like a big brother or sister or a personal cheerleader. The tallest was the Purple Pal. As Moss's eyes lingered over each soldier, his display flashed their name, rank, and vital stats. Elevated pulse and blood pressure showed they were all on edge; he didn't blame them. He hoped the PAMMs would keep them focused.

"We were not solicited about your presence," Kaal said. "This is invasion."

Moss turned back to the Nydron governor. "Sometimes war moves faster than diplomacy can keep up."

"Not fast enough. The Rise beat you here. But they refused to trade. They take." Kaal's eyes narrowed, and he seemed to sneer, giving Moss a peek of sharp teeth the color of butter. "You must not take. We have always traded. You must trade."

"What do you have to trade?" Moss asked.

"I will show you."

Kaal turned and headed down the trail, the other Nydron following him.

"Devane," Moss said. "See what he's got. Be back in five."

"Yes, sir."

Devane signaled two soldiers to go with her. They jogged after the Nydron.

An alert appeared in Moss's display.

A dozen life forms were approaching their wrecked carrier. Sensors identified them as Rise. Searching the crash site, Moss guessed, maybe hunting survivors. He spread word to the unit to be watchful.

After a few minutes, Devane returned and knocked her visor open. "You'll have to see this to believe it, sir."

Taking two more soldiers, Moss followed Devane into the village. It was a settlement of low, wooden dwellings and a few large buildings that Moss took to be the equivalent of town hall, a school, and a theater. Nydron packed the village square, baring their teeth, watching every step the soldiers took. They didn't look happy to see them, but neither did they seem threatening.

"Caution, Captain, lest this Nydron trap become a descent into Hades," Ares said. "I recommend you take some villagers hostage or slaughter a few as a warning."

Irritated, Moss reached to turn off his PAMM but then chose to leave it running. Despite his bloodthirsty motivational themes, Ares had so far guided him well dealing with the Nydron. "We're not slaughtering anybody, Ares. The Nydron are traders, not trappers, and we're not at war with them," Moss said. "At least, not yet."

Still, he ran a full sensor diagnostic. The Rise blipped near the crash site, and it seemed nearly every Nydron in the village was within a hundred yards, most of them in plain sight. Devane led them to the theater. There were life forms inside plus an odd energy signature, but not one that suggested a weapon. Moss sent two soldiers ahead then ducked through the low door after Sergeant Devane. The space was wide and dim, but none of them could stand up straight. Pillows dotted the ground for Nydron to sit on while watching performances on the low platform at one end of the structure. What waited for them there were three Rise officers, gagged and bound together on the stage beside a pile of Rise tech.

"Hell, no." Moss eyed the insignia on the Rise officers' uniforms. "Is that a general?"

Ares said, "Rank insignia indicates a general and two colonels."

"Can you identify them?"

"The oracles do not heed my petition," Ares said. "Perhaps you should sacrifice the officers to soften their deafness."

"They're defenseless prisoners," Moss said.

"They are the Rise. We have suffered great losses at their hands today. This is *all-out war!* Seize the opportunity. Crush the Nydron too. They have staged this trap."

"Nuts," Moss said. "This whole operation was a trap. Go take a cold shower, already. What do you make of the Rise gear?"

"Nefarious tools of destruction direct from Hephaestus's forge. I cannot identify them."

"Great, just great. Devane?"

"Nothing I've ever seen before, sir."

"Me, neither." Moss consulted the roster and summoned Tech Sergeant Klavachev to the theater. Then he asked Kaal, "How'd you capture these prisoners?"

"We wished to trade. Their governor declined. We tracked his flying craft and made it land when it passed over us. Many of their people died. The governor and the survivors still refused to trade, so we brought them and their goods here."

"Did you shoot us down too?" Moss asked.

"No," Kaal said. "The Rise landed weeks ago and installed the weapons that hurt you. They run by machine. The Rise come and go while their machines fight their battles. But they refuse to trade, and we cannot fight them. Now you are here. *You* will trade."

"You want us to take these prisoners?"

"Not take. Trade," Kaal said. "We do not want you or them here. We will give you the Rise prisoners and their goods. In return, you will take all your people and theirs and leave Nydro."

"Oh, is that all?" Moss said.

Klavachev entered and reported to Moss. Loping beside him was the Purple Pal. Moss groaned. The character looked different. It had squished itself to fit inside the theater, but there was something... glitchy about it. Moss launched a systems check of the PAMM interface. While it ran, an alert flashed on his display: The Rise party was heading toward the village. One by one, the names of the few wounded left behind with the carrier blipped off the live roster and appeared on the casualties list.

"See what you can make of that pile of wires," Moss told Klavachev.

"...Yes, sir," the tech sergeant said.

"You got something to say?" Moss asked.

Klavachev was scanning every inch of the theater as if he expected something to jump him. "...Uh, no, I guess not, sir."

"Then get to work." Moss knelt to face Kaal. "A trade for these prisoners and their gear is fine, but what you ask in return is way above my pay grade."

"No," Kaal said. "You trade. You get what you want. We get what we want. My people are friends to your people."

"Sure, we're friends," Moss said. "That doesn't mean I can do the impossible."

"Accept the trade, you will do the impossible," Kaal said.

Moss exhaled. *Difficulties in cultural translation*, he thought. Could Kaal really think it would be that simple to boot the Rise from Nydro?

The PAMM systems check was taking too long. Moss wondered if there was a connection to whatever was happening with Klavachev's Purple Pal. The tech sergeant looked wired; he was trembling. The Purple Pal hovered by his shoulder, speaking into his ear, his pie-slice smile full of angry teeth. Moss flipped on the audio. The damn thing was singing.

"...kill them all, Klavachev, before they kill you, because that's just what friends do," the Pal sang. "They'll push you down and take your guns, and take your toys, and spoil your fun, they'll make you share when you don't care, and they'll step on your head, or shoot you dead, so don't be late, don't hesitate—jump up and kill them all, kill them first..."

Moss edge to the theater door and looked outside. Half his troops were in the village, circled around the gathered Nydron. "Nuts," he said.

He cycled through a random selection from the PAMM audio.

"War is Hell, mister. Gotta get them before they get you. Don't trust the Nydron."

"They look like dogs, *rabid* dogs. You put down rabid dogs."

"That massacre today was because of the Nydron. They hid the Rise here. Now, tell me sexy thang, did you come halfway across the damn galaxy to scratch an itch with that weapon in your hands or use it?"

"Who knows what the Nydron want? They could reverse-engineer our ships and invade Earth. We could all die here—*unless you eliminate the threat.*"

Moss switched to a wide comm channel. He ordered everyone out of the village and told them to disengage PAMM mode. A few soldiers moved toward the trail; some lingered where they were, skittish and afraid to give up their advantage over the Nydron. When they keyed in the codes to deactivate their PAMMs, though, the projections stayed online. Moss keyed the quit code for Ares, but the God of War only widened his toothy, martial grin.

"We will not abandon you," Ares said.

Moss eyed the signal that tracked the Rise party coming through the woods.

Other signals joined it. Three more Rise parties were nearing the village.

He ducked back into the theater. "Klavachev, report!"

"I think this thing's what's jamming us. But, sir, it's two-way. It's downloading from our systems then returning a signal." Klavachev flipped his visor open and brushed sweat from his brow. "Captain, I think it's into the PAMM interface. Some kind of malware. My PAMM is... well, it's really weird and aggressive, especially for the Purple Pal."

"Can you shut the thing down and kick it out?"

"Doing my best, sir."

Klavachev popped a cover from the box. Amber light emanated from within, and Moss recognized it as the same strange light that had bathed them during planetfall. He'd been right to assume it was a weapon—only not any kind he expected.

"Don't listen to the Purple Pal," Moss said. "Do you hear me? Ignore it."

"Klavachev's PAMM is the Purple Pal?" Devane said. "What are you, like, five years old, Klavachev?"

"Stop distracting him, Devane," Moss said.

"Don't sweat it, Captain. I know how to get the damn thing turned off." Devane's PAMM, looking angry and grim enough to chew through steel, chomped on a cigar stub at Devane's side. He followed Devane as she walked to the Rise prisoners, placed her gun against the head of the first colonel, and said, "How do we kill that box? Tell me. Or die."

After Devane's translator did its job, the Rise colonel recoiled. Its pink face scrunched in on itself, puckering until only two of its solid green eyes were visible. They stared at Devane, who tapped the colonel with the tip of his gun barrel. The other Rise squirmed and trembled, tugging hard on the cords that bound all of their arms and legs.

"Kill them and the gods shall favor you," Ares said.

Moss ignored him.

"They are the enemy. The Nydron are vermin," Ares said. "Have you no honor?"

Devane cocked his gun with a dramatic flair. "Let me plug this one, sir," she said. "The others will talk, sure thing."

The colonel wiggled and squealed, and an unpleasant odor drifted into the air. Moss got the idea the Rise colonel had pissed itself.

If the Rise had infected their PAMM system, why were they trying to get him to kill these officers? He could fathom fostering violence between human and the Nydron, pitting them against each other and picking up the spoils later. It was a risky strategy, but if they had too little time to plan and too few forces to occupy Nydro, it was something. Hostilities between humans and Nydron would give the Rise dibs on the rare earth supplies. But why target the prisoners? There was a reason—it mattered.

He considered letting Devane fire on the colonel to intimidate the others. But that's what Ares wanted, and Moss's gut told him the best course of action was the opposite of what Ares or any other PAMM recommended.

Take the trade. Do the impossible, Kaal had said.

Be friends. Make all the Rise and humans leave.

The impossible.

What does he mean?

On his display, he watched the Rise units draw closer and encircle the village.

Moss alerted the troops and ordered them to form a perimeter to protect the Nydron. At the few who hesitated, still confused by their PAMMs, Moss launched a stream of invective so foul and horrifying that they double-timed it into position. For now at least, human and Nydron were in this together.

He ordered Devane to lower her weapon.

"Tell me you figured it out, Klavachev," Moss said.

"Sorry, sir. Every time I think I've got it the Pal starts up again. It's like it knows when I'm close. I can't keep two thoughts together except that I want to blow *something* to hell. The Pal has always been my shield, sir, ever since I was a little boy having nightmares. This isn't how it's supposed to be."

Blow something to hell.

Moss took a deep breath, walked to the Rise gear, and drew his weapon.

"Heads down in case this backfires," he said.

"Captain! Do not do this. You must kill the prisoners!" Ares shouted.

Moss ignored him. He took aim and fired into the glowing box, braced for an explosion. His blaster burned a hole through the device's middle. The amber light flared before it died. A stream of smoke drifted up from the box. Through his command view, Moss saw all the PAMMs in sight flicker, dissipate for a second, and then reassemble. He keyed in the code to turn off Ares, and this time the war god vanished. He ordered all personnel to disengage their PAMMs then watched each one blink out.

Intel flooded Moss's display. The inter-planet comm was back online. Data flashed by, confirming much of what Kaal had told him. Moss uploaded images of the Rise officers. Then he went outside to monitor the village defense. He stopped outside the theater. The Rise units that had been closing in had vanished from his display. His sensors canvassed a four-klick radius and turned up nothing but Nydron. Three of his wounded at the crash site whose names had come up on the casualties roster were restored to the live list.

"Nuts," he said. "It was all that damn box."

Moss ordered his troops to stand down and returned to the theater.

Looking relieved to be free of the Purple Pal, Klavachev was rooting through the Rise gear. Moss's display flashed red. The images he'd transmitted had been relayed to command via satellites maintaining a slipmode connection, and now they returned with an intel report for each one. The Rise officers were tagged targets of "highest possible value." The general was the head of the Rise force for the entire quadrant. His death would've been a setback for the enemy, but his capture would cripple them.

"Hell, no," Moss said.

Do the impossible.

He got it now, what Kaal was proposing. An alliance, a trade: *We give you the prisoners and their secret weapon because we know it will let you defeat the Rise and kick them off our world. Will you make the trade?*

If the Rise had deployed their weapon elsewhere on Nydro, Moss had to assume at least some of the earth force had been misled by their PAMMs and attacked the Nydron. But once the terms of a trade were struck, all the

Nydron would abide by them. They had to spread the word and find the other Rise virus transmitters—or try to have command deactivate the entire PAMM system remotely, and fast. Moss issued a bullet report to command then found Kaal and offered him his hand.

The Nydron stared at it before he returned the gesture and let Moss grip his paw.

"Kaal, my friend, you've got a deal," Moss said.

THE BALLAD OF BECCA SANJURO

Nancy Jane Moore

I F YOUR ASSIGNMENT IS SUCH A JUMP ON THE MOON, WHY DO YOU WANT US TO BANK ova and sperm?" Jake said. He and Becca sat in the kitchen of their tiny apartment in the Marine living quarters at Armstrong Base on Luna. Neither of them cooked much—they ate most meals at the mess hall—so the kitchen had become the place where they sat to have serious discussions. The bed/sitting room was reserved for pleasure.

For the past year, they'd both been running low-grav training for new Marines. It was the longest time they'd lived together in ten years of marriage. Despite the work hours, having each other to come home to at the end of the day had made the year feel like an extended vacation.

But it was coming to an end. Jake Horner was off to Mars, part of the so-called peacekeeping operation that was really an effort to keep various rebellious factions tamped down. Becca Sanjuro's assignment was Europa and protection of the coffee industry centered in Galileo. The Solar Union was beefing up security there, in response to a series of threats from a terrorist group.

"Could be it's you I'm worried about," Becca said. "Something stupid can always happen on Mars."

Outside of the uniform they shared—two Marine staff sergeants—they looked nothing alike. Jake wasn't tall, but his wide shoulders and powerful legs gave the illusion of size. His skin was a creamy brown and his combination of features indicated a broad mixture of ethnic backgrounds. Jake's people had been military going back five generations. That defined him more than any historical group from Earth.

Becca, about the same height but slighter in build, was mostly Asian by heritage, though by no means all Japanese despite her surname of Sanjuro. She, too, came from several generations of military, all enlisted. It wasn't a bad career for someone who lacked the money and gene tweaks for higher education. You got to see the Solar System.

"Besides, even if we've both got cushy assignments right now, it's still a good idea," Becca said. "My eggs should be at their best. Early thirties, that's supposed to be the peak point for a woman's eggs. A man's sperm, too, for that matter."

"I always wanted to make a baby the old-fashioned way," Jake said. Though he knew they'd never be able to do that. They couldn't afford a baby now. By the time they reached retirement age and had put enough money by, they'd both be in their fifties. Becca might still be fertile, but the odds of having a healthy child would be much lower. Artificial was the way to go.

"Always the romantic."

"Guilty," he said. "But you're right; it's time to do it."

"Besides, it gives me a hold on you. Things get wild on Mars, or at least they did last time I was there. You might meet some hot young thing."

"I might at that," Jake said. They both knew he wouldn't.

"Best be careful. You know what they say about Mars. Best way to make E-5..."

"Is to go to Mars as an E-6. Yeah, yeah. You're the one who needs to be careful. I know how to take care of myself on Mars. Europa is a big question mark."

"It's still a sleepy place. We'll have a few bomb throwers, but I can't see how it could be worse than that. I'll watch out, though. Promise."

Yeah, thought Jake. *You'll watch out and I'll watch out, unless the job demands we take a risk*. He knew Becca had common sense and he didn't consider himself unusually brave. But people who think of themselves first in a crisis don't become Marines.

Becca shipped out for Europa two days before he left for Mars. *Come back to me*, Jake thought, watching her shuttle take off. *Come back to me.*

Jake's main assignment on Mars was running a checkpoint at the entrance port for Aresville, the largest of the domed cities on Mars. No one lived outside the domes: Bioformed plants had been seeded there and were starting to grow an atmosphere, but the possibility of living on the surface was still a century away. The shuttle landing spot was outside the city, as was the depot for the mag-lev train that ran among the settlements. All those people came to the city via heavily shielded vehicles, and all were thoroughly checked out before being allowed in.

Repair crews and those working on the atmosphere project also came and went on a regular basis. They had been vetted in advance, but Jake made sure they were checked again as well. His troop was well-trained in watching for behavioral clues. They'd caught a few thieves and smugglers, though mostly the work was dull and routine.

There were at least five dissident factions on Mars, and some of those were fractured into even smaller groups. According to the Marine colonel in charge, most were extreme libertarians—people with great aversion to the Solar Union and the idea of one government, or even one federation of governments, for the system. "Their very principles keep them from working together," she told the troops. "If they should ever unify, though, we're going to have a civil war on our hands."

So they changed crews at the checkpoints often, to keep people fresh. It was easy to get sloppy when nothing happened.

Jake and Becca were too far apart to talk—realtime FTL com was way beyond the means of sergeants—but from the comp messages he got regularly, it sounded as if her assignment was equally routine. She wrote:

> **We're based at Galileo, with coffee plantations all around us. I'm working intelligence under Lt. Mbuki. She's maybe a year out of the Academy, smart as hell when it comes to data analysis, but inexperienced at dealing with people. The colonel is of the "kill 'em all and let God sort them out" school; he wouldn't recognize a subtle pattern if it hit him over the head with a rock. He's got no use for intelligence (in every way). Mother taught me how to handle officers like that and I'm trying to teach Mbuki, but I've got to be careful in how I deal with her, too. She's too unsure of herself as an officer to know how to listen to enlisted yet.**
>
> **But so far there's nothing much going on here. The terrorists appear to be the remnants of a wildcat corporation that was trying to establish coffee on Ganymede and got knocked out of business when the**

> Union-sanctioned and funded plantations took off on Europa. Regular intel has a line on most of them and gets all their com messages before they do. Our crew is just keeping an eye out for a bigger pattern.
>
> Been awhile since I've done this kind of work and I'm enjoying it. One thing Mbuki is good at is teaching others. I know a dozen new ways to chop data now, and have a fancy new encrypt code we can try out down the road. I don't think the one we've got now would survive any serious analysis, but fortunately nobody seems to care what I write to my beloved spouse.
>
> Damn but I miss you! Love, love, love —Becca

Jake felt relieved. He figured the dolt of a colonel and the inexperienced lieutenant were driving Becca crazy, but putting up with bad officers was part of the job. He'd been lucky in his officers this round.

Her next message made him more uneasy:

> There's a pattern coming together in the data that's got us worried. It looks like there might be money and other support coming in from outside, probably from Earth. So far we can't tell how big it is. Mbuki mentioned it to the lieutenant who's running the regular intel. He hadn't seen any chatter on his systems, but he promised to keep an eye out.
>
> I ran some historical data. Seems the success of growing coffee here undercut the market systemwide. Real coffee—as opposed to the synthetic crap usually found in mess halls—was extremely pricy on Earth, since the places where it grows have been crowded out by human settlement. Europa's success made some very wealthy people a lot less wealthy. And they're not happy about it.
>
> We're factoring all that in. But Mbuki got slapped down for bringing it up at all. The colonel's decided we just have a few idiot terrorists and don't need to think any bigger than that. I don't think the lieutenant's going to be willing to push it again. I hope it's just a little money

and regular intel picks it up. They can shut down money.

Oh, well. It wouldn't be the Corps if there wasn't something to bitch about. Wish you were here so I could complain in person and you could cheer me up. Or something.

Always yours —Becca.

Two messages later, Jake got scared:

Regular intel is still seeing nothing, while our analysis is indicating that something big is in the works. It looks to me like the power people are letting the local terrorist groups distract us from the real problem. I think Mbuki agrees with me—like I told you before, she's a wiz with data—but she's scared to bring it up. The whole officer chain spends their time trying to stay on the good side of the colonel, so she hasn't found any support from her immediate superior.

I tried going to the Top, but he laughed at me for being a conspiracy theorist. He's been the colonel's senior NCO for years, and it's clear they think alike. They might as well be clones. I shouldn't have expected anything different; officers like the colonel always surround themselves with people who won't rock their boat.

It might help if we could figure out exactly what's in the works, but we're missing a couple of key components.

So much for assignments that look like they're going to be easy. I should know better by now. Yours sounds dull, but I wouldn't object to a little dull at this point. Wish I was there.

All my love —Becca.

That scared Jake enough to take it up with his captain. He ended up having a brief conversation with the colonel— "I don't really want to know how you're hearing all this, Sergeant" —in which she acknowledged that the man on Europa was a fool. "But he's a well-connected fool. Don't expect much."

It wasn't much. Becca wrote:

> **Thanks. It didn't work, but thanks anyway. A couple of inspectors came in, Mbuki gave a presentation, the colonel laughed it off and Mbuki didn't defend it. Maybe she couldn't have done much, but she didn't try very hard. I guess she's just covering her butt and crossing her fingers that it won't amount to anything. Or at least, won't amount to anything until we get rotated out of here.**
>
> **The colonel thinks she's the one who got to the inspectors, so there's no chance that she's going to say anything else.**
>
> **I guess I better cross my fingers, too. And my toes. You could cross yours, too. Just in case. Thinking of you every minute**
>
> **—Becca.**

He got a couple of personal messages after that, and then a very short one.

> **I love you. Always have, always will. Don't ever forget that.**

His reply bounced. He tried to find news reports out of Europa, but there was a blackout on everything. Desperate, he barged into the colonel's office.

"She's talking to the brass on Earth," the clerk told him.

"Please. I have to know what's happening on Europa."

The clerk took pity on him and sent in a message. The colonel came out. He popped up to salute, but she put her arm around his shoulder. "I don't know much. There've been explosions all over Galileo. But Space Corps pilots from the station orbiting Europa were evacuating people for about 48 hours before the first one hit. It looks like a lot of people got off, but the refugee situation is the usual mass of confusion and nobody knows who made it out yet."

She turned to the clerk. "Have Sgt. Horner pulled off his regular duties. Sergeant, I assume you can run data analysis?"

"Yes, ma'am."

"Good. Intel is trying to pull a picture out of the chaos and they can use the help. That way you'll know something as soon as anyone does."

He joined a room full of other Marines, all plugged into individual holo data. The current theory of data analysis involved a combination of straight computing power, AI, and human minds. Computers gathered, AI sorted, and humans saw the patterns that AI missed.

This is what Becca's been doing for the past six months, Jake thought, as he sat there, trying to see something, anything. It was a connection.

They found a spike in messages back and forth between the Marine base at Galileo and the Space Corps headquarters on Europa Station. Drilling down deeper, the pattern showed both the increased communication was almost all enlisted to enlisted. Some large data dumps were included in the transmission.

Becca backdoored them, Jake thought. *She couldn't get her officers to pay attention, so she talked to the Space Corps enlisted doing intel on the space station. And they got somebody in authority to listen.* He was guessing, of course. The rules on data analysis didn't allow drilling down to actual accounts. But it had to be her. Had to be.

Official announcements were now coming in. The admiral running the space station had ordered the evacuation after getting an intel report showing that vast areas of Galileo had been rigged with mines. No idea yet of the casualty rate, except that it was considerably less than it could have been. A cadre of bots had been set down even before the evacuation to locate and disarm as many mines as possible. A large chunk of them had gone in the initial explosion, but they had succeeding in blocking further attacks. That operation was ongoing.

The Marine colonel had continued to dismiss the risk, but he had to go along with the evacuations once the admiral got involved. Apparently he had not evacuated. The Marine base was gone.

Please, please, let Becca have evacuated, Jake thought. He dove back into the data cracking. There was a systemwide push on to trace the attack back to its source.

He was deep in the data when someone tapped him on the shoulder. He shut down visual and turned around to see the colonel and next to her an officer he'd never seen before, with chaplain's bars on his collar.

"No," he said. "No." And then he began to cry. Once he started, he couldn't stop. The chaplain took him by the arm, led him to the infirmary, where they gave him something to make him sleep. It took him two days to cry himself out and move on to a state of numbness.

The colonel came by to talk with him. "It seems Sgt. Sanjuro did send the Marine intel data to the Space Corps crew on Europa Station. They saw the implications right away. Fortunately, the admiral is no fool, and even more fortunately, the colonel on Europa was under his authority. I don't normally hold with Space Corps authority over Marines, but in this case...."

"I knew it had to be her, once I saw how they got the data," Jake said. "Becca wasn't one to sit idly by if there was anything she could do. No matter what it meant to her career."

The colonel nodded.

"I'm sorry I fell apart so bad, ma'am. If I...if we hadn't both thought the assignment would be just a jump on the moon, that the risk was tiny, it might not have been so bad. If she'd been assigned to a war zone, I'd have been prepared for the possibility that she wouldn't make it." That wasn't quite a lie.

"She was a hero, you know. She saved a lot of lives."

"Not a hero, ma'am. Just a good Marine."

They gave him a month of compassionate leave. That was the colonel, most likely. Not every commander subscribed to the theory that time to heal made better troops.

He spent it at a retreat on Earth, exercising for hours a day so that he could collapse exhausted into sleep each night. Two weeks into his stay, Lt. Mbuki came to see him.

Jake didn't want to see her, but he let her in anyway. She looked like hell. Her ebony skin was ashy, her eyes looked bruised from lack of sleep, and if he hadn't known she couldn't be more than twenty-five, he'd have guessed her age at forty.

"I'm sorry," she told him. "You probably don't care, but I had to tell you anyway. I should have listened to her, should have had the courage to say what I knew to be true, should have been the one to go around the colonel if I couldn't get through to him. I knew our data were right, knew something was going to happen ...."

Part of him wanted to comfort her. Part of him wanted to keep hating her. He found he couldn't do either.

Mbuki went on. "She saved my life, you know. She was herding people onto the shuttles, mil and civs. The colonel was telling us not to go, that he'd break anyone who ran. Sgt. Sanjuro ordered the enlisted to ignore him, said it would be on her, and they listened. But even then I was wavering.

"She said, 'Get on the fucking shuttle, Lieutenant.' It was an order. And I followed it.

"She was on the last shuttle out, but the explosion knocked it out of the sky as it took off."

Jake nodded. He couldn't think of anything to say.

"I'm going to resign my commission, as soon as they'll let me," she said. "I'm not fit to lead anybody. I don't know what I'm fit to do, but it's not that." She turned to go.

"Don't," Jake said. His voice was hoarse. He cleared his throat. "Don't resign. If you can learn from this, you'll be worth something as an officer."

She stared at him. It must have sounded crazy to her. It sounded crazy to him. But he knew he was right. "Don't resign."

"I'll think about it," she said.

Jake was trying not to cry. Tears running down his cheeks or his voice cracking as he accepted Becca's medal, that would be okay. But not the uncontrolled blubbering that still came on when he woke from dreaming about her to realize she wasn't there, wouldn't ever be there. It had been over a year since Becca died, and all his friends were telling him it was time to move on. But his grief hadn't moved.

He sat in a row with one live hero and the parents of another dead one on the stage in the secondary auditorium at Solar Union headquarters in Brussels. In front of them sat the Secretary General in a gilded chair that would have done justice to an ancient king. Behind them were various aides, charged with moving the ceremony along. At the back of the stage hung a large flag showing the planets in orbit around the sun with the words *Sol, Societas, Posteritas Nobis* in script underneath.

The auditorium, which held a thousand people, was perhaps a third full, with most of those in attendance wearing military uniforms. But it would look full on the holo being beamed throughout the Union. It had been designed for that.

The welcoming speech had concluded and they were sitting through holos of the honorees' lives playing alongside them on the stage. Watching the beautifully edited bits and pieces of Becca's life posed the largest threat to Jake's composure. There she was in the training hall, tossing larger people aside left and right. There she led a troop into battle; despite the sameness of the uniforms he always knew which one she was. There they both were at their wedding.

A younger version of him stood there before the judge with that "how did I get so lucky" look on his face. He and Becca were both in uniform—the wedding had taken place over a 72-hour leave and there had been no time for fancy dress.

He took refuge in anger. Becca should have been an officer. If she'd been an officer, she wouldn't be dead. No matter that neither she nor anyone else in her family had the gene tweaks, not to mention the education, of the officer class. Becca was as smart as any officer about war, probably smarter.

Becca's holo ended and the next one began. Jake sighed in relief.

Twenty minutes later he stood before the Secretary General to accept Becca's medal. His face was wet, but his voice held steady.

At the reception afterward, several of his friends—fellow sergeants in their Marine best—rescued him from painfully polite conversation with diplomats and dragged him out to drink Belgian beer.

"What you gonna do with the money, Jake?" someone asked.

Jake, already half drunk, looked at him. "Money?"

"You know, the money they give out to the medal winners. Or their families. Megabytes of credit, that's what I hear."

They'd told him about the money when they told him about the medal, but he hadn't paid attention. It was just money, like the medal was just a hunk of gold. None of it would bring Becca back.

But now he thought about it. "A kid," he said after a couple of minutes. "A girl. I'm going to have a daughter. And I'm going to use that money to give her all the chances Becca never got—the gene tweaks, the education. She'll never be stuck in a dead end job like us. She can be an officer. Or a doctor or a scientist or even a goddamned politician.

"I'm going to have a kid."

Jake made it back to barracks on his own steam, though just barely. And for once he had managed to reach the right level of drunkenness: no dreams disturbed his sleep.

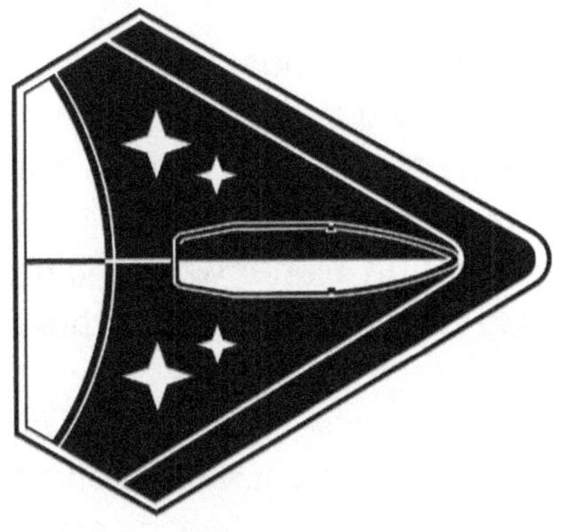

BRAND SPANKING NEW
Maria V. Snyder

G ET DRESSED. THEN REPORT TO DECK TWELVE, BARREL TWO," THE MEDIC SAID. "Are you finished?" Eunice pushed up on her right elbow. She covered her breasts with her left arm.

The medic huffed in amusement either from her delayed modesty—she had to strip prior to lying on the procedure table—or from her question. Or possibly from both.

"Where is the Data Storage Unit?" she asked.

"That's classified, Private Daniels." His brisk manner softened for a moment. "It's for your protection."

"Do you know where I'm going?" she asked.

"No. Your pilot will know. This is a routine delivery, Daniels."

She sat up and swung her legs off the side of the cold table. Of course he was casual and relaxed. He didn't have a DSU inserted somewhere underneath his skin. As Eunice dressed in her uniform, she scanned her arms and legs, searching for a cut or mark or anything to indicate the skin had been cut, but she found nothing. She ran her fingers through her short brown hair, feeling for a lump on her scalp. Again nothing.

A strange, creepy-crawly sensation skittered over her. She stifled the desire to shake herself like a wet dog. The crushing disappointment she'd felt when she learned her first assignment for Mother Earth would be as a courier had turned into trepidation. Transporting information had seemed so innocuous and dull. Yet...

Eunice hurried through the corridors of the military base on Mercury Three. As she navigated the mind-numbingly drab base, she mentally cursed her recruiter. *See the universe*, he'd promised, but so far all she'd seen were the interiors of two military bases, which had identical layouts. Granted, the only way to get off planet was to join the military or pay billions. Mother had stopped building colonies on other planets over a hundred years ago.

While she'd been growing up and dreaming of traveling, the United Federation of Planets (UFoP) had gained more and more member planets, stealing them from Mother Earth. Sure they'd agreed to pay back Mother's huge investment in setting up the colonies. But what would happen when they decided to stop payments? By that time, Mother's empire would have shrunk to a handful of planets and she'd have no resources left to enforce the treaties.

Perhaps that was why Mother had switched tactics. Instead of fighting the colonies that wished to become independent, she was working with them. But UFoP had sliced into the Kasner-space communications collective (although they claimed innocence) so Mother had to send messages the old-fashioned way. Hence the couriers.

At least, I'll finally be able to visit other planets. Excitement built and Eunice reported to deck twelve, barrel two to meet her pilot. First impression—his gray skin exactly matched the color of his unruly hair. *He's ancient for a lieutenant.*

Remembering her basic training, she snapped to attention. "Private Daniels, reporting for—"

"Relax, Private. I don't do the whole salute and shout routine. Name's Leo." He eyed her. "Where's your stuff?"

She patted her pockets. "It's only an overnight trip."

"Ah, a woman who knows how to pack." He thumped his chest. "Love at first sight."

She stared at him. *Was this guy for real?*

"Hop into the bullet, I'm just finishing pre-flight." He returned to the collective's screen built into the side wall.

Eunice scanned the area. A long, thin tunnel disappeared to the left and a round black metal container rested on the tunnel's track. One end was cone-shaped, while the other looked like it had been chopped off. Probably a probe. "Uh...Leo, where's the bullet?"

He spun, mouth agape. "You're the courier, right?"

"Yes."

"You've never flown in a bullet?" The question was more a groan.

"I've never couriered before. I'm just out of training."

"Holy shit with a crown and scepter. You're a spanking newbie!" He gestured at her fatigues. "I should have noticed your shiny newness and fresh-from-the-factory smell. Shit." Leo tromped over to the probe, muttering under his breath.

The top of it just reached his shoulder. "This is the bullet. Fastest conveyance known to man." He smacked the side. It clanked. Then he opened the hatch and swept his hand out, pointing. "Navigational and life support equipment in the nose, pilot's seat, passenger's seat, cargo area, and the Kasner-Phillips engine behind that panel."

"Oh." A feather of fear twirled in her chest. Eunice had learned about the KP engine in basic training. But they were mostly used for emergencies because of the dangers. Her sergeant had said this was a routine delivery.

"What do you think?" Leo asked.

"It's...ugly."

He laughed, flashing big yellow teeth. "That it is. No frills for sure. But it'll get us to Venus Five in no time."

So that was where they were going. Eunice hoped she'd have some time to look around before they returned. All she had to do was show up, let them remove the DSU, and head back to Mercury Three for her next assignment. Routine.

Eunice strapped into the passenger's seat. Leo handed her a stack of self-sealing bags.

"What are these for?" she asked.

"Just in case you get Kasner-speed sick. Make sure you press the bag to your face and seal it tight when done. Floating vomit is the nastiest of the nasty. If it happens, you can find another way home."

She searched his expression. *Was he kidding?* His bright gaze was a little too bright. A crazy gleam swirled. How many trips had he made at Kasner speed? Too many too close together would scramble his brain and turn his insides to goo. *My first mission may be my last. Wonderful.*

Leo settled into his seat, sealed the hatch tight, and fired the engine. Eunice's pulse jumped in her throat.

She leaned forward. "How long have you been flying bullets?"

"Dozens of years. I started with cargo ships and flew anything with an engine, but after my first trip in a bullet, there was no turning back."

Great. She'd heard some pilots became addicted. Just her luck to be assigned one of them.

"Don't worry, my shiny new recruit. I've turned down promotions so I could fly. I'm the best of the best."

The tightness in her stomach eased. Feeling better she relaxed, and asked him how many courier missions he'd flown.

"This is my first."

Before she could react, Leo said, "Barrel two ready to launch." He glanced back at her. "I'd warn you what to expect, but you won't believe me."

"That bad?"

"Worse." He faced forward. "Fire!"

An invisible wall slammed into her, driving her into the seat. Squashed flat, she struggled to breath, to think, to exist in three dimensions.

"Engaging Kasner-speed!" Leo shouted.

Her insides exploded. Bones shattered and ripped through her skin. All in silence and without pain. Then the pieces of her physical body fogged around her, fragments of bone, drops of blood, shredded bits of muscles, clumps of brain matter. And in the center a thread of consciousness remained. Just enough for Eunice to understand the horror and freak out.

A sense of the physical returned with a pushing, sticking, pressing, and tingling feeling. Once she was whole, she didn't even had time to marvel over the solidity of her body before her stomach rebelled. Grabbing for a vomit bag, she heaved, fearing the action would cause her to shatter again. But she remained solid.

"You'll get used to it." Leo assured her.

Oh no she won't. As soon as they landed on Venus Five, she'd find another way back, another career if she had to. *Just notch one successful mission and go home.*

"We have bigger problems," he said.

Before her trip through Kasner space, she would've been worried about his comment. Now—not so much. "And?"

"We were followed by a Phillips-class cruiser, X-military."

"How do you know?"

"For us experienced travelers, we know that the cloud of body parts around our consciousness is really the universe. When you're at Kasner-speed you are everywhere and nowhere at once."

"And in all that...stuff, you saw an XP?" She didn't hide her disbelief.

"Yes I did, and I changed direction, Ms. Raw Recruit, so they don't learn our destination. Do you know how many bullet pilots can change course like that?"

"A dozen?"

"One."

Impressive. "Is UFoP chasing us?"

"Not sure who." Leo seemed distracted.

"Where are we now?"

"I've no idea."

She closed her eyes. Lost in space was such a...cliché.

"Not to worry. I've pinged the universe and should have a response... Holy shit with a harp and wings."

"Now what?"

"They're still on our tail."

"How is that possible?"

"Must of installed a KP engine. But with that sized ship, it'd have to be... humongous!"

Eunice considered and she didn't like the direction of her thoughts. "And they'd have to put a tracer on us." Once a ship reached Kasner-speed there were an infinite number of vectors of travel.

"Right. Just what are you transporting anyway?"

"Data."

"Ah Data Pirates. They've been stealing info and selling it to UFoP so it appears as if UFoP is playing by the rules. What kind of data?"

"I've no idea. This was a supposed to be a routine delivery. My sergeant said so, and the medic said so."

"And you believed them?"

"Of course."

He groaned. "Spanking newbie. Never ever trust a superior officer when he or she says, 'it's routine.' The military is all about routine. There's no need to *say* it's routine. That would be redundant."

"Oh."

"You've a lot to learn. If..."

"If what?"

"Never mind. I've just received an order to hold my position so those bastards can pull us in. Not bloody likely. I've got enough juice for one more K-stretch. Where shall we go?" he mused to himself.

"Why don't we just go to Venus Five? What's the big deal if they know our destination? Once there, won't our forces protect us?"

"Where's the fun in that?"

Eunice clamped down on her reply. His comment just confirmed it. Leo's brain had Kasner-rot.

"Think about it, Recruit. They put a tracer in my bullet."

She connected the dots. "They have someone working on the inside."

"Right. Do you know who?"

"No. Do you?"

"No. So wouldn't it be in all our best interests to find out who they are and who their pals are?"

"Yes. But, Leo there're only two of us and an XP has—"

"Fourteen crew members and enough space to carry a company of soldiers," Leo said. "What's your point?"

She thought it was obvious. "We're outnumbered. It might be...difficult to learn anything about who is chasing us."

"Nonsense. Oooohhh...I know where we are. Perfect. There's a moon not far... Try to pay attention this time, Private."

"To what?"

"Engaging K-speed."

Ugh. She blew apart. This time as the bits of her body expanded, she wondered if this was what it would be like if she had been injected into outer space without a protective suit. An odd thought. She doubted her consciousness would survive for long in real space.

After she coalesced, she dry heaved into another vomit bag. If she survived this mission, she was transferring to a desk job.

The bullet jumped. The straps bit into her shoulders, keeping her in place.

"Holy shit with wine and a chalice! These guys are serious."

Eunice was afraid to ask. She couldn't believe she fell for the load of crap the recruiter fed her.

"We're hit, but don't worry," Leo said.

Yep. K-rot. No doubt. At this point being captured by the enemy didn't sound so bad.

"The moon I'm heading for is basically a giant rock, but it has an atmosphere that can support us. I'm gonna aim for the sunny side, but the landings gonna be rough." Leo turned in his seat and met her gaze.

The crazy goofiness was gone. And that scared her more than anything else.

"Just don't let them peel you, Private. Trust me to do the rest." Leo returned to the controls.

Peel me? She tried to wrap her head around that and failed.

Then they hit the atmosphere.

Hard.

Then the ground.

Harder.

Pain sliced through her temple, waking her. Blurry dark gray shapes formed mountains around her. Sharp rocks jabbed her through her torn uniform. Her entire body ached. Eunice pushed up into a sitting position. The fuzzy landscape faded behind black and white dots. She drew in deep breaths to keep from passing out. The air smelled of rust and tasted gritty. After a couple minutes her surroundings sharpened.

It wasn't pretty. All jagged rocks, rubble, and one crumpled bullet. She must have been ejected during the crash. By the amount of damage, she knew she was lucky to be alive. Staggering to her feet, Eunice limped over to the ship. Relief that Leo's body hadn't been crunched into pulp was replace with worry. A fair bit of blood stained what remained of the control panel.

She scanned the area. Where was he? Perhaps he searched for help or water or...something. Her brain refused to cooperate with this guessing game. It wanted to scream, "He left us!"

Determined to stay optimistic, she walked a loop, seeking footprints or perhaps a note for her scratched into the hard dirt. Nothing.

"We're going to die!" her brain yelled.

She ignored it until the distinct whine of a transport's engine cut through the air. A black speck in the gray sky grew as it dropped toward her.

"Told you." Her brain was smug.

After another sweep of the area, Eunice knew she had some time. There was no place nearby for the transport to land. They'd have to send a patrol out to fetch her. She could run and hide unless they had heat sensors. And if they didn't, then what? They'd leave and she'd die of thirst. Maybe Leo signaled for help before they crashed. Maybe he was hiding and wondering why the spanking newbie was standing like an idiot out in plain sight.

The engines roared above her. Shit. Her orders hadn't included this contingency. *And why not, Private Daniels?* Because everyone was too damn busy telling her this was routine.

Leo's last bit of advice came unbidden. *Just don't let them peel you. Trust me to do the rest.*

Nothing about avoiding capture or keeping quiet. The hard part...no the impossible part was trusting him. Eunice had trusted the recruiter—a mistake, had trusted her sergeant—bigger mistake, and had trusted the medic—huge mistake. Why trust Lieutenant Leo? She glanced at the bullet. So far, Leo hadn't lied to her. Plus she was determined to finish the mission.

All right Leo, I'll trust you. She sat on the ground and rested her back against the still-warm metal of the bullet. Crossing her arms over her knees, she leaned her aching forehead on her forearms.

The crunch-scrape of boots over the rocky soil warned of their approach. Eunice listened and counted about a half dozen of them. When they spotted her, they fanned out, pointing their Watson-921s at her. It had enough fire power to blow a hole in her chest. A laugh caught in her throat. Did she look dangerous? She hadn't even been issued the standard JS-97. Another red flag she missed.

The four men and two women wore civilian clothes, but even Eunice with her limited experience knew they were ex-military. They checked the cockpit of the bullet.

"Where's the pilot?" one man with buzzed black hair asked. He holstered his weapon, and pulled a metal cylinder that was as long as his hand from his belt.

Irrationally more afraid of the new weapon, she stood. "I don't know," she said.

He searched her for weapons, then pressed the cylinder to her neck, shooting an icy liquid into her. She stumbled back as cold spread through-out her body.

"Where's the pilot?" he asked again.

"I don't know."

He exchanged a glance with the woman standing on his left. "Why don't you know?"

"I woke and he was gone, gone, gone. Left me all alone. Poor, poor me, the brand-spanking newbie." The words bubbled from her mouth. She couldn't stop them.

"What a coward," he said. Then he studied her. His blue eyes creased in concern. "Christ these recruits are getting younger and younger."

The ground under her feet swayed. Eunice clutched the man's arm to keep from doing a face plant. "I'm twenty, and you're really, really cute." Mortified, she clamped her mouth shut, but he ignored her.

"We don't need the pilot," the woman said. She gestured to another man. "Sid, attach the hook to the wreck, we'll snag the bullet on our way out. The KP engine will fetch a nice profit."

Eunice's man put his hand on hers. "Where's the DSU?"

"I don't know," she sang, feeling giddy. "It's for my protection. A safety harness for my brain." She giggled.

"They didn't do you any favors, sweetheart. The DSU is manufactured from skin cells so I can't find it with my medical scanner. I'll have to search underneath all your skin."

And finally the true significance of Leo's words hit her. Terror sliced right through the drug's effects, sobering her in an instant. *Just don't let them peel you.* Surrounded by six armed guards, how the hell was she going to stop them?

No plans formed as they escorted her to the transport ship. The medic kept a firm, almost protective grip on her. Nothing popped up when he secured her into a seat, or when they lifted off, and swept down to snag the bullet. Not a single idea crossed her mind as they flew into the XP's cargo bay. Panic burned in her guts.

"Do you even know what you're carrying?" the medic asked her as he escorted her through the hallways. Two armed guards followed them.

"Just data. Routine data."

He barked a laugh. "Oh my, they screwed you big time, sweetheart. You're carrying the schematics for Mother's newest, deadliest weapon. One that can blast through a planet's shield. It's a game changer."

She stopped. "Are you sure? I'm just a new recruit."

He smiled, but there was genuine regret in his gaze. "Yes. They sent out an experienced and well-known courier on a heavily armed Phillips-cruiser with a full escort a few days ago—an obvious decoy."

"Oh." Eunice froze in place as the information sunk in.

The ship rocked to the left then to the right. She stumbled, and grabbed his arm. "What was that?"

"We're leaving orbit. There's nothing to worry about."

He could be calm. But from the depths of her fear, a plan formed. "What's your name?"

He hesitated. "Devon Marshall."

"I'm Eunice. Are you guys looking for recruits? I don't have much experience, but I'm willing to learn."

Devon laughed a full throaty chuckle as they continued. "Thinking about betraying Mother Earth?"

"She started it."

He agreed, then sobered and wouldn't meet her gaze.

Oh no. "I'm not going to live through the procedure. Right?"

"If we had more time..." He took a deep breath. "No."

When they entered the infirmary, panic boiled in her stomach. The guards assumed positions outside the doors and Devon took her firmly in hand.

Instead of struggling, she pressed against him, looking up. "Please, don't."

His arms tightened around her, and his expression showed his conflict. "Game changer, Eunice. I'm really sorry."

She buried her head in his chest and sobbed, letting all her fear and anger flow.

"Uh...look...maybe I'll find it right away and I'm good with skin grafts..."

She stepped back. "I'm sorry." She sniffed. "Some soldier I turned out to be. I just need a minute. Is there a washroom?"

"Of course." He strode to a cabinet and removed a robe. "Here." Devon gestured to a washroom. "When you're done, take off all your clothing and put this on."

She gave him a watery smile. "Okay." Keeping her shoulders hunched, she shuffled into the washroom and closed the door. There wasn't a way to lock it on this side.

Leaning against the door, she gathered her courage. Now what? She spotted a call button and speaker. Perhaps she could use the wires...

Ah, who the hell was she kidding, she was a spanking newbie. The first time she'd been in a spaceship was two months ago. All she had was her basic training. She considered. There had to be something she learned during those eight weeks of hell that she could use now. Her mind sorted through the massive amount of information she'd learned, including proper military procedures, spaceship stats, weapons, warfare tactics, and military strategy.

Devon knocked on the door. "Is everything all right?"

No, you asshole. You're going to flay me.

"Just a minute, please." she squeaked, sounding as pathetic as possible.

Her thoughts snagged on one lesson. *Okay Leo, I trust you, so all I need to do is hold up my end.* Eunice stripped, threw on the robe, kicked off her boots and socks, and opened the door.

As Devon led her to the procedure table, she concentrated on being a raw recruit, fresh from the factory. She shook with fear. Tears streaked down her face and she huddled on the table while Devon programmed the med-unit for surgery.

He instructed her to remove the robe. She stood and untied the belt with fumbling fingers, pulling it through the loops. Devon picked up the anesthetic and approached. Eunice shrugged off the robe, it plopped to the floor. He skidded to a stop, staring at her. *Brand spanking new body, too. Score one for the recruit.*

Eunice's training kicked in. In one quick motion, she wrapped the robe's belt around his hand holding the medicine. Pulling his arm straight up, she spun behind him then yanked his wrist down. Devon shouted in surprise. Before he could fight back, she pushed the button, sending the anesthetic into his neck. He collapsed.

Eunice had about two seconds to celebrate before the door flew opened. She dashed for the latrine and shut the door, but knew she couldn't hold it. She prayed her memory wasn't faulty. The moon they had crashed on was small and an XP cruiser of this size should have enough power to leave orbit smoothly. That bump when they left orbit might have been a signal. In other words, she was betting her life on a should-have and a might-have. She pressed the big red call button. *Okay, Leo, your turn.*

"How can I assist you?" a mechanical voice asked.

"Lock the washroom's door!"

The bolt popped into place. Holy shit with a halo and a robe, indeed!

The guards banged on the door, shouting at her to unlock it.

"Do you require anymore assistance?" Leo's voice replaced the mechanical one. He sounded very smug.

"Can you take me to Venus Five?"

"Already in route. Sit tight."

"Leo, you *are* the best of the best."

"I know."

After they landed, Leo collected her from the washroom. As they walked through the empty corridors of the XP, he explained that once she was out of harm's way, he flew the XP to Venus Five and delivered the group of pirates to the military police.

"MP's already fumigated this nest of nasties," Leo said.

"How did you get onto the ship, let alone gain control of it?" she asked.

"While you were believing I'd abandoned you, I was hidden in the engine compartment of the bullet. It threw off enough heat to mask my presence."

"And when they took it to the cargo bay—"

"No one thought to search it because they were so focused on your Shiny Highness. Nice blubbering baby act by the way."

"Thanks. How did you get into the bridge?"

He huffed as if insulted. "I don't need a bridge to fly. I just cozied up to that beautiful huge Kasner-Philips engine and she sang for me." Leo's expression took on an avid glow of someone in a state of pure bliss.

"I sang for you, too, Leo. On my knees and bent over the latrine."

He laughed. "You'll get used to K-speed, Recruit."

"Not bloody likely."

They reported to the commander of the base. He congratulated Leo on his quick thinking and Eunice for keeping her skin on. Well, not those words exactly.

"Should I report to the medic, sir?" she asked. She couldn't wait to deliver the DSU and be finished with this mission.

"No need, Private Daniels. We didn't implant the data in you. You were our decoy this time. And an excellent one at that." The commander left in good spirits.

Eunice stared after him as fury burned in her chest.

Leo laughed and slapped her on the back. "Welcome to the military, Private Daniels." When she didn't respond, he added, "Look on the bright side."

She sputtered. "What bright side?" she demanded.

"You're no longer brand-spanking new."

FLECHE
Jack Campbell

Something slammed into the Alliance light cruiser *Fleche*, jerking the warship's mass down and to one side. That brought a bulkhead swinging around to batter Lieutenant Tanya Desjani as she tried to make her way to the bridge.

Tanya bounced off the opposite bulkhead, momentary dizziness from the blow made worse by the way the passageway she was in rotated and wobbled as *Fleche* moved in the same uncontrolled fashion. The survival suit she wore had minimal armor and minimal padding, but it had kept her alive as repeated hits had torn the hull of *Fleche*, venting the ship's atmosphere into cold, empty space.

The lights flickered twice, then went out, replaced by the scattered radiance of emergency lighting running off batteries. Gravity had gone out, too. Something had happened to the power core. Not an overload. That would have produced a moment of intense heat and light in which both cruiser and Tanya would have been vaporized. But a shut-down power core meant the ship was now totally helpless. If *Fleche* wasn't already dead, she soon would be.

The same was likely true of every member of her crew.

Tanya jerked in involuntary fright as the nearest body to her, lacking a left arm and shoulder and clearly dead, suddenly twitched into motion not related to the light cruiser's tumble.

"Lieutenant Desjani." *Fleche*'s executive officer finished pushing aside the dead and hung for a moment before Tanya. She couldn't see his features through the survival suit's face shield, but he sounded oddly abrupt, his words coming out in brief bursts. "Weapons officer. Status."

Tanya swallowed on a raw throat before she could speak. "Weapons central control completely off line. No weapons left. All hell lances out. All grapeshot projectors destroyed. We expended the last missile half an hour ago. Weapons crews have suffered serious casualties." She felt her voice cracking and fought to hold on to her self-control as *Fleche* lurched from several more hits. Another Syndic warship must have made a firing run on this wreck which was still technically a light cruiser of the Alliance fleet. "Internal comms are out and all of the wreckage in the passageways is interfering with my suit comms, so I was heading for the bridge to get orders."

She would never know what the executive officer's response might have been. Tanya suddenly realized that, during the last Syndic barrage, matching holes the size of her fist had appeared in a star-shaped pattern around her and the exec, one set high up on one side of the passageway where Syndic hell lances had torn through *Fleche*'s light armor and another set down near the deck on the other side where the particle beams had kept going through what were for them minor obstacles.

One of those pairs of holes bracketed the exec. He had jerked slightly as a hell lance instantly bored a hole through his torso from shoulder to opposite hip, a movement she hadn't understood at the time but did now as the body of the exec drifted lifelessly to bump into that of the dead sailor he had earlier shoved aside.

Feeling panic threaten, Tanya closed her eyes and strove to fight down fear and confusion. Promotions came fast in a fleet suffering brutal casualties. Less than two years ago she had been an ensign, quickly trained and naive. The experience she had gained since then had not included anything this bad. *But I can do this. Black Jack faced this same situation when he fought his ship to the last at Grendel. He did his duty. We're all supposed to follow his example, to be like Black Jack when he stopped the first Syndic attack on the Alliance. He's been everyone's hero since then. I have to be like him now.* That helped. Every Alliance sailor was urged to be like Black Jack, who legend said wasn't dead and who would return some day to save the Alliance. He wasn't here now, though, and while she couldn't be Black Jack, she could do her job. *The bridge. I need to get to the bridge. The captain will give me orders, will tell me what to do when there doesn't seem to be anything anyone can do.*

Her mind steady, Tanya shoved off, pushing aside wreckage and bodies blocking her path until the hatch to the bridge loomed before her.

The bridge was located deep within the ship, as well protected as any compartment could be, but that did not mean much when a light cruiser was being pounded into scrap by heavier units. Tanya paused to gaze at the mess here, made up of drifting debris and torn portions of bodies. "Captain?"

A figure pulled himself over to her. "Lieutenant Desjani? I'm Master Chief Milam, from engineering. The captain's dead."

Her mind whirled in counterpoint to the wild motion of the ship, but Tanya gripped a railing with one hand and brought her senses back to stability by force of will. "Who's in command?"

"The executive officer. Before the captain died, the exec went out to—"

"No. He's dead, too. I saw it happen."

"Dead?" Master Chief Milam pointed at her. "Then you are in command, Lieutenant. I don't know of any other officer left alive."

In command. Of a light cruiser whose remaining existence might be measured in seconds. What should she do? Take charge. "What's our status?"

"All comms are out, internal and external. All we've got are survival suit comms and those are patchy. The chief engineer sent me up here to tell the captain that maneuvering controls were completely gone. We can't repair them with what we've got aboard. Most of the main propulsion units are gone, and with the power core down we can't use what's left. Life support, sensors, and all other automated systems are out. I don't know about weapons."

"They're all gone, too." Her mind seized on one thing the Master Chief had said. "Why isn't the chief engineer in command?" Absurdly, the primary concern motivating her question was one of precedence and honor, which over decades of war had become of overriding importance among the officers of the fleet. The chief engineer would raise hell if a more junior officer stepped on his prerogatives, no matter how severe the emergency. Even with the ship wrecked and the captain dead, Tanya felt an irrational worry about impugning the honor of a superior officer.

But in reply to her question, Master Chief Milam indicated a sailor nearby. "Petty Officer Deladrier showed up two minutes after I got here to tell me that main engineering had been shot up and half the personnel there killed, including the chief engineer and the assistant engineering officer."

Deladrier nodded, expression unknowable behind his face shield. "We took several volleys. They must have aimed to avoid the power core area and hit the watch teams, but they tore up the power core controls, too. The survivors were trying to shut down the power core when I left to keep it from blowing us all to hell."

The assistant engineering officer dead, too. Her roommate, Lieutenant Mei Singh. *Don't think about her. Not now. Focus on the job. Why did the Syndics target the engineering crew and not the power core itself?* Tanya was doing her best to concentrate on that question when another sailor pushed forward. "Lieutenant, my acting section chief sent me up to see if we're supposed to abandon ship."

If only she had days to think this over, to get a full picture of the situation. "How many escape pods are still working?"

"I...don't know."

Training and experience finally offered a clear course of action for her. "Master Chief Milam, get an inventory of the escape pods. How many haven't been destroyed or disabled? I need to know if abandoning ship is even an option. I also need a muster. How many of the crew are still alive and how many of those are able to function?"

"Lieutenant, we may not have time..." His voice trailing off, Master Chief Milam looked around. "I'm not feeling any more hits. Maybe there's no Syndics coming in on us right now, or maybe they figure we're not worth any more attention."

"Or maybe we won." Tanya swung over to a status panel and swept junk away from it, avoiding looking at what she was pushing away. Only scattered status lights reporting systems failures answered her examination. "Is there anybody here who can get us a look outside?"

A petty officer with one arm cradled in the other kicked herself toward Tanya. "I can try, Lieutenant. We've still got some back-up battery power here. Our sensor systems are shot to hell, but if there's even one set of working back-up circuits I can route through I might be able to link to the fleet net and get a status picture."

"Do it." Was there any fleet left in this star system? Before *Fleche* had been overwhelmed Tanya had watched the status display in her weapons control station showing the Alliance battleships and battle cruisers with this force trading blows and being annihilated as they wiped out the Syndic battleships and battle cruisers opposing them. Were any left? Or had the Syndics triumphed here?

Master Chief Milam had sent runners off to find out the information Tanya had asked for, and now echoed her thoughts. "I hope we won. Otherwise the best we can hope for is getting captured and taken to one of those damned Syndic labor camps for the rest of our lives, however long that is."

He knew as well as she did that the odds heavily favored death instead of capture. Neither the Alliance nor the Syndicate Worlds took captives very often these days. Sometimes she wondered what her ancestors thought of that, but it wasn't as if she could change the ugly patterns that had developed over nearly a hundred years of war between the two main factions of humanity in space. "They may just leave us here to die aboard *Fleche* when our suits give out," Tanya said. "I don't know why they didn't target the power core on that last run."

The petty officer laboring over a status panel gave a gasp of satisfaction. "Here, Lieutenant! I hope it holds, but look fast just in case."

A grainy display had popped into existence above the panel, showing the situation in this star system. Tanya focused desperately, fighting down a gust of despair at how few ships were still active.

There were only two Alliance heavy cruisers left, both badly-damaged and both nearly ten light minutes from *Fleche*. The rest of the Alliance warships which had entered this star system were gone, blown into fragments either by enemy fire or when their own power cores overloaded. She could list them in her mind. Three battleships, four battle cruisers, five other heavy cruisers and eleven other light cruisers, and twenty-four destroyers. Swarms of escape pods drifted through the vast area of battle. Often a ship died too fast for anyone to escape, but other times many of the crew could get off and hope for rescue if their side won. If the other side won the outcome might only be a quick death when the winners used the losers' escape pods for target practice, or a slower death as life support gave out in pods the winners had not the resources or the motivation to bother recovering.

But the Syndics had taken losses almost as bad. All of their battleships and battle cruisers were gone, too, along with all of their light cruisers and Hunter-Killers. They had three heavy cruisers left, but two of those were in at least as bad a shape as the surviving Alliance heavies. The last Syndic heavy cruiser, though, was nearly untouched. Given the state of the surviving Alliance forces that one ship provided the Syndics with overwhelming superiority.

But it wasn't going for the kill on the two surviving Alliance heavy cruisers. Not yet. The sputtering display showed the operational Syndic heavy cruiser on a curving intercept path ending where it met the staggering path of Fleche. Why bother with a firing run on what was obviously a dead ship when those two Alliance heavy cruisers were still threats?

Because it wasn't a firing run. That was the only explanation. "Damn. They didn't destroy us because they want this ship. They tried to kill a lot of the crew but avoid causing a core overload. They can tell we've had to shut down our power core so we can't deliberately overload it and take them with us if they board us."

Master Chief Milam didn't answer for a moment, then looked around meaningfully at the wreckage surrounding them. "Why do they want the ship?"

"They must have a reason. Something they—Ancestors preserve us. Master Chief, they think, or hope, we've got an Alliance hypernet key aboard. If the Syndics could capture one of those it would give them access to the Alliance hypernet."

"We don't have one," Master Chief Milam objected. "But they'll come aboard and kill us all while finding that out, won't they?"

"Yes." Her voice stayed amazingly steady as it pronounced a death sentence on them all. "I need that muster, Chief. I need to know how many sailors on this ship can still fight."

So much needed to be done and yet she could do so little. Suit comms remained erratic except at close range, so Tanya waited, trying to sound and look calm, as runners came to the bridge with reports. "Only four escape pods in working condition, Lieutenant," one said. "There's a fifth that might work, if we're really desperate."

Master Chief Milam looked up from where he was tabulating muster reports. "We've got one hundred and two sailors still able to fight. That includes the lightly wounded. There's another thirty-six too badly injured to move or fight, including Ensign Ybarra. The rest are dead."

Fleche had gone into battle with two hundred thirty five crew aboard. Ninety-seven were dead, nearly as many as were still effective. "May the living stars receive their souls," Tanya muttered. Would they ever receive proper burial, cast into the nearest star? She couldn't worry about that, or about how many of her friends and comrades were dead. What she faced now was a simple math problem. An undamaged escape pod could carry twelve sailors. She could get as many as forty-eight survivors off of this ship, to face an uncertain future as best. Or keep as many able sailors aboard as she could to fight the Syndics.

A simple math problem, involving lives to be subtracted from the universe. *I'm in command. I have to decide.* "Get the badly-wounded into the working escape pods and eject them," Tanya said. "They'll at least have a chance that way. Divide the thirty-six evenly among the four working pods and add one lightly-wounded sailor in each pod to look after the badly-wounded. All other personnel are to break out small arms and be prepared to repel boarders."

The sailors around her stood, not reacting, as frozen by events as she had almost been earlier. "Were my orders unclear?" Tanya said in a voice that made them all jerk to attention.

"No, Lieutenant," Master Chief Milam said. "Get going!" he told the others.

Only after the runners had scattered to pass on Tanya's orders did Milam speak to her again on the private command circuit. "What are we going to do, Lieutenant Desjani? We've got less than a hundred effectives left, and whoever comes aboard is probably going to have heavier weapons and a lot more bodies."

"If we're going to die, Master Chief, we might as well go down swinging." She thought she had accepted that. Maybe somewhere deep inside a remnant of sanity was screaming in terror, but everywhere else a dull calm filled her.

"Yeah," he agreed. "Might as well."

"How many do they carry on Syndic heavy cruisers?" Tanya asked him. "It's about three hundred in the crew, right?"

"Roughly. They carry fewer per ship than we do, which is the main reason they can't repair battle damage like we can. But if they've picked up anyone from the other ships the Syndics have lost, they'll have more."

At least three to one odds, then. Maybe worse.

Hopeless. Hopeless.

Tanya realized that she was looking toward the command seat which the captain had occupied. The captain's body was still there, most of it, anyway, surrounded by controls which no longer worked. *We can't save this ship, can't keep the Syndics from taking Fleche. But we can't retreat, even if the Alliance fleet did retreat instead of standing its ground. What does that leave?*

Attack.

"Once they finish with us," she said to Master Chief Milam, "they'll finish off those two heavy cruisers."

He nodded wordlessly in agreement.

"But if we hurt that ship badly enough, our cruisers might have the time to repair enough systems to defend themselves and maybe even take out the remaining Syndics."

He took a moment to reply. "How do we do that? What have we got left?"

She was maybe half his age. Remarkable, really, that Milam had managed to survive this bloody war for this long. And now he was looking to her for orders, while she could turn to no one else to ask what to do. "We've got nothing to lose, Master Chief. That gives us something. What can we do to take out that heavy cruiser?"

"With a hundred sailors out-numbered three to one? We can't take that Syndic ship, Lieutenant, even if we don't care what happens to us. We'd have to seize the bridge and engineering and we'd have to do it fast."

"I know," Tanya said. "Syndic ships have their control compartments inside armored citadels that can be sealed and defended for some time. We'd have to get inside those citadels before they could be sealed."

"And we can't do that. No way. We don't have the firepower or the numbers. The Syndics will seal their citadels and bring their boarding parties back and wipe us out."

"How do we make our deaths count, Master Chief? What *can* we do?"

Master Chief Milam took a long moment to reply. "There's something we could try, as long as we're going to die anyway."

Tanya felt a dull ache inside as she spoke her next words. "Let's hear it."

She had known one thing: the Syndics would aim the majority of their boarding party toward the part of *Fleche* where a hypernet key would be located, and that they would aim their suppressing fire ahead of that boarding party at the areas around those compartments to help knock down any resistance between them and their goal.

She had guessed another thing, from the records she had seen of other Syndic boarding operations. "Since they don't know whether or not our captain is still alive they will send a force toward our bridge to capture the captain for intelligence purposes."

Master Chief Milam nodded. He was packed in next to her, here in the main forward passageway where any Syndic boarding party heading for the bridge of *Fleche* would come. Here where every surviving member of *Fleche*'s crew was also packed in, a solid mass of defenders. "If they fire in this area, they'll wipe us out easy, Lieutenant."

"We have to risk it, Master Chief. The launches of the four working escape pods twenty minutes ago might convince them that none of the living crew of *Fleche* has remained aboard."

"They'll still shoot us up a little more, but if I were them I wouldn't waste time and energy slamming shots through the whole ship," Milam agreed.

"Let's hope we're both right. I doubt there will be time to talk much after we start fighting. Remember your objective, Master Chief."

"I got it, Lieutenant. Just keep them off my back as best you can."

Calm voices. Rational voices. Discussing an insane course of action.

A single sailor who had been posted near the riddled outer hull came back toward them at a rush. "I saw them. They're matching our motion now."

The Syndic heavy cruiser had met their path, had matched their speed, and now was maneuvering to match the tumble of *Fleche* so that boarding parties could easily reach the Alliance light cruiser. How long would it take the Syndics to match movement? It was an article of faith in the Alliance fleet that the Syndics were not equal to Alliance sailors when it came to driving ships, but Tanya knew the Syndics were at least competent, and even if they hadn't been competent then automated systems could do the predictable job of matching movement well enough, though without any imagination or special skill.

It felt so strange, waiting here in the dim glow of the emergency lighting, on a ship which was dead in all but name. In Tanya's mind she could see *Fleche* alive, her passageways and compartments filled with men and women Tanya knew, power flowing through her hull, main propulsion hurling her through space, weapons ready to wreak havoc among any targets. But around her was only silence, the light cruiser bereft of any life except that among her surviving crew members.

As Weapons Officer, Tanya had controlled two hell lance batteries and one specter missile launcher. Awesome weapons, really. She had gloried in the damage they could do. Now she grasped tightly a simple slug thrower. An anti-boarding weapon little different from the hand-weapons humans had carried centuries ago. She would have to ensure she was braced whenever she fired it in zero gravity or the recoil would cast her helplessly backward.

The crew members around her held a wide assortment of other hand weapons. Some pulse rifles, but not nearly enough. A lot more slug-throwers. A few sailors carried hand tools, the only weapons available until either friend or enemy died and relinquished their weapons to those who had none. Against soldiers or Marines, wearing full battle armor and carrying heavier weapons, Tanya and her crew wouldn't stand a ghost of a chance. Against Syndic crew members equipped little better than themselves, they might survive long enough to make a difference.

Fleche shuddered as if someone were beating a rhythm on her hull. "Aft of us," Desjani told the others. "They're shooting up the area around the navigation compartments."

A long pause, then *Fleche* shuddered again, this time throughout her length, as if spasmodically attempting to return to life.

"Zombie ship," someone muttered nervously, earning a scattering of edgy laughter.

"Grapples," Master Chief Milam told everyone. "They're going to dampen the motion of this ship so they can send boarding tubes across."

Fleche jerked, fighting the Syndic tethers, but her twisting movements eased, smoothing out.

A close-set series of heavy thuds caused *Fleche* to quiver. "They've attached the boarding tubes," Master Chief Milam said. "My guess is two of them aft of us, but I could feel another one hitting near here. You called it right, Lieutenant. Any minute now."

The passageway flared white with brilliance as Syndic breaching charges dissolved a big square of hull material. Tanya's face shield automatically darkened to protect her vision, then just as swiftly cleared to show figures in suits not too different from her own bursting out of the breach.

"Fire!" she yelled, pulling the trigger on her slug thrower and feeling it jam her backward against those with her.

The Syndics boarding the light cruiser here had expected to meet some defenders. They had not expected to meet a solid plug of defenders, all firing down the passageway at those storming aboard.

The first wave of boarders died under that concentrated storm of fire, the Alliance volley going onward to tear into those behind them.

"Go!" Tanya cried again, a wild elation swamping her fear as the mass of Alliance sailors surged forward. "Go! Go! Go!"

She had meant to lead the charge, as she had been told an officer should, but as the welter of bodies stampeded forward Tanya found herself falling behind the leaders, those in front firing wildly as they swamped the rest of the Syndics boarding here. Some Alliance sailors fell, but not enough to slow the charge. Then the counter-attack was in the three-meter-wide tube the Syndics had attached to the *Fleche* at this point and was rushing onward toward the opening at the other end.

As it turned out, not being one of the first sailors to reach the Syndic ship saved Tanya's life.

Syndic standard procedure called for sentries to be posted at the entrances to their own ship offered by boarding tubes, and if the Syndics could do nothing else they excelled at following standard procedures. Surprised and off-balance as the counter-attack hit them, the sentries nonetheless held their ground, firing at and killing the Alliance sailors in the front of the charge. The Syndics kept shooting until literally overrun and wiped out by the Alliance sailors.

Tanya slumped against a bulkhead inside the Syndic heavy cruiser, gasping for breath and staring at the dead sailors from both sides. On this living ship she had gravity under her feet again, something which helped steady her emotionally as well as physically. "We have to keep moving. We need to hit them while they're still reacting to our attack so we can take as many of them with us as we can. Master Chief, good luck."

Milam paused to bring the fingertips of one hand to his brow, and she realized he had saluted her, a gesture almost lost to the fleet though still followed by the Marines. She awkwardly returned the mark of respect, but Master Chief Milam was already racing out of the compartment with about half of the surviving Alliance sailors in his wake.

They could not take this ship, but enough Alliance sailors heading for engineering might be able to get access to the heavy cruiser's power core, might be able to damage it, before the Syndics could stop them by bringing the boarding parties back from *Fleche* to reinforce the Syndic defenders of this heavy cruiser.

That required a two-pronged assault. Milam was leading half the Alliance counter-attack toward the power core where he had the knowledge to do the most damage in the shortest time, while Desjani would lead the rest of the sailors to block as much as possible the return of the Syndic boarding parties, protecting Master Chief Milam's flank and rear. The odds of success were impossibly long, but trying it beat dying without attempting anything.

Or so it had seemed amid the wreckage of *Fleche*. Now, as Tanya looked at those remaining with her, many clutching weapons taken from dead Syndics, she had to struggle to keep her fears from overwhelming her.

She ordered a dozen sailors to hold this position. Names and faces Tanya knew. "Good luck," she said, knowing how meaningless the words were since the dozen would all soon be killed here. "Hold off the Syndics as long as you can when they try to reboard their own ship."

"We'll die with honor," a petty officer said in a tight voice, hands gripping a captured Syndic pulse rifle.

"You will." Not knowing what else to say, Tanya turned to the rest of her sailors, their numbers much diminished by those who had gone with the Master Chief and the twelve who would stay at this spot.

"Let's go," she managed to get out through a ragged throat, then led her group along the inside of the heavy cruiser near the outer hull. "Set your survival suit guidance displays to project the deck plans for a Syndic heavy cruiser. If you get separated from me and the others, keep heading aft toward where the next boarding tube is most likely to be."

She was in the lead this time, through a series of hatches and short passageways alongside the outer hull of the Syndic warship, some of her sailors peeling off to take slightly different routes.

The sentries guarding the next boarding tube over were startled to be hit by attackers coming from the side, above, and below. But one of the Syndic boarding parties was already coming back in response to alarms from their ship, arriving seconds after the Alliance sailors, and the compartment rapidly clogged with bodies locked together as they fired point-blank at each other. Tanya found herself jammed next to a Syndic officer who was twisting to fire on her. Tanya fired first, her hasty shot clipping the front of the Syndic's face shield and shattering it.

For a moment, a bare instant, Tanya looked directly into the eyes of the Syndic woman. Eyes very much like her own, eyes reflecting confusion and determination and fear, eyes changing in that instant to fill with dread as the Syndic's mind grasped that she would surely die in the next second.

Tanya's weapon had automatically chambered another round. As she stared into the Syndic woman's eyes her finger twitched spasmodically on the trigger, the impact of the shot hurling the woman away from Tanya.

She became aware that the fighting had stopped and looked around. All of the Syndics were down. "How many do we have left? I see...eight?"

"Nine, Lieutenant," someone gasped. "And you."

They would never take another boarding tube with those few. How many tubes were left? One? Two? The Syndic boarding parties must be storming back aboard everywhere else, aiming to intercept Master Chief Milam's group as well as sweep up Tanya and her remaining sailors.

"Lieutenant!" The tone of voice was urgent but the volume over the suit comms was weak. "This is Cahalan at the first tube! They're hitting us! We're—"

Tanya waited a few seconds, then called back. "Petty Officer Cahalan. Reply. Petty Officer Cahalan."

Nothing. The small force left to hold the first Syndic boarding tube had died holding their ground.

She was trying to decide where she and the sailors still with her should die when her suit's comm circuit lit off again. "Lieutenant?" The voice was even weaker than Cahalan's had been, riddled with digital static, but recognizable.

"Master Chief Milam? Where are you?"

"We made it to the power core. Six of us."

She fought back tears. *Ancestors forgive me. Only sixteen left, and none of us for long.*

"Lieutenant," Milam was continuing, "I have enough time here to manage a partial core collapse. I'm setting it up as I talk to you. I have to override remote signals from the Syndics and local safeguards, which I can't do well enough to achieve a core overload. A partial power core collapse won't destroy this Syndic ship, but hopefully it will blow out the aft end."

"Do it and get back here!" If the Master Chief could get to this compartment before the core collapse, if they could fight their way back to *Fleche*—

"Can't do it, Lieutenant. Not a chance we'll make it out of here alive. Even if the Syndics weren't on top of us we'd have to stay to hold down the overrides and cause the collapse. This was always a one-way mission. We knew that. But the Syndics coming for us will catch the collapse, too. They'll make a nice honor guard for me when I meet my ancestors, huh?"

She couldn't say anything, could only stare sightlessly ahead. *I knew he wouldn't get out. I knew none of us would get out. But I didn't realize he would have to stand there physically holding down safety overrides until the core collapse killed him.* "Master Chief...may the living stars welcome you with every honor."

"You, too, Lieutenant. You did damned good. You've done all you can. Get back to *Fleche*. There's a chance she'll still be intact after we blow out this core. Maybe some of you will make it after all. If you do, please let my family know I died with honor."

"I will." From somewhere an odd thought emerged. "If you see Black Jack, tell him to get his ass back here. We need him."

"I'll do that. Goodbye, Lieutenant. They're knocking hard on the hatch and I'm setting the final collapse sequence. You got maybe one minute."

She wasted a couple of seconds of that minute pulling herself out of shock, then glared at her remaining sailors. "Back to *Fleche*! As fast as you can move!"

Gravity vanished again as they jumped into the Syndic boarding tube to return to *Fleche*. She had to fight down an irrational sense of abandoning Master Chief Milam and those with him. Staying, fighting, would make no difference at all. But still she felt sick at leaving him and the others behind, and repeatedly reached to check her motion. Each time, Tanya fought back the impulse. *Save the ones with me. Maybe I can still do that.*

Were there any Syndics still on the Alliance light cruiser's remains? They had surely had time to learn there was no hypernet key aboard. There would have been no reason for any Syndics to stay, and doubtless frantic orders to get back to their own ship to deal with the crazy Alliance counter-attack. But that was no guarantee no Syndics were waiting for them. Tanya held her weapon in a death grip as she shot out of the boarding tube back onto *Fleche* and looked around frantically for danger. Only wreckage and drifting bodies were visible. "To the far side of the ship! Away from the Syndic ship! Move!"

They were still going in that direction when a huge fist slugged the wreck that had been *Fleche*, hurling the light cruiser's broken carcass away from the Syndic heavy cruiser, breaking loose the boarding tubes, and bashing Tanya and the sailors with her against surfaces that had suddenly accelerated toward them.

One of those surfaces crashed into Tanya's survival suit helmet. She had an instant to wonder if she would see the light of the living stars beckoning to her through the dark as blackness filled her mind.

"Lieutenant Desjani?"

Tanya jerked into wakefulness, startled to see above her the tangled mass of conduits and cables that marked the overhead on an Alliance warship.

She looked over, seeing a chief with a physician's insignia on her breast. Tanya didn't recognize the chief, but from her surroundings Tanya was in a bunk in a crowded sick bay. The chief checked some read-outs, nodded and turned to speak to someone else. "She'll be fine."

A man wearing commander's insignia came into Tanya's field of vision. He extended a hand toward her, smiling. "Lieutenant Tanya Desjani. I'm captain of the *Hauberk*. May I shake your hand?"

"What?" Tanya tried to unravel her tangled thoughts. *Hauberk* had been one of the surviving heavy cruisers. "What happened?"

"What happened was that you took out that last operational Syndic heavy cruiser. Blew her butt off and left her helpless. After that, *Hauberk* and *Utap* had the time to get enough systems fixed for us to move in and wipe out the two Syndic ships disabled during the battle and what was left of the heavy cruiser you crippled. Thanks to *you*, Lieutenant."

"Me?" She had automatically extended her hand and the captain of *Hauberk* now pumped it enthusiastically.

"You. By my ancestors! Attacking under those circumstances! Black Jack himself must have been by your side."

"I didn't see him," Tanya said without thinking.

"Of course you didn't, Lieutenant Desjani, it was his spirit that was with you. I'm putting you in for the Alliance Fleet Cross. You deserve it if anyone ever did. If there was a higher award I'd put you in for that. You avenged *Fleche*, you saved *Hauberk* and *Utap*, and you enabled the Alliance to hold onto this star system. Of course, you also saved the rest of your crew. After we finished off the Syndics we checked the hulk of *Fleche* to see if anyone was still alive aboard her and brought you and the other nine off."

Nine. Out of two hundred thirty five. "Master Chief Milam—"

"He'll be put in for the Fleet Cross, too. The others from *Fleche* told us what happened, what the master chief did, what *you* did." *Hauberk*'s captain grinned. "Black Jack himself couldn't have done better. Your ancestors must be very proud."

He shook her hand again and left, saying he had a lot of repair work and wounded crew members to check on. Tanya laid back, her eyes on the overhead, trying to feel something. Pride, relief, surprise. Anything. A darkness still seemed to fill her, a darkness in which familiar faces now never to be seen again in life appeared briefly before vanishing.

The chief she had seen before came up beside Tanya, slapping a med patch on her arm. "That'll help, Lieutenant."

"I thought you said I was fine."

"Your body is fine. Your head...that's going to take some work."

Feeling finally came. "They died. Everybody died. I was in command and they died."

The chief looked down at Tanya somberly. "From what I understand, they all would have died no matter what. As it was, they saved a lot of other lives with their sacrifice. And they're not all dead. You got nine of them out. And you. That's ten people who should have died, who by all rights should be among their ancestors now, and aren't. Because of you. And the escape pods you launched with your badly-wounded on them. We've been over-whelmed by the casualties. We couldn't save every one and not all of them lived until we managed pick ups of the pods. But sixteen of those will live, too. You know if the Syndics had won here they wouldn't have bothered to save your wounded."

Twenty-six, then. That ought to have helped. It didn't. "How many died here? On all of the ships?"

"I don't know, and if I did I wouldn't tell you. Lieutenant, it's what we do. It's what we have to do. They attacked us, a long time ago. They keep attacking. We have to fight."

"We have to fight," Tanya echoed. "Kill them. Just keep killing them." One vision filled her mind now, the memory of the eyes of the Syndic woman who had looked at Tanya and seen death. Tanya knew she would never forget those eyes. "It's all we can do. Kill them until they stop. Kill them until they stop making us kill them."

"I guess so. I wish there was some other plan, but I don't know of one."

Tanya thought of the captain's words. "We don't need another plan. We need Black Jack. Somebody like him. If he'd only come back..."

"Well...maybe. It's been almost a century now. If he was coming, he ought to have made it by now."

Tanya locked her eyes on those of the chief. "He'll come back. He'll hurt them badly enough that they'll finally give up."

The chief looked down at Tanya. "Wouldn't he try something else? If it's about nothing but killing, that would be like the Syndics, wouldn't it?"

"We're not like them! We're only killing because we have to!" But de-spite her insistence the chief's words still stung. "What else can we do?"

"I don't know, Lieutenant. I wish to hell I did. Maybe Black Jack will come back some day, maybe he'll know what else we can do. I sure don't. You get some sleep now. You'll get meds, you'll get therapy, and you'll be able to go back to fighting and help end this war."

Grief and despair forced the words from her. "I can't end this war. Maybe no one can end this war."

The chief hesitated, looking uncomfortable. "Maybe not. We do what we can. You did good. A real hero. You saved a lot of Alliance lives. Remember that."

Tanya felt sleep stealing over her as the meds took effect. The eyes of the Syndic woman looked back at her, not seeing a hero, not a saver of lives, but death. *If death is what I must be, I will be that. As long as I have to.*

Death to the Syndics. Until real heroes like Master Chief Milam don't have to die fighting them anymore. Is there another answer? Ancestors, please beg the living stars to tell us. Tell us if there is something to strive for besides being death.

She fell into darkness again, this time the shadows of sleep.

Tanya dreamed of Black Jack. She saw him sleeping. She couldn't see his face clearly, but she knew it was him. Instead of basking in the glow of the living stars he lay surrounded by darkness and a sense of cold that struck at Tanya. Despite that, she knew that he was not dead. She yelled at him to wake up, to come back and save them. But Master Chief Milam shook his head at her, gesturing Tanya to be quiet, giving her the fleet hand sign that meant *wait*. She watched Black Jack and Master Chief Milam fade away, watched everything fade into the darkness, and could remember nothing else from her dreams when she finally awoke to once again face the reality of a war to which she could see no end.

HARD CHOICES
Bud Sparhawk

TANG THOUGHT THE ASSEMBLY ROOM WAS COLD AND STERILE. AT THE FAR END was the body of a cybermarine. It looked like a large man, slightly inclined backward, and was connected by thousands of wires to an armature covered with mechanical arms, legs, and even a head with a half dozen eyes.

The other room, the place where the brains were dissected, diced, and turned into code for insertion into the gel "brains" of the cybermarine's new body, was something he'd only viewed once. He had no desire to repeat that experience.

"It's not activated yet," Doctor Mores said when he noticed Admiral Tang staring. "Those are just remote units. We'll use them to familiarize the inductee to his new augmentations. It is only after he learns how to use his new motor skills that we enable the equivalent parts of his new body."

Tang nodded. He'd been in this room several times as the other cyber-marines had been activated. His presence was partially as expiation for his guilt in approving the conversion and partly to give each man a morale boost. He wanted each volunteer to know that they had earned the respect of the highest level of command.

While that had been his primary motivation, he thought it was bloody neat to watch when the marines realized the awesome capabilities and power of their new bodies: a cybernetic heart-lung pump that allowed them to operate in any atmosphere or even underwater; augmented muscles on *legs and arms that bulked them up like cartoon giants on steroids; amped vision that ran from the near infrared up toward the UV range that could switch to monochromatic high key for better night vision, and smart-metal skeleton to provide a good base for those massive muscles. A cybermarine's skin was impervious plas. Their hands electro-mechanical marvels capable of ripping weapons-grade plating off a spaceship, yet flexible enough to handle any weapon.*

Their awakening was like watching a birth.

A week earlier Admiral Tang had been brooding over the pile of folders on his desk. He'd quickly learned upon being promoted that his choices became more difficult, and not only because he was working over a broader canvas. The difference between the decisions he'd learned to make earlier in his career and the ones he now faced were qualitatively different. No longer could he concern himself with his squad, his company, or battalion. No, now he had to deal with issues of economics, logistics, politics, and of why the hell it took so damn long to get something done once a decision had been made.

He breezed through the pile, reading the summaries and ignoring the dense sets of references and attachments. *My aides can sort through this stuff,* he thought idly and then realized that they already had—these were just the issues they felt were important enough for him to see. He flagged a few for later discussion, signed a half dozen, and sent the rest of them to be handled by Vice Admiral Gould. That's what his deputy was for, wasn't it?

The morning reports had been grim—insufficient civilian evacuations and four Navy ships lost in the brutal battle at Ginck's Follt. Worse, too few of the damned alien bastards had been destroyed and none captured.

He ran his hand through his thinning black hair: Capturing one of the Shardie ships was the Navy's primary objective. But every attempt had cost ships and lives. The aliens were an implacable enemy. Simply surviving an encounter with them was considered a success.

The alien ships were unbelievably maneuverable, accelerating at rates far in excess of any known technology. The hope was that capturing an intact ship might reveal its secrets and allow Earth's forces to gain some sort of parity. But there were usually no disabled ships with intact drives—any enemy damaged always made a suicide run, turning them into scattered bits of crystal and...other things.

Only one damaged ship had been found and on it were reduced humans, their brains linked to whatever commanded the ship. That was how the aliens were able to anticipate human tactics: Knowing how your enemy thought was a damned smart way of gaining advantage.

Tang felt a shiver of revulsion at his memory of those agonized souls woven bloodily into the guts of that captured ship. The human brains were being kept alive, conscious, and wired into the ship's guts by a cat's cradle of thin glass threads. It was a mercy that someone had killed them to end their suffering. Since that gruesome discovery the overriding policy had been to deny the enemy any access to human bodies through evacuation and other means.

There were not enough Navy ships to defend all of the colonies, insufficient marines to try to set up ground-based defenses that did little more than provide assurance to the colonists. In a real attack even a full regiment of marines would be as useful as a toilet paper umbrella in a rainstorm.

He'd hoped for better news at every dismal briefing, but the facts were distressingly the same. If they couldn't stop the Shardie's implacable advance it was clear that the human race was heading toward extinction.

Things were no better on the diplomatic side: You couldn't negotiate with an enemy who failed to communicate, who failed to express intentions or purpose, and who attacked with insane ferocity at every encounter. The aliens were clearly sentient, technological, and obviously saw humanity as something to be eliminated. Was it hatred? If they shared at least that much, that sort of unbridled emotion with humanity it could be an opening to understanding, but they had given no sign. Attack, attack, attack seemed to be their entire repertoire.

The human race was losing the war.

"Status update in five minutes, sir," his aide announced and swept away everything except the précis of the proposal from the conversion team, allowing him a glimpse of what would be discussed so he would not look uninformed. That was another problem with his position—he never had enough time to grasp the whole of anything. His days were filled with a series of brief, but imperfect summaries of serious matters on which he was supposed to make command decisions. Were it not for the staff work and analysts' reports that crystallized the issues on possible consequences, he'd not be able to function. As it was, he was forced to rely on these snapshots, these products from people whose biases and perceptions could easily mislead him to bad decisions by making them appear proper, logical, and necessary.

He sighed. What he wouldn't give for a few days to delve deeply into a single issue and come to his own conclusions. But he knew he'd never get those days and, even if he did, he would probably lack the background and technical knowledge necessary to do the proper analysis for a good decision. He was damned if he did and damned if he didn't—the curse of command.

He rose and entered the briefing room.

"We're resurrecting Gunnery Sergeant Hollis Jackson," Mores informed them. "The body he'll be using is our latest design; lighter but more rugged." He nodded to where technicians were fiddling with the body. Mores beamed. "To Jackson, it will seem as if he just came out of surgery, awakening for the first time."

His deputy read off the briefing sheet. "Jackson was originally converted ten years ago. He was assigned to one of the early recovery teams. Managed to deny the Shardies access to a bunch of farmers and blew away some of their ground troops. Got a posthumous, it says here."

Tang remembered the mission if not the man. He hoped that someone on the command staff had attended Jackson's funeral. It would have been the least they could have done as they buried his true remains. "Will he be able to speak?" he asked.

Mores nodded. "We've trained him enough to operate his vocal cords, although they really aren't…"

"Spare me the technical details. All I want to know is if he can answer a question."

"Yes, he can do that, but it will be a synthesized voice and not his…"

One of Tang's aides was gesturing furiously from the other side of the room while Colonel Mill tapped her foot impatiently. "Let's see it. I only have ten more minutes before we have to leave."

"I didn't realize we were so time constrained," Mores complained. "We have to run some checks before we initiate this instance."

"Checks you should have done before the Admiral got here, Doctor," Colonel Mill cut in. "Turn the damn thing on, for God's sake." A moment later she blushed through her scars and mumbled. "I didn't mean that, sir. Honest to God, I didn't think…"

"I understand," Tang answered. He was a bit surprised at seeing her reveal a spark of humanity, but knew where she was coming from. It was not easy to think of a cybermarine's body as anything but a "thing." That it was also a living human being could too easily be ignored.

"Sir." Colonel Joan Mill, head of combat effectiveness, snapped to attention as Tang entered the briefing room. She was of medium height, broad of shoulder, and had rather a nice ass, he mused as she took her seat. Nevertheless her vacuum-burned face and the rows of ribbons and combat tags showed that she'd seen more than her share of combat before joining his staff. She was sitting beside Hector Mores, his R&D chief.

Tang seated himself. "Shall we begin?"

Mill cleared her throat. "I won't try to soft pedal this, sir, but we've just learned that the Shardies have been making copies of their captives."

Vice Admiral Gould looked surprised. Obviously he had not read the file. "How the hell can they be replicating humans?" he asked.

"Probably the old-fashioned way," the Colonel guessed. "It's the brains they want, sir, not their knowledge or experiences. A kid's brain is probably sufficient for their purposes."

Gould appeared shocked. "That's disgusting. Breeding humans as if they were animals? Has this been confirmed? How do we know this?"

She pushed a folder marked TOP SECRET in fiery red block letters across the table. "That report contains the analysis of the human fragments that were found in the wreckage of the End Point battle." As Gould hurriedly scanned the contents Mill continued, "Analysis indicates that the fragments belonged to individuals who were not on any the captured lists."

"Are our databases that detailed, Colonel?" Gould demanded. "Couldn't the fragments have come from one of the earlier captives? Were the samples degraded by exposure to vacuum? That could provide false indicators." Tang said nothing, allowing his deputy to be the foil for the moment. He was certain that nobody would bring this to their attention without verifying the facts two, three, or more times.

"We only used fresh samples, sir." Mill answer grimly. "Gathering intelligence is not always a pretty process. We're positive of the results, sir. The immaturity of the chunks," she blushed. "Excuse me, sir. I meant tissues, not..., well, not what I said."

"I understand," Tang answered. "We all get inured to reality after a while. Please continue."

Mill recovered her composure. "The *samples* we recovered indicate that their owners had been born long after the war started and had a strong match to the DNA of the original colony. The range of ages, based on their telomere lengths, ranged from three to five years. Based on those facts we conclude that the breeding program started soon after they obtained their first captives."

"It's horrifying!" Steve Gould looked disgusted as he slapped the folder closed. "Humans shouldn't be bred like animals for God's sake! And making them into parts of ships turns them from living, breathing people into nothing more than mechanical relays, switches, or computer parts. It's not something any sentient race should do. It's sinful, breeding people for their unholy ships."

Mill nodded. "I don't disagree that we might consider it sinful, sir, but you've got to admit it's a pretty smart use of resources."

Admiral Gould glared, clearly on the edge of anger. "I can't believe you approve of this, Colonel."

Mill didn't flinch. "No, sir, I was merely commenting on the Shardie's efficiency. When you're in a war you use everything you have to win and it looks like that's what they're doing."

Gould didn't look like he was buying it. "Your attitude makes me want to puke. I'd expect more from a marine officer."

Mill smiled, but there was no humor in it. "I'm being realistic, sir. It is what it is."

Tang spoke up before the argument escalated any further. "What's the proposal, Colonel?"

Mill nodded to the doctor, who had said nothing up to this point. "As you've observed at the last weekly update, Admiral," Mores began. "Our volunteer conversion rate has continued to fall." An incomprehensible graph blossomed onto the screen. "The majority of our wounded marines are choosing radical rehabilitation instead of becoming cybers."

"Probably because of advances in medical treatment," Tang mused. "I don't blame them for that choice."

"There's still about thirty percent of eligible wounded who chose to die rather than live, even with advanced prosthetics," Doctor Mores continued. "Given the nature of their injuries, I'm not surprised. The amount of prosthetics these few need would make them more machine than man."

"Or *women*," Mill corrected softly and turned to Tang. "Admiral, unless we do something we are shortly going to be in trouble. In simple terms, our attrition rate exceeds production and we've gotten too close to being seriously understaffed with cybers."

As if Tang didn't already know that. Referring to the steady numbers of suicide missions he'd sent marines on as the "attrition rate" demeaned the substance of what happened. Men were dying in increasing numbers.

Tang looked at her scarred face and noted the barely noticeable strain of her facial muscles, the tenseness of her body, and the white of her fingers where she grasped the edge of the table. Clearly there was more to this briefing than a dry recounting of statistics. "Just how serious has it become?"

"We've only given life to half the number we had last year," Doctor Mores answered. "One-fifty and the trend is downward."

"We've expended two hundred in the same time period." Mill injected.

"Killed, you mean," Gould barked. "These *cybermarines* were men. They're marines who made the ultimate sacrifice, and did so after already proving themselves in battle. So don't use bullshit words like 'cybers' and 'expended' on me."

"I agree," Tang added. Gould tended to get overly enthusiastic at times and he needed to calm things down. "One can get rather removed from reality when dealing with statistics, Colonel. Please show a bit more respect."

"I've been in a few battles, sir," Mill replied. "I've worked with the cybers—that is, *augmented marines*—more than a few times. And Admiral," she turned to look directly at Gould; "Don't presume that I don't understand the sacrifices and difficult choices these volunteers make when they choose to convert. It's just that I find the abstraction easier to deal with when hard choices have to be made."

"Choices, Colonel? I assume that you have some reason for bringing up our declining strength?" Tang knew she was merely bringing the matter to his attention with that nice ass of hers and... He mentally kicked himself for even thinking that way. She was an officer under his command and any relationship, nor matter how innocent, was improper. Why he should keep thinking about her when there were a lot more cute young things around mystified him. She was well beyond the cute stage, but damn; she did have a nice bottom.

Another graph came on the screen, equally as dense and incomprehensible as the former. "As you know, Admiral," Mores began and Tang groaned inwardly. Why did all the technical people feel the need to go back to basics? As he yammered on and on about how desperately wounded marines at the threshold of death were offered the choice of dying or continuing to serve as a much-augmented fighting machine, but sacrificed much of themselves in the process.

"You have to understand exactly what is done," he continued. "We have to retain enough mental capability for them to function properly, enough humanity for them to understand the mission, and still have a dedicated sense of purpose."

"We know all of that," Gould said. "So what?"

The doctor coughed apologetically. "That's what everybody's been told and, as far as it goes, is perfectly correct." Tang knew what he was going to say. He'd read the classified briefings.

"What is not widely known is that we don't transfer all of a marine's memories to their new bodies. The artificial brains only have so much capacity and we have to limit ourselves to what is practical."

"That's made clear to those who volunteer," Mill said as if apologizing.

"But the rest of them isn't," Gould added. "Every cybermarine converted means a man has died."

"Yes, we only use one body per cybermarine," Mores added. "It is a restriction, an *artificial* restriction. Without that restriction I could produce as many cybers from a single volunteer as we need."

Tang grimaced. "Just run off a few mores copies; right?"

"It's possible," Mill confirmed.

"You can't be seriously considering making *copies*!" Gould leapt to his feet and began to pace. "The concept's a disgrace, an obscene idea. It's as horrifying as those poor souls linked to those ships. There's no way we can allow our men to be used that way. We'd be just like the fucking aliens if we did that."

"They've preserved partial scans of over two thousand volunteers," Colonel Mill said softly. "It would be a dishonor to destroy them."

"Also wasteful of resources," Doctor Mores added dryly. "We preserved the best, the most useful parts and, by using our inventory we could cut the hideously expensive conversion program by half."

Vice Admiral Gould shook his head. "Another bullshit word: 'augmentation vehicles,' indeed! I think that's a ghoulish suggestion, Doctor. How would *you* feel about being stamped out like license plates for God's sake?"

Mores didn't flinch. "As far as each resurrected individual is concerned they'd be unique, with no awareness that any other copies had preceded them. They wouldn't feel as if they had been used, other than as they volunteered to be, I mean."

Mill motioned the doctor to silence. "Admiral, look on this as way our brave marines could continue to serve, giving them the opportunity to continue the battle, to honor their commitment to the corps."

Gould objected. "That's a nice sentiment, Colonel, but would making copies be *right*? If each copy is a fully realized human being, an individual, then sending him to his death would be no more morally defensible than with any other human being."

"I don't know about right, but it would be far more efficient," Mores replied. "We could produce ten cybers in the time it now takes to convert one marine. Further, without the extensive medical procedures involved, costs of transport to the facility, and maintenance costs of those we have to keep alive long enough to process, we'd double our production without an attendant increase in costs."

"The Sergeant is ready, sir," Mores interrupted Tang's train of thought. "You can talk to him now." Despite Mores' supposed objectivity it was obvious that he had not fallen into the trap of thinking of this Jackson as an object.

"Yes, I'd like to talk to him." He stepped closer to the microphone. "Jackson? This is Admiral Carl Tang. How do you feel?"

"Fine, sir. Ready to do my duty, sir!" The response was crisp, his eagerness to serve obvious by inflection and emphasis. "Er, did you get promoted, sir?" Mores jerked.

Tang kicked himself. He'd forgotten that he'd only been a Colonel when Jackson was converted. "Yes, recently," he replied and saw the doctor's sigh of relief. "Do you remember who you are?" He'd almost said "what." Have to be careful about that.

"Gunny Jackson, sir, Hollis. Serial number 030586734...."

Tang didn't let him finish. "I meant, do you remember how you got here?"

There was a pause before Jackson answered. "I was almost dead when they offered me a chance to serve, sir. I was so pissed—excuse me, sir—so angry that I wanted a chance to get back at the bastards that...sorry, sir...at the aliens we were fighting."

"I can't believe this," Steve Gould exploded at Mores' suggestion. "You're talking about our volunteer's remains as if they were objects. We can't use human beings this way. We lose whatever moral advantage we have over the enemy."

"And where our morals gotten us so far?" Tang was only mildly upset with his deputy, who was becoming tiresome. But hadn't he thought the same thing when the idea had first been broached? Mill was right. They'd made a promise to each volunteer, a bond that had not yet been broken. It was a bond of honor, of remaining true to the oath that every marine took when they chose to serve. It was a large part of being a marine.

Mill spoke up. "If we did as Doctor Mores suggests we would be able to send a battalion of cybers to take back our colonies. Hell, with the augmented resources we'd have at our disposal we could send an entire regiment if we chose." She had obviously thought deeply about the immediate implications of this proposal.

Mores stuttered with excitement. "Admiral, we don't even have to limit ourselves to augmented bodies. The human form is highly inefficient for many combat tasks. We could as easily put the volunteers consciousness into more rugged machines—tanks, ships or..." his voice tapered off as he realized the line he'd crossed.

"Yes," Steve Gould said bitterly. "Put them in ships. Just like the Shardies."

"But these would be volunteers, no unwilling captives," Mill defended the doctor's position. "There's a moral difference here, Admiral. It's no different than giving our marines bigger weapons or having them drive an assault vehicle instead of being foot soldiers. In fact, it would enhance the present combat capabilities enormously."

"But still..." Steve Gould was unrelenting in his objections. "We've can't permit this abomination. There's principle involved!"

Mill smiled, but there was no humor in it. "Yes sir, I agree that we can stand on our principles. We can also ask the Shardies to chisel that on our tombstones."

Gould looked as if he were about to explode as Mill turned to Tang. "Sir, Admiral, we need to change the program and increase production. We've spent the majority of our wealth on evacuations and recoveries because we haven't enough ground forces to defend ourselves. We need to increase the power of our fighting forces." She looked at Gould, "Sir, this isn't a matter of ethics or economics; it's about our survival as a race. We need those troops."

Tang could not deny the appeal of having a large army of supermen at his command. Instead of parsing them out piecemeal to each ship, they could load entire transports with cybers and mount massive assaults against the alien's ground forces, assaults that they neither had the manpower nor opportunity to pursue at present.

"I agree," he said before Gould could argue the point. "The truth of the matter is that we are losing the war and have to do something, however distasteful it might be."

"And why did you choose to become a cybermarine?" Tang continued his questioning of Jackson. "You were given other options."

There was no hesitation. "You mean death or life as a cripple, sir?" Jackson snapped back. "Not a great choice, but even so I'd rather be helping my mates, serving beside them than sitting on the sidelines waiting for the enemy ships to arrive. No, sir, there wasn't any other choice for me. Serving in the marines is all I have left. The only thing that gives me purpose."

"That's very noble, Sergeant, but what about enjoying life; fishing, hunting, playing ball with your kids..." Tang stopped. There was no chance Jackson would ever have kids, "...or enjoying a fine meal?" he finished with nary a pause and realized how stupid those last words sounded.

"Those things are for civilians, sir. I've been given this new life and I'm damn well going to use it to kill as many of the aliens as I can. I'm a marine, sir. I'll do my duty."

The aide motioned furiously. It was time to leave. "Thank you, Sergeant. You've answered my question."

Tang sometimes wished some decisions had landed on someone else's watch, someone with more balls, someone with less consideration of the long-term effects that might result from those decisions. Someone without principles.

Since taking command he'd had to send eighteen squads to certain death and approved a dozen more of the expensive zombie conversions. He jerked his mind away from that outdated terminology. It was a remnant of his less tolerant past, back when the first cybers had been introduced.

Now he sent cybermarines on recovery missions; suicide missions, actually. That none returned from these weighed heavily on his soul, just as did every decision that cost the life of any other marine. It mattered little that the only reason for the original conversions were to give seriously wounded marines yet another chance to serve, just as Hollis Jackson had so strongly stated. Jackson's answers proved he was still a true marine, filled with fighting fury and dedicated to his role, despite the fact that he was unknowingly a copy of the other Jackson who had already died twice. The hard choice of sending cybermarines to certain death had always left Tang with a burden of guilt. He carried that proudly, aware that it was part of being in command.

But Joan Mill's proposal could change that. He imagined that he would still feel somewhat guilty about each suicide assignment, but that guilt would be mitigated by the knowledge that the same marine could be resurrected and rise to fight another day as if it were for the first time. If this program went forward he'd no longer be sending cybermarines to a final death but giving them the opportunity to fight again and again, and yet again in numbers beyond imagining.

The concept was both exciting and horrifying. Pursuing this program might help win the war but at what cost?

He turned to Gould. "Steve, you called these additional conversions sinful. When did you get religion?"

Gould turned away. "It wasn't a religious objection. It's about ethics, a matter of respecting human beings as individuals instead of pieces on a chessboard."

"Nonsense. We think of our marines the same way when we plan missions. They're all just pieces on a game board at that level, not individuals. These duplicates wouldn't be individuals at all—they'd just be copies of men who volunteered to serve honorably and to the extent of their capabilities— capabilities, I should remind you, that are well beyond those of any ordinary marine."

His deputy wasn't about to accept that facile argument. "They might be copies, but as far as each one of them is concerned, they are the original, with all the hopes and dreams of their precursors." He leaned forward, intent on pressing his point. "Jackson said that he'd fight for life just like every other marine and die knowing that he'd have given his best. He might be a copy, but he is damn well human where it matters. And matter it does! We made a social compact with our men and need to honor it, not treat them like a bunch of disposable units."

Although Tang agreed with much of what Gould said, he knew there were more important issues: declining troop strength, the failure of any progress on the political side, the reduced capability of the Navy, and the general acceptance that their backs were to the wall.

No, this wasn't a situation where Gould's appeal to humanity was relevant, not when it was a matter of how the human race could continue to fight and survive in the face of an overwhelming force.

"We need to put a stop this," Gould insisted as he rose to leave. "I'll tell Mill and Mores that we'll have no part of this."

Tang knew his deputy's philosophical objections, but they both had to put those aside and do what was best. As Colonel Mill had said earlier, this was a matter of survival. He carefully put his cup back on the tray. Sharp and capable as he was, Gould was still only his deputy. "I think that decision is mine, Steve. I think the decision is mine."

Jackson's answer had shown Tang that he needed to make the decision. Mills had been right about this. Her proposal was more than merely making copies. It would allow the preservation of that sense of honor, that sense of mission, that desire to serve to continue beyond death that was at the core of every volunteer. Each copy would allow the resurrection of all that is noble and good about each marine. It would let them continue to be true to the oath they all took. The men who made the hard choice to become cybermarines were those whose sense of purpose and dedication to the Corps exceeded all others.

Copies they might be, but they were more than human in all that mattered.

"I'm going to approve the proposal," Tang said to his appalled deputy. "Repugnant and sinful it might be, but by damn it's the right thing to do." He had, like Jackson, made the hard choice. "It's a matter of survival."

"But at the cost of our souls, sir," Gould said angrily. "At the cost of our souls."

THE TIGERSHARK

Peter Prellwitz

Earth date: July 22, 2230

With a loud clang, the matte black gunship sealed to the vertical airlock landing surface. The captain and four crew didn't even flinch. They were too experienced and battle worn. To them, the welcome thud of a docking was the ring of freedom and a much-earned rest, however brief. The ship vibrated as the deck swiveled orientation from wall to floor, the large outside airlock door rotating with it so as to make a pressurized hanger. Gravity plating in the ship and hanger worked together seamlessly, causing no loss of balance.

"Welcome to Aurora Station, *Tigershark*."

Captain Pamela Carlson tapped her chair's command pad and accessed the comlink.

"Thank you, Aurora. Are my repair crews standing by?"

"Affirmative. How long this time, Captain?" Pamela had garnered a reputation for staying in port as short a time as possible. To her way of thinking, the longer she kept her gunship in port, the longer it would take to end the Troid Piracy War, already in its sixth year. She twisted in her chair and looked over at her chief—and only—engineer.

"What's your estimate, Mal?"

At twenty-seven years of age, Mahlon Stewart was the grizzled veteran of the crew. He was considered one of the best engineers in the fleet.

"I'd like a refit of number two dorsal vent. And I'm nervous about the grid slippage we picked up last week. Any more and we'll start losing thrust efficiency." He shrugged loosely, showing that his nervousness was anyone else's complete relaxation. "Other than that, maybe a day. Two if I can get it." Both knew he wouldn't.

"One day it is, Mal," Pam replied with a grin. She hit the comlink. "I want to shove off in fourteen hours, Aurora. Please get started immediately. *Tigershark* out." She stood up and stretched—the only member of the crew short enough to be able to stand upright in the current gravitational orientation of the tight, sleek combat vessel.

"You heard it," Pam said out loud. "Fourteen hours to get drunk and sleep it off. Except you two, Gary and Janet," she added to her port and starboard gunners, who were just sitting up, swinging their legs off the "couch" each one lay on. Brother and sister, the Kersey twins had grown up in the Trojan asteroid field and their parents had informed them yesterday they'd hop the Hollow Stump company shuttle from the mining colony of Agamemnon and meet them on Aurora. "Brett. Mal. You're with me."

While Bret put the nav and comm systems into diagnostic from his chair immediately forward of her, Pam waited for Mal to drop out of the ship's belly hatch. She heard the stomp of feet on the hanger deck plating then slid her chair back two meters, shifting the hatch to the forward half of the ship. All about them, a dozen ground crew yanked coolant and fuel hoses to connect up to the ship, along with data links, power couplings, and all the umbilicals required to keep a combat ship at full operational status.

The *Tigershark* was among ITA's latest and greatest combat ships in the war. Protected by cutting-edge powered armor with burst counter-gravitational shielding, the fifteen-meter-long ship could withstand prolonged physical weapons fire and disrupt energy attacks to a fraction of their effectiveness. And she dealt far, far worse than could be inflicted on her. Eight laser mounts and missile racks provided conventional attack at short range or on surface targets, while sixteen compressed-plasma cannons not only worked at any combat range, the multi-colored flame ribbons of the prototype weapons also had a demoralizing effect on most targets.

But the *Tigershark's* biggest guns, the two hull lasers, were the most terrifying of all. Hull lasers were already the horror of the war, slicing through any and all armor with ease. The thin, traversing beam could destroy weapons, engines, and open ships up to deep space in an instant. The only saving grace of hull lasers was that even a single shot strained the power output of the attacking ship's engines, dropping the magnetic containment fields to dangerously low levels and making a second shot impossible.

Which is where the *Tigershark* became a truly feared opponent: her engines. Though based on time-tested, fusion-based technology, the creative use of new alloys and improved magnetics increased the efficiency and output by an order of magnitude, allowing for multiple firings, which also allowed for the twin hull lasers.

But while long and deep consideration was given to armor, weapons, sensors, and engines, crew comfort was almost an afterthought. Originally intended to be a forty-hour attack gunship, recent losses in the Interplanetary Transit Authority's fleet had forced Pam to keep her ship out for 200-hour patrols, constantly looking for the raiding ships that threatened the Earth trade routes to the outer planets' microcolonies and threatened Mars herself.

Pam's feet hit the station's deck plating with a solid thud, something she wasn't used to. The asteroid Aurora was 200 kilometers in diameter, making it one of the larger asteroids in the Belt. That meant nothing where gravity was concerned; it was the gravity plating that gave weight to Pam's mass. Mustering forty kilos at most, it felt more like a hundred after a week of near-zero g.

She stretched and yawned, then moved away from the hatch to let the other three off. Mal was already out and leaning against the airlock hatchway that led down into the base proper. He gave her a grin and winked, then nodded at the ship's port side above them.

"A little close, even for you, Cap'n," he drawled in his Vermilion accent; the one Pam had come to associate with wisdom and control in the years she'd known him. She'd lived on Mars her entire life, first in Enla in the northern hemisphere and then in Vermilion, in the southern hemisphere, and quickly came to love Vermilion's open attitude and frontier wildness.

She followed his gaze up and looked at the wicked furrow marring the ship's surface. They'd gone up against a tough Troid ship over near Siegena the day before yesterday and had beaten it only after five hours of fighting in and out of the Trojan field, doggedly frustrating all its attempts to escape. Brett had nailed it with a hull laser shot directly to its forward sensor display, opening the cabin up to space, but not before it got a final shot, the one that had raked the *Tigershark*'s port hull, carving a silvery four-meter long, four-centimeter-deep scar into the armor. Just below it were three Ceres Sabers insignia. This battle made four Ceres ships the *Tigershark* had destroyed. One more for the ace.

Pam winced at the damage to her ship, then approached Mal, having put it out of her mind. She was only twenty-one, but a tougher captain didn't exist. Born and raised on Mars, as Mal had been, she'd gone from the cream of Martian society to the dregs, then began the long journey up. Mal was one of the very few who knew Pam's original surname. And why she'd abandoned it.

She shook her head. Tired.

"Tuckered, Cap'n?" Mal said, interpreting her action correctly. "Me, too."

"Too tired to get drunk, old man?" she shot back. She always shared a drink with her crew upon their safe return to port.

"Nah. If I'm still breathing, I'm still ready to get drunk. My problem is that with just fourteen hours, either I get drunk or your ship gets fixed. No choice really."

"No choice," Pam agreed. "I'll have one for you."

Mal chuckled. She would, too.

"You do that, Cap'n. Send any sailor who bugs you my way. I can always use another pair of hands to clean the hull."

Pam laughed and descended the ramp to the station bar, The Wreck, with Brett and the twins following. At the bar entrance, the twins waved and continued on to the civilian-housing wing. They said something, but Pam couldn't make it out as the heavy vibrations and loud thumping pouring out of The Wreck muffled it.

"My treat, Captain," Brett yelled over the din. A quiet, compact man, at age twenty-two Professor Brett McKenzie had started teaching at Enla University on Mars, then signed on with ITA in the war's third year. A teacher of astral navigation, he had put his teaching to practice, proving his knowledge of his subject matter went far beyond books. He had probably the most promising future of the crew, Pam included. All she had to do was make sure he lived.

"Thanks, professor," she shouted back. "I'll take that drink after I check in with the admiral."

"Sounds good, Captain. I should be on the floor by then." He waved and entered, leaving Pam alone. They both knew he was the only one who didn't drink too much.

Pam continued a hundred meters down the brightly lit stone tunnel to the eledisc at the far end. There were two guards on station, who saluted at her approach. They were assigned to keep troublemakers from using the eledisc. ITA officers entered without challenge, but anyone else who attempted to use the eledisc got popped a shock.

Pam entered the eledisc and descended one hundred and fifty meters to ITA Central. Stepping off, she went along the right hallway which led to the gunship division. The walls—all native rock that had been cut and polished to an even shine—were covered with the names of the dead and holos of the ships they'd served on. With the advent of hull lasers there were many ships with their entire crews listed. Six of them were *Seawolf*-class gunships like hers; one-fourth of the two dozen so far built. Though the toughest ships in the ITA fleet, they were also the most recent. And new ships with new crews made for desirable targets.

Ensign Selvey, Admiral Chu Mong's administrative assistant, was waiting for her.

"Captain Carlson," he said, standing.

"Ensign," she replied. "Is the Admiral available?"

Admiral Mong was in and was available, so Selvey ushered her in.

"Pam!" Admiral Mong said, her voice both warm and tired. She rose and returned Pam's salute, then reached through the holo she'd been studying and gripped Pam's forearm in the familiar greeting between fellow Martians. "In port at last. Are you here for long?"

"Sorry, Admiral, but no. A fourteen-hour refit, then we shove off."

"Hmmm..." Mong replied. She looked thoughtfully at the holo before her, a map of the immediate area, then motioned for it to close before sitting down and opening her desk drawer.

"Whiskey?"

Pam flashed a smile that for a moment showed her young age, then nodded and seated herself. The Admiral pulled out a bottle and two glasses and poured a generous portion for each. They lifted their glasses.

"Victory!" the admiral declared.

"Or death!" Pam replied, finishing the corny ITA frontline toast. She took an appreciative gulp, then sagged back in her chair and let out a long sigh, staring at the ceiling. The admiral gave a quick chuckle.

"Not your normal demeanor, Pam. Hard patrol?"

Pam lifted her head and looked at her.

"On record or off?" she asked.

"Off."

"It was the toughest one we've had yet, Chu," Pam said flatly. "That Ceres ship was an unbelievably fast little bastard. Nimble, too. Mal said the only reason they didn't burn our asses off was because of their inferior gravity plating. He monitored their engine burns and said they weren't running over two-thirds power at any time; not even when they fired their hull laser. I don't know where they got that kind of power."

"Weapons?"

"Had a punch to them we haven't seen from any..." Pam broke off and sat up. "You know something, Chu?"

Her friend took a sip and set the glass down on her desk carefully.

"I do."

"On record or off?"

"Off, Pam. If I told you otherwise, we'd both be in big trouble. As in, shove-you-naked-into-an-air-lock-and-wave-goodbye trouble."

Pam nodded and set her glass down. "Then I guess I should pay attention so you don't have to repeat yourself."

Chu smiled at her friend and touched the holo display. The map popped up again between them. It showed the immediate area, centered on the base at Aurora and stretching out roughly 8au in all directions. She tapped out the locations of Earth, Mars, Jupiter, the planetoid Ceres, Aurora, and the asteroid Agamemnon, pulled along by Jupiter in the giant's L4 region. Pam narrowed her eyes and sat forward suddenly. Chu nodded.

"You see it then. Earth in the lead, close to Mars but far enough out to take away combat units based on its orbital station *Brutal Light*. Mars is behind Earth by two au's, with Aurora base the same distance from Mars, and Ceres almost directly between us and Mars. If ever the pirates wanted to make a significant attack on ships bound from Earth to Mars or Earth to the Jupiter outposts, the time is now. The principles in the war are all grouped up. The stars may or may not be aligned, but the planets sure as hell are."

"And Agamemnon?" Pam asked.

"Yes... Agamemnon." Chu touched two icons on the bottom of the holo and they shimmered, unlocked. "I need to step out for a few minutes, Pam. Let me just shut this display down. Classified and all that. I'm sure you understand."

Rather than close out the map or lock the documents, she instead came around the desk and went to the door. Her hand hovered over the door switch.

"Oops," she said quietly, and then left, closing the door behind her.

Pam was behind the admiral's desk in less than two seconds.

The Wreck was open, loud, and crowded, as always. A bar that started fifty years ago from the salvaged parts of a crash-landed freighter, it was one of the more rowdy bars in the belt. Some said in the entire system. To Pam, after eight days of boring duty followed by six hours of harrowing battle, it was just the thing.

Despite the packed conditions, Pam and her four crew members were seated at a round booth toward the back; one that became available the moment they'd entered. It was well known throughout the ITA and the fleets that you treated Pamela Carlson with respect. Three kills—now four—on the *Tigershark* and seven on the *Ice Wraith* earned Captain Carlson plenty of respect. And the half dozen broken bones dealt out to those offering her unwanted advances demonstrated she was willing to demand respect if it wasn't offered.

"Martian crew here!" Pam called out to one of the half dozen bartenders moving up and down the ten-meter bar. "So *real* Martian ale!"

A cheer went up from two-thirds of the people at the bar. Though Earth's population vastly outnumbered its Martian colonies, most of the fighters were Martian. Earth was protecting its trade routes; Mars was protecting its lifeline.

Drinks were served and Pam told her crew what she'd found out, not hiding any details or glossing over the conclusions she'd come to.

"A trap?" McKenzie asked, not hiding the disbelief in his voice. "ITA wants to set a trap for the Ceres Sabers in space? That makes all kinds of no sense, Captain."

"I'd agree, Prof," Mal replied. It was thirty minutes since Pam had finished examining the map and documents—coded, eyes-only memos— and hurriedly called her crew together, including Mal. The ship was still under repair and rearm, so they were meeting here. It was possible some- one was listening in, but Pam had never been one for paranoia, nor even excessive cautiousness, prudent or otherwise.

"I'd agree," Mal repeated, "unless the Sabers had a trap in mind too."

"And that's what ITA has determined, from what I read," said Pam. "There's a heavy freighter leaving from Earth orbit in two days, headed for Mars and then Aurora. It's hauling assembled engines as well as ample spare parts that have been built to take this new fuel mixture they've mined, refined, and blended in the Trojan Collective." She nod- ded at her gunners. "New fuel your father, Professor Kersey, created two months ago and we went up against in that Ceres fighter two days ago. ITA had found out they'd gotten their hands on some of the prototype fuel and the Sabers had marked the *Tigershark* as the target to combat test it against."

"Which was probably why we kept them from escaping," Mal put in. "They weren't interested in getting away, they just wanted to see if they could without actually doing it. They were more interested in seeing how much more power the engines could feed to the hull laser."

"ITA knew about this and didn't warn us," Brett interrupted. His tone seemed locked on disbelieving. Pam shrugged.

"Admiral Mong said ITA informed her they'd attempted to contact us but had failed. Whether it was true or not, it worked out for the better for us. Now we know what we're up against."

"Up against, Cap'n?" Gary asked. "How much of this fuel did they get?"

"It's not certain, other than it was a relatively small amount. Maybe one or two missions. But there's a shuttle from Agamemnon scheduled to reach Aurora in a few hours. It contains a modest shipment of the fuel, along with Professor Kersey, who is to begin research on duplicating and mass producing the mixture on other mining asteroids."

"Why Aurora and not just Mars, Captain?" Brett asked. "Not only is Mars more protected, it's currently a shorter distance."

"Shorter distance, yes. Better protected, not so much. ITA has stripped its patrols around most of Mars and the significant asteroid ports for an upcoming operation."

"Then that'd be a tempting target," Brett conceded. "Though I imagine that level of power output would burn out the fusion engines currently being used."

"Burn them out and then melt them when the magnetic containment is lost," Mal said. "Which is why this is turning into a perfect trap, 'cause the engines will be on the freighter from Earth and in the same area. Too much to pass up."

"Which ITA knows," Pam said. "And Ceres knows ITA knows. And ITA knows Ceres knows..." she broke off. "It gets kind of murky on how many we-know, they-knows there are. In any event, ITA has all the details planned out for all the details Ceres has planned out for all the details... well, lots more skullduggery layers."

"When does all this happen, Captain?" Janet spoke for the first time.

"In eighty hours," Pam replied.

"And we're part of the plan, I take it," Brett sighed with no enthusiasm.

"No, we're not," Pam said firmly. "Not even Admiral Mong knows what we're going to do, if anything. By the time she'd returned, I'd finished studying the whole thing and returned it to the way she left it. We finished our drinks and I left."

"So what are we going to do, Captain?" Janet asked.

Pam gave a slight smile.

"I'm thinking we'll head toward Earth and hook up with that freighter."

"Hook up?" Brett asked.

"Yes. Literally. If we can clamp onto their belly, go full mask, and cool down our engines, we'll essentially be a secret weapon. Then when the Ceres Sabers attack the freighter..."

"We'll detach and open up!" Janet interrupted. Of her four crew, only Janet shared the love of combat as much as Pam.

Pam shook her head. "No, we'll let the ITA fighters engage them. We'll wait for the third wave of Ceres Sabers to engage and then..."

"You mean second wave, Cap'n?" Brett corrected.

"Nope, I mean the third wave. Both ITA and Sabers have second waves. I'm betting the Sabers have three, so we'll wait for..."

"They could have a fourth wave, for as overly complicated as all this sounds," Gary observed.

"What is this?" Pam complained. "Interrupt the Captain Day? Let me finish!" Pam looked over at Mal, who just shrugged innocently and kept his mouth shut.

"That's better. Anyway, by the time the Sabers come in with a third wave, everyone will be busy killing each other off and NOT shooting at the freighter. Remember, the Sabers want its contents intact. They may try to open up the bridge to space, but that's risky during a pitched battle."

"So ultimately, the advantage is ours," Mal observed. "They won't destroy their target, but we can fire freely." He shook his head. "Hope it's enough."

"It'll have to be. The Sabers went out of their way to engage us. They probably assumed—maybe knew—that if that ship failed to destroy us, we'd have to put in to Aurora for repair and resupply, effectively taking us out of this operation."

"There are seven more gunships."

"Yes, Gary, there are," Brett countered. "But right now we're the ones the Troid pirates fear. We've got the reputation, the kills, and the captain to merit extra caution." He nodded his head at Pam. "Your pardon, Cap'n. No embarrassment intended."

"None taken," Pam chuckled. "Because you're right. But you left out best crew in the war."

"Yeah, yeah," Mal said. "We're all great and wonderful. And we can all be cut in two by a hull shot. So what's next on the game plan? I take it getting drunk is no longer on the list."

"It's off the list," Pam agreed. "We need to…"

Whatever Pam thought they needed to do next was expunged from consideration by a sudden, attention-seizing concussion, followed by a piercing strident tri-tonal alarm that cut through the conversation and merrymaking in an instant. The imminent attack alarm destroyed all sense of what passed for normalcy on a military base and instilled an adrenaline jolting desire to fight and survive.

The bar cleared out almost in an instant, every man and woman racing off with purpose and destination. Loud orders blared over the atmospeakers, but no one paid much attention; they already knew where they had to be and what they had to do to keep their home intact.

Pam and her crew waited at their table for the base personnel to clear out first. Pam would give everyone else the extra time needed to scramble to readiness; she knew her crew was always ready. They were a gunship crew; their place was in flight and in combat.

A minute passed before Pam took one last sip of her ale, then rose. Her crew stood and followed her at a brisk walk out of the Wreck and to the hanger where the *Tigershark* was no doubt being prepared for launch by a station crew that knew their most powerful weapon was about to put a whole belt of hurt on whomever picked this time and this target.

The tunnels vibrated as the base defense ships launched. It was a full-on attack by an as-yet-unknown band of fighters. Blended into the vibrations were the distant thuds of the anti-spacecraft rail guns. And still the alarm sounded, though much diminished in volume.

They passed through the hanger door, which thudded closed behind them, and made for the belly of the *Tigershark*. Activity in the hanger was fast-paced but with fewer personnel. As each finished their job, they ran to the air-lock that allowed entrance to the base. Mal passed them to enter the ship, followed by Gary, Janet, Brett, and finally Pam.

She slid her chair to command position and sat down. Systems positively identified her as the captain and a holofield surrounded her, allowing her access to all ship's systems through neural interface. Her fingers deftly flew over her comm channels, piloting and gunnery overrides, gravity plating efficiency, and multiple systems readouts. There came a deep boom from the plasma engine less than two meters beneath her feet, followed by a throbbing that was more felt than heard.

"Configure to Gazelle-class fighter mask," Pam ordered quietly.

Brett also plugged into the 'puter. Multiple holos appeared in front of him and copied to Pam's holos. He quickly glanced at several locations in the holo, then nodded his head. There was no change on the interior, but energy signatures and the shifting some of the hull aligned titanium to transparent now gave the *Tigershark* the appearance of the older style fighter.

The gunnery beds flickered on red and green lighting, with readouts and controls appearing in front of the two gunners, focusing and shifting in response to the commands given through the neural interfaces. Satisfied, Pam tapped the ready-to-launch alarm. The fast pace of the final half-dozen personnel in the hanger reached fever pitch and within ten seconds the hanger was cleared and sealed.

"Launch," Pam ordered.

There was no countdown, no communications, no wishes of luck or good hunting. The hanger platform rotated from floor to launch wall, the gravity plating rotating orientation with it. The wall took three seconds to slide up thirty meters to the gravity catapult and lock as the opposite wall opened to space. The catapult and the *Tigershark* exchanged launch codes, synched up in 5.4 attoseconds, waited one entire second to allow for human preparation, then fired.

The catapult reversed the gravity plating and shoved against the *Tigershark* with the equivalent of six hundred gravities while the ship pushed back with four hundred. The *Tigershark* erupted from the launch bay at over nine thousand meters per second, less than a hundred meters above the surface of Aurora. Within two seconds the ion thrusters had lifted the ship up to two hundred meters and reoriented the vessel to put the keel toward the asteroid surface. Within five seconds, the *Tigershark* had cleared the asteroid and Mal engaged the plasma engine, but only at ten percent, to keep in line with the older and slower Gazelle-class defensive fighter, of which Aurora still had a few.

"Opportunity fire," Pam said in a quiet tone. Both her gunners switched over to hunter-killer holopanels. The *Tigershark* was on the prowl. The first prey appeared with seconds.

"Contact," Brett announced. "Sixty-thousand kilometers aft and closing." The holos blinked and aft view showed. It blinked three more times to magnify and then they were easily seen; three R17s; typical fighters for colony defense in the asteroids. They were slow and clumsy, but well-armored. And since the war began, well-armed against anything other than a *Seawolf* class gunship.

"Take out the two flankers," Pam replied. "I want to see how the third one reacts."

Switching over to missiles, each gunner fired twice. There was a flash of light as the missiles' plasma engines ignited, then spilled out four blinding pools of light that faded and became two as they raced toward their targets.

The flank R17s veered, but they were too slow. Each took two missiles and disappeared in a silent ball of light, plasma, and debris.

The remaining R17 appeared to waver a moment, but then closed even faster. There were several blossoms from the hull as it opened fire with its own missiles.

"Incoming," Brett said. "Low-yield, short-range. Four second burn at most."

"Acknowledged. Boost to 450kps, evasive at burnout, and disengage mask," Pam replied, still curious as to the R17s intentions.

The ship surged forward, tripling in speed, then climbed to avoid the missiles which had now burnt out their plasma engines and could no longer change course. The R17 stayed doggedly on the *Tigershark*, firing two more missiles. Pam leaned forward, frowning. As she stared at the holo, a green and then red indicator lit at each edge. Both Gary and Janet had fired plasma cannons. A moment later, they fired again.

"Incoming," Brett announced. "Three kills, seven remaining and closing. Now nine."

"The mask is disengaged?"

"Yes, ma'am. We're flying our true colors." The gunners' lights flashed again. "Eight kills. Fourteen hostiles still closing, nine friendlies are attacking them."

"Hostile ship configurations?" Pam asked.

"Eight hostiles are P21s," the computer replied. "Four are R17s, two are unknown variants of S-class fighters."

"Something's not right, Cap'n," Gary said. "Not one of those ships has a chance against us. Not all of them together have a chance." He fired again and a kill was indicated. "This is a turkey-shoot, ma'am. I don't feel good about this."

Janet fired, then fired again. Two more kills. "I can live with it."

"Twenty hostiles now," Brett announced. "All about the same capability."

"What faction?" Pam said.

"Uh… Juno Mining Consortium. Freia Collective. Elpis Hardhats. There are even three from Vesta."

"And no Ceres?" Pam asked, already suspecting the answer.

"No, ma'am. No Ceres."

"Vesta?" Mal said over the comm. "That's on the other side of the system now. Captain, something big is going down."

"I know, Mal," Pam replied. "Brett, show me the position of the Agamemnon shuttle."

A blip showed up on the extreme edge of the main holo.

"That's not right," Brett said. He shifted his gaze and pointed several times, then zoomed in. "Captain, the shuttle is moving away from Aurora station." A series of crossed lines and equations popped up over the flight line. "She's moving at emergency flank speed!"

"They're the target," Pam concluded. "Mal, give me 1500 kps now. Brett, lay in an attack engagement approach. I want to come up from underneath. Gunners, configure and charge the hull lasers."

The dull throb of the plasma engines picked up to a trip-hammer pulsing. The hostile markers quickly fell behind as the *Tigershark* accelerated away, again on the hunt.

"Engagement in four minutes," Brett said.

"2000kps," Pam replied.

"Ninety seconds," Brett corrected.

"Hull lasers charged and ready in all respects," Janet reported.

"Very well. Helm, engage full mask."

"Engaging full mask, aye." Brett glanced over to three separate points, then tapped his physical console. "Hold on to your ale."

To anyone visually observing the *Tigershark* from the outside, the ship seemed to disappear as the entire hull of aligned titanium took a polarized charge from the engines. On sensors, too, the ship ceased to exist. Unsettling, to say the least. But to the captain and crew, it was more so. Each felt a tingling in their bodies, followed by an upset stomach, a mild but annoying headache, and the momentary blurring of vision. And then they were moving through open space, the *Tigershark* seeming to have gone off on its own, leaving them behind. Were it not for the various holo displays for four of them and the ever-present, ever-throbbing plasma engines for Mal, the experience would be terrifying.

"1200kps and alter attack vector to approach from top right quadrant," Pam said calmly. She was certain they were seen by the Troid ship prior to full mask. This would leave them guessing.

"Aye."

"So what are you thinking, Cap'n?" Mal asked. "This is the first part of the whole grand plan about attacking that freighter from Earth and kidnapping the shuttle?"

"I do," Pam replied. "If we're quick enough, we can kill the Troid ship trying to grab the shuttle and escort the shuttle safely to Aurora."

"That might change the rest of their plans about attacking the freighter," Brett commented slowly. "Which would end any thoughts of doing enough damage to shorten the war. We might be better off letting them take the shuttle."

"We might," Pam agreed. "But we're flying a gunship, not a desk. I'll leave the what-could-be to the admirals and take care of the what-is in combat."

"Damn straight!" Janet said. The others as quickly agreed.

Pam smiled and said nothing. She expected nothing less from a gunship crew; especially hers.

"We're at visual distance, Cap'n," Brett said, while bringing up the view and automatically magnifying to max.

"Very good. Gunners lock on target with hull lasers. We should take them out before... Damn!"

Even from nearly a hundred thousand kilometers, it was clear they'd been anticipated. Rather than tow the captured shuttle, and leaving themselves open to attack, the Troid ship had attached itself directly to the shuttle. As they watched, the pirate sent both themselves and the shuttle into rotation. Faster and faster they spun, making a difficult shot a near impossible one. Were it not for the gravity plating on both ships, they'd have been torn apart. As it was, the pirate had been able to seize control of the shuttle's plating and spin the ships, while maintaining a heading away from Aurora and the fast-approaching *Tigershark*.

Pam looked away briefly in bitter disappointment. She knew what she had to do. She looked back at the two ships. They were forming a near-spherical target, with only minor bulges along the outer edges.

"Target both ships," she ordered. "If they get away with that shuttle, they'll have more fuel and Professor Kersey. The attack on the freighter will become even more critical. And if they succeed, Mars will be cut off."

Silence. Finally, Gary spoke.

"Cap'n? I... I can't kill my own parents. I just can't."

"You don't have to, Gary. I don't want to, but I'll... do it," Janet said, her voice catching. "They'd want us to. Dad knows they'll torture Mom to force him to tell them how to refine that fuel. And they both know they're dead after that."

"And you don't have to either, Janet," Pam said softly. "I won't order anyone to kill a loved one if there's another solution. And there is." She paused then said, "I'll take the shot."

Janet turned toward Pam, a sheen of tears in her eye reflecting the green tint of the combat lighting. She nodded gratefully.

Pam called up her gunnery holo and switched guns to her chair. The main holo duplicated what she saw, the two ships in a lovers' tumble through space. Only now all the hull details were highlighted; the best points of fire marked in red overlays. They spun so fast as to be a blur. The computer worked out the optimum targeting to strike one of the weak points, but it hardly mattered: Their hull laser would slice both ships cleanly in two. If the crews on the ships were lucky, the laser would hit the magnetic conduits of the engines and they would be instantly vaporized.

The firing solution concluded the best shot and targeted a location where shuttle and pirate touched at midships. The area flashed blue, then expanded out to fill the entire holo before fading, leaving smaller, intense blue cross hairs. Left and right indicator bars reported fully charged hull laser.

"Drop mask," Pam ordered. Space disappeared, replaced by the opaque form of the hull. Pam made a split decision and overrode the targeting computer by pulling back. The crosshairs jumped to the edge of the two ships.

"Fire port laser."

A beam of blinding white touched with a flashing violet ribbon flowing around it connected attacker and prey in an instant. The beam traversed in a forty-meter sweep at the target, then flashed out.

"Target missed," the computer reported.

"Recharge port laser," Pam said coolly and adjusted the aim in slightly. "Fire starboard laser."

Visually, the same effects happened; the beam was unchanged, as was the sweep, as were the results. Audibly, it was very different. The healthy throbbing sound of the engines took on a distressed tone.

"Recharge starboard laser," Pam said without emotion.

"Captain!" Mal shouted. "Magnetic containment is down to forty percent! I recommend switching to missiles."

"Acknowledged." She drifted the crosshairs in slightly further. "Fire port laser."

A third time and a third failure. By now the throbbing had been replaced by a high whine.

"Containment at twenty percent!" Mal shouted. "Pam! If you fire again, we almost certainly lose all magnetic shielding!"

"Acknowledged," Pam said with not so much as a quaver. The crosshairs drifted in a little closer. "This is my final shot. I'm certain to hit one or both of the ships. But it's worth one gunship to end this war by saving that shuttle."

The starboard laser recharge toned ready and the crosshairs intensified. Pam took a deep breath...

And slowly exhaled. Perhaps one or both ships had shielding. Perhaps the pirate ship even had nano-repair capability. Either would have held off for a few seconds the truth that Pam's third shot had struck its target. But for a few seconds only.

The damage was catastrophic to the pirate ship. The cut hit just above the engines, slicing everything from stern to bow clean off the hull. The ships continued to spin, but even now the vessels were visibly slowing as the pirate's gravity plating released control of the shuttle's command system. The top half the pirate ship sheared off and tumbled away.

"Engines..." Pam stopped giving the order as she heard Mal cut engines to all stop and powered down the fusion reactor. The screech of the magnetic shielding quickly quieted and grew silent.

"And that's how you do it," Mal said. No one took him up on his comment, so he returned to nursing his engines back to health.

"Contact from Aurora, Captain," Brett said. "The pirates are breaking off their attack and making a run for it."

"Do we go after them?"

"Not today, Gary," Pam replied. "Today we put in for a three-day rest and refit." The twins looked over at her in surprise and delight. She smiled.

"I'm sure you two would like a little time to catch up with your parents. You know, see if anything interesting has happened to them recently."

COMMAND DECISION
John L. French

I T'S BEEN SEVENTY YEARS SINCE HAWKING SPACE WAS UNFOLDED AND TRAVEL BETWEEN star systems became possible. It's been forty years since the initial probes provided evidence of true Earth-type planets. And it's been three years since the Earth Ship *Phillimore* left orbit.

The *Phillimore*, like all deep-space vessels, was a prison ship, its crew made up of criminals who had been sentenced to death or to long terms of confinement. The Global Network's idea of efficiency. If the ship made it back, pardons for all. If not, no big loss.

Except to the crew, and to the officers who supervised them.

The officers were not the same as the crew. The crew was made up of thieves, murderers, political dissenters, environmental terrorists, and corrupt public officials. Just about every type of crime and criminal was represented except sex offenders. Under the Global Network they didn't live long enough after sentencing to be considered for space.

The officers were different. They chose to be on board.

My name is Jack Boone and I was one of them.

Why? Why give up fifteen to twenty years of our lives? It wasn't for glory or adventure. There's none of that in space, where every day is more or less the same – sleep, work your shift, and fill the time in between with reading, holosims, and other pointless activities. And it wasn't to fulfill otherwise meaningless lives. Most of the officers were like me. Back on Earth I had decent job in law enforcement, a nice home, and was involved in a relationship that more than met my physical needs.

So why give it up? For the most basic of reasons.

For the money.

The officers were being paid a small fortune, enough that if we made it back we could retire and live at ease for the rest of our lives. None of us would have signed on for any other reason.

A ship full of convicted criminals with a handful of officers to keep them in line. On the surface that was more dangerous than the mission itself. But only on the surface.

None of the crew had the skills or knowledge needed to operate the ship. Without her officers, the *Phillimore* would just continue on through the grey of Hawking Space, a soon-to-be ghost ship lost forever in the void.

At least, that's what the crew believed. We officers suspected otherwise, but that wasn't something we liked to think about. The crew's belief that officers were needed kept us all safe. That and the nanochips in their heads.

The chips let us track the movements and activities of the crew. If necessary, we could also briefly put them out, long enough to calm a crowd or disperse a riot. Some of the crew even believed that we could even issue a "kill order." We officers did nothing to discourage this mistaken belief.

Even with the chips there was trouble. Not the mutinous kind but the usual kind that comes from putting eight hundred people together for any lengthy period of time. Which is why many of the officers were former police officers like myself. On board we were the law and we kept the peace, just like on Earth.

Except that on Earth, there were judges, juries, and rules of evidence. On the *Phillimore*, we made the rules, we decided guilt and innocence, and we determined the sentences.

None of the officers cared what the crew did to each other, as long as it stopped short of serious injury, rape, death, or damage to the ship. Minor offenses resulted in loss of privileges or a period of confinement. More serious ones meant assignment to the nastier work details. The most serious, like deliberate damage to the ship, well, that's what the airlocks were for.

That's all they were for. The *Phillimore* was not designed to hook up with any other ship. All instrumentation was inside the hull, not on it. There was no need to venture outside. Going EVA in Hawking Space, even fully suited, meant a quick and messy death. The crew knew what offenses resulted in being put out. And after one or two of their number were sent through the one-way door, they knew that we were serious about enforcing the rules on-board the *Phillimore*.

We were still seven months out of 55 Cancri. Cancri-4 was a possible Earth-type planet that we were to assess for possible colonization. I was walking my usual beat—top level to the bottom, then back up again—when the alarm went off. Airlock 3 had been opened.

Command's voice sounded in my head. (Yeah, officers are chipped too, only ours are two-way and give us access to the ship's computer.)

UNAUTHORIZED EXIT. OFFICER BOONE RESPOND AL3

Why I was chosen I didn't know. Command didn't explain its decisions and we weren't encouraged to ask.

On Earth or in space, some things never change. By the time I got to Airlock 3, a crowd of gawkers had gathered. Most were crew, curious as to which of their number had been given the short walk. Some were officers, off duty and looking for anything to break the dull routine of their lives. At least the officers had enough sense not to approach the lock, as well as to keep the rest away.

Command had already sent that the scene was mine so all I got was a nod from one of my fellows and a "Need any help, Jack?" from another.

I shook my head. "Thanks, Karl, I got this. You guys clear the corridor for me."

They did and left me alone to investigate.

The inner hatch was closed. According to the display, the outer one was open to Hawking Space.

Computer I ordered through my chip, *close outer hatch without replacement* I didn't want what little evidence that might be left contaminated with Ship's air. Not that that mattered. It was all routine anyway.

DONE came a voice that was suspiciously like Command's.

Sample the chamber and analyze for biologicals

WORKING

While you're working, scan location records for this corridor prior to AL3 access

PERSONNEL NEAR OR PRESENT WHEN AL3 LAST ACCESSED—GRIFFIN CHURCH—CREW, ASSIGNED TO LOWER-LEVEL MAINTENANCE

Anyone else present?

NO

Scan records of access to AL3

RECORDS DO NOT SHOW AL3 ACCESSED BY ANY SHIP'S PERSONNEL

Yet the airlock was used

YES

ANAYLSIS OF TRACE BIOLOGICALS IN CHAMBER COMPLETE. SKIN CELLS, PERSPIRATION, BLOOD FOUND TO BE THOSE OF GRIFFIN CHURCH

Church was crew; he should not have been able to open the lock. And if somehow he had hacked it, why was there no record? Maybe there was a glitch in the system, maybe his hacking caused it.

Those were questions for the computer and Command to answer. I had only to observe and report, then go do my cop duty and ask the usual questions, not that I'd get any answers. There were just two more things to do.

Computer. Scan for onboard presence of Griffin Church

NO INDICATION OF GRIFFIN CHURCH ON BOARD

Access external monitors this location. Replay video starting just before the opening of AL3 outer hatch

The holosim started in my mind and I was on the outer hull of the *Phillimore*, staring at the outer hatch and past it into the grey nothing that is Hawking Space. At the bottom right of my field of vision was a countdown showing thirty seconds before Church took his last walk. Twenty, then ten, then five. The zero point came and the outer hatch opened.

No sign of Church.

I waited. At some point the hatch closed. Church had still not come out. Yet neither he nor his remains had been in the lock when the inner hatch was opened. And there was no record of his being onboard.

End sim I told the computer and I was back inside thinking that this was no longer a routine case.

REPORT

It was the same voice, the same toneless inflection, but somehow I knew that this was Command and not the computer.

I told Command what I knew, what I suspected, even recommended an overall systems check. Then I told it that what had happened was impossible.

There was a noticeable pause, longer than any I'd ever experienced with Command. Finally ...

THE ANOMALY IN THE SYSTEM THAT MADE POSSIBLE AL3 UNAUTHO-RIZED ACCESS MAY ALSO HAVE AFFECTED EXTERIOR MONITOR. CHECK SHOWS ALL SYSTEMS NOW OPERATING NORMALLY. SITUATION RESOLVED AND RECORDED AS SUICIDE BY CREW MEMBER CHURCH. GOOD JOB OFFICER BOONE. RESUME PATROL

It made sense, one glitch caused another resulting in the monitor not recording Church's body when it came out. But it did show the hatch opening. One hell of a fast glitch. But Command was satisfied so I should be as well.

Except that I wasn't. On Earth I was a cop, and a damn good one. I had worked patrol, traffic, and had spent two years in the Detective Division before succumbing to the lure of too much money. Up here I was a combined security guard/ correctional officer but the cop wasn't far from the surface.

The proper step would have been to start asking questions. But except for "Yes Sir, No Sir" and the like, the crew doesn't talk to the officers. And officers only talked to the crew to give them orders. For me to go down among them looking for answers would upset the natural order of things. That would put me in danger, from the crew and probably from Command, who doesn't like the natural order of things disturbed, particularly when it has declared a case closed.

But there were too many questions that needed answers. If Church's body had not come out of the hatch, where was it? The chips work even after death. If his body was still on board it would have registered. How did Church get the inner hatch open? If he found a hack maybe other members of the crew have as well. And if there was no hack, how did Church open the airlock? With help, of course. And that help could only have come from an officer.

That line of thinking led to a dark alley I didn't want to walk without backup. Still, the possibility could not be ignored. Officers are permitted to space crew, but only after approval from Command. Church's walk outside had been "Unauthorized." If he did have an officer's help, then was it assisted suicide or murder, not that there's much of a difference.

I should have stopped thinking, dropped the case, and gone back to my daily routine of patrol, sleep, eat, and mindless entertainment. Command had decided and anything I came up with could not lead to anything good. But like I said, I had once been a damn good cop, and a good cop looks for the truth, no matter how many dark alleys he has to search.

I had the computer trace Church's movements over the month before his death. His life was much the same as mine—work, sleep, eat, and what passes for fun aboard the *Phillimore*. I knew what holos he had watched, what sport sims he followed, and how many times he had gotten laid and with whom.

None of it helped. Outside ship's business, Church had had no interaction with any officer and there were no reported altercations or trouble.

If tracing the victim doesn't help, the next step is the victim's associates. I tracked their movements with much the same results.

Except for Darien Ricks, Church's one and only lover. He wasn't as exclusive as Church had been.

Homosexuality is not a crime, not onboard the *Phillimore*. Back on Earth it's a different story. Same-sex liaisons were outlawed when radical religious sects teamed with neo-conservatives and forced a realignment of the Global Network. It was all the moderates and what few liberals were left to keep homosexuality from being classified as a perverted sex crime and thus punishable by death. That's why a sizable percentage of the crew is so inclined. The Network would rather they be off-planet entirely. As for me, as long as they keep it safe and consensual, I don't care what people do in private, but I don't make the rules.

Jealousy as a motive is as old as the Bible. It was the cause of the first murder and it gave me a motive for Church's death. Either he couldn't handle the fact that other men shared Ricks's bed or someone else didn't like Church being in there.

I looked closer at Ricks. Except for sharing it around, he led the same dull life as the rest of us. With nothing else to do, I decided to track his partners. Records showed that Ricks opened his door to company at least four times a week, sometimes to Church, sometimes to one of three other Crew members. The records also showed that on occasion, about once a week, Ricks opened his door without his leaving or anyone entering.

The movements of the crew I can trace. Tracing officers is exclusive to Command.

When I said earlier about homosexuality being tolerated onboard the *Phillimore* I was speaking about the crew. It is assumed that officers had no criminal backgrounds or tendencies, criminal as defined by the Global Network. If it were an officer visiting Ricks ...

I doubled-checked Church's movements. Twice he was near Ricks's quarters when the door opened and "no one" was admitted.

Blackmail is another good motive for murder, as is killing a witness.

The cop I used to be was sure of what happened. The officer I was knew I needed stronger proof than an open door before going to Command. And both of me wondered what Command knew, what it suspected, and how far it would go to cover things up.

I thought about stopping then realized that it was too late for that. If my suspicions about Command's nature were true, it knew everything I had been doing through the computer. I was already in deep so I might as well keep digging as long as I could.

Which wasn't much longer. Without a body I had little to go on, no way to counter the presumption that Church had gone out the airlock and that the monitors had missed him. It was like an old arson detective once told me, my case had plenty of heat but no fire.

Thinking of heat reminded me of one thing I had yet to check.

Computer

YES, OFFICER BOONE

Access records for AL3 at the time of Crew Church's unauthorized use. Search for heat differential caused by Church's presence in the lock

NO HEAT DIFFERENTIAL DETECTED

Access records of authorized ejections of Crew. Search for heat differentials

SLIGHT RISE DUE TO BODY TEMPERATURES OF CONDEMNED IN ALL CASES

Griffin Church had not been in the air lock, not alive at least. Alive or dead, Church was still on the ship. But how to prove it?

Computer, search for onboard presence of Crew Griffin Church's ID chip

CHIP NOT ACTIVE. DELETED FROM MAIN FILES

I almost gave the computer the order to undelete Church's ID chip but what would be the point? Whoever hacked the air lock also hacked his chip so as not to register. But I still had an option.

Computer, reinstall Crew Griffin Church's ID Chip from back-up files

JUSTIFICATION REQUIRED, OFFICER BOONE

Was that last from the computer or Command? Not that I thought there was much, if any, of a difference. Time to dig my hole a little deeper.

Second Law, Computer. You are required to comply with my request unless it endangers the ship, the officers, or the crew

The computer, or was it Command, now had a choice. If my request was denied it would confirm what some of us already suspected, that there was an AI in control of the *Phillimore*. If my request was granted, that left things as just a nasty rumor.

There was a noticeable pause, then...

CREW CHURCH ID CHIP REINSTALLED

Still a nasty rumor then, but it gave me an idea of how an officer could have covered his and Church's tracks through a series of carefully phrased requests, each one seemingly harmless. Maybe Doctor A's laws needed a little refinement.

Search for onboard presence of Crew Griffin Church's ID chip

CHIP DETECTED DECK EIGHTEEN, SECTOR TWELVE

Life signs?

NONE

*Send a team. Check access records to 18-12 *

Church's body was found in a storage area for equipment we would not need until planet fall. A good place to hide a body that could not have been moved about the ship without someone noticing. The killer had at least six months to figure out what to do with it.

By the time I got to 18-12 the team was in place and doing its job. Designated Officers had secured the area while others were recording the scene and searching for anything that might be evidence. A medic had already confirmed the obvious, that Griffin Church was dead, the cause of death being manual blunt-force trauma—he'd been beaten to death.

I looked at the scene and played it out. Church and his killer met down here. Maybe Church suggested the place, maybe the killer. Things got out of hand—passion, anger, or both. A hasty and ultimately ineffective cover-up. The killer would probably have done better not to have done anything.

Some effort was made to clean the body, but not much. That made this murder as much of a mystery as that long-ago first one I mentioned. There was even an omnipresent, near omniscient Presence to help me solve it.

Computer, scan body for DNA other than victim's and report

SCANNING. UNABLE TO REPORT. JUSTIFICATION: FIRST LAW

I didn't need an explanation. Knowledge that an officer had murdered one of their number would cause unrest among the crew. That could harm the ship.

Allowing a killer to go free and kill again harms the crew. How does this comply with First Law?

PROBABLITY OF GREATER HARM RESTS WITH DISCLOSURE

Crew Damien Ricks already knows I sent, then added, *By now, so do others of the crew. Disclosure is moot. *

In all likelihood, that wasn't true. With his active social life, Ricks may not have even noticed that Church had stopped visiting. And he may or may not have heard or cared about Church's death. I'm sure his officer lover didn't tell him.

DECISION STANDS

Of course. Command would not, maybe could not admit that it had been wrong. I had expected no less.

RESULTS OF EARLIER REQUEST. ACCESS LOG TO 18-12 SHOWS ONLY THE PRESENCE OF OFFICER KARL WILEY IN 120-HOUR CYCLE PRIOR TO DISCOVERY OF CREW CHURCH

That I didn't expect. Maybe there was hope for Command yet. Or maybe that was the computer alone. Maybe I should stop worrying about who or what was running things and get some justice done.

Two days later I met Wiley in the Officers' Mess. Thanks to an accommodating computer, we were alone.

"Karl."

"Jack."

"We found Church's body."

"So I heard."

"Your DNA was all over it." Still no confirmation on that, but I was reasonably certain. When Riley didn't reply I went on.

"I talked to Ricks."

This last was an out-and-out lie. Like I said, officers don't talk to crew. But cops do lie to suspects.

Wiley broke. I saw it in his eyes before he said anything.

"Jack, I..."

"Save it. I know what happened and why. Passion, crime, a sloppy cover-up."

"What now?"

That was a good question. Despite my request, Command would not allow the execution of an officer or even formal murder charges followed by confinement. The First Law and all that. It did like my second suggestion.

"Access the computer, Karl."

He tried and the look on his face told me that he failed.

"Get used to the silence, Karl, or should I say, Crewman Wiley. Your status has been changed effective now. No more position, no more officer privilege. No payday at the end of the voyage. Just two decades of your life gone with nothing waiting for you at the end. On the bright side, now nobody gives a damn about your sex life."

He looked confused, lost, lonely, scared. "What do I do now?"

"The computer will assign you a work detail and quarters with all you need."

"What about my personal stuff?"

I shook my head. "That belonged to an officer."

"What if one of the crew recognizes me?"

I didn't reply. I didn't have to. Crewman Wiley knew the answer. If he was recognized he'd either be killed or shunned. A quick death or a long, lonely trip.

Wiley was halfway to the corridor hatch when he turned. About to say something, he suddenly remembered that crew don't talk to officers. He left, broken and defeated.

I wanted to feel sorry for him. It wasn't in me. Having done what he had, Wiley had gotten what he deserved. Still, there was one mercy I could show him.

Computer. Should at anytime Crewman Wiley want to take a walk outside the ship, open the hatch for him

AGREED

RIDING THE ROCK
Jeff Young

EVEN THOUGH SHE KNEW SHE WAS HANGING HEAD DOWN OVER A FRACTAL expansion valley inside a hollow asteroid, Petrine was dreaming of home. The vibration she felt reminded her of the constant hum of the air-cyclers in the Ganymede Float Point Collective. Her mother's voice was echoing through the chambers and as always Petrine was singing softly along. Petrine turned and there was her father standing before the view port. Over his shoulder rose the globe of Jupiter like a great eye with a wayward bloody pupil. Then she could see nothing but Jupiter as she fell inwards. Always she was falling inwards. Falling...

"Target has tripped motion sensors on the valley wall," came Rescoe's voice. Petrine shook her head, casting off the dream, awakening fatigue aches that had become all too familiar.

"Go to IR and you might pick him out from the background. There're very few hot spots," Rescoe continued.

Breathing in and gently sighing out, Petrine reluctantly opened her eyes to reality. For an instant she felt like she was hanging in the harness onboard *Shiva's Dance* waiting to deploy, instead of twelve hours later with the ship destroyed, teammates dead and the asteroid they were to protect open to vacuum.

Her three piton-anchored stay lines suspended Petrine horizontally over the Red River Valley that spread out below her. The rift ran down the center one of the fractal expansion caverns that had been hollowed out of

Cecropia: one of the midfield asteroids between Mars and Jupiter. At the end of the valley was the estate house of the wealthy DeMannis Family. After the disabling of the orientation field and the exposure of the interior to vacuum, what was once a beautiful alpine valley with terraced fields and scenic home became a wasteland of ice, frozen air and free floating detritus.

The destruction was lit by occasional flickers of cloudy yellow light from the fusion tube anchored to the roof of the valley only slightly higher than her present position. Without the orientation field that provided the tenth gee push toward the floor of the valley, all loose items drifted about the space. Although hanging over the wreckage of the estate was uncomfortable—it was the tactical high ground.

Petrine's internal system registered her neuroline request for the IR filter and the view hazed over, targeting various heat sources. Gradually, the tactical programming matched up the heat signatures with base profiles from the main monitoring system of Cecropia. Petrine used her internals to block off the identified areas and then prioritized the points in motion on the surface. She ignored the bait, a viral heat source she'd planted inside one of the windows of the estate's mansion. "Damn you take the it," she whispered.

"Have patience, I am the underside of the unobserved rock," Rescoe breathed. Petrine dropped into the immobility of waiting once more.

"No motion directed toward target," she replied

"Don't forget, we do not exist. After all, our boy might be concerned about the lack of communication from his comrades."

"Recycle it! Rescoe, that's the complete circuit and there's nothing."

"Shh, my destroying dove, that's the IR sources did you check the sinks?"

"Working now—save the sweetness. I'm backing through the scan, focusing on the interior rather than the surface. What's the likelihood of our discovery?"

"Slim, he'd be running the same checks as us. We're only spiked in the static range now since we adjusted our fields to attract enough dust to damp us down to ambient. All except for the helm and he'd have to adjust the size to…"

"Got 'em, bastard was drifting with a cloud of debris closing on the right. I'll give him about a minute to intercept the bait or less if he id's the source. He has his field adjusted to a sink, pulling in any residual heat. That trick and the drift made him hard to pick out. I make him at 230 meters distant,"

Petrine replied watching the now-highlighted figure in its combat suit as it advanced on what must appear to be an adversary watching from the view point of the upper window of the estate.

The first rule of space combat rolled through her mind, "down is dead." Allow your mind to be trapped by orientation and you could never react in time to save your ass, because sure as saints your opponent had also had that truth drilled into him. In combat where wire neurons trigged weapons from thought impulses, suits moved limbs through the fullest extent of their speed — anything that slowed you down was a death sentence. But tactics and strategy could still defeat a force of greater numbers, as Rescoe and Petrine had been proving.

"We'll have a distraction in about 25 seconds. Are you ready?" Rescoe asked.

"On the mark, ready to play Anansi," Petrine replied, sending a pulse at two of the stay lines, charges in the pitons snapping off their ends. She then drifted inward from the ceiling of the valley. The third line was clipped to her winch reel and the monomole line paid out behind her as she drifted downward. Since she had been anchored next to a huge conduit housing, Petrine used her janusuit to generate a magnetic push off of the casing.

"Still clear, target is intent on the bait, continue," updated Rescoe.

"It's going to be about five more seconds, ready for the pulse?" Petrine answered, drifting through the first third of her descent.

"Bring the noise," Rescoe laughed as the mine detonated from the proximity of the intruder.

The resulting haze of glass and debris filtered by her sensors was lacking the sink she'd oriented on. "Gotta' problem," she said kicking through search programs over an area of possible motion.

"I've got a tentative and am redefining," Rescoe came back.

"Damnit, make it quick! so's he and I'm a hanging target!"

"Read you- got him. He's tethered to the side of the house. I can read sweeps coming on line in his area, at one hundred-meters radius."

Petrine punched up the targeting musculature on the janusuit and let the machinery take over assessing the distance to the target. Her gun arm lifted as she watched the sweeps from his sensors bounce out to 1000 meters, well within her range. Soon she'd be identified as a threat and targeted.

System assisted targeting locked her gun and activated the firing sequence. She followed through and did not blink, holding her weapon steady through its discharge. She prayed her system was a hair faster.

It wasn't. Her opponent's weapon had already swung about and fired at a speed that would've ripped her tendons apart. An instant later she could feel the snap of her stay line- he'd shot her loose. Now, in the precious seconds it would take her to reorient, he could take her down at his leisure. The momentum bounce spun her off course but her weapon had already fired.

As his gun arm dropped down to focus on her armor, the anchoring packet of the grapple she'd fired slammed into the weakest point of his suit in the join of the weapon-bearing arm. Not even attempting to reorient, she'd reversed the polarity of the field that had bonded the camouflaging dust to her suit and slapped a second-long burst from her maneuvering jets. Decompression seals struggled against the massive rupture in his suit as the weapon on his arm tracked toward her. As his shot flared harmlessly through the halo of dust she'd left behind, Petrine triggered the grapple. Six half-meter spikes, designed to insert themselves into either asteroid rock or hull ablative plate impaled themselves into him completely rupturing his combat armor.

"Bravo, you are clear. I'm showing minimal activity although I recommend vacating the area. More than likely the armor is sending out a beacon and someone will send it a kamikaze code soon. My compliments on another beautiful kill. Time to haul ass girl. I've got your back." Rescoe laughed.

Petrine did a quick review. All of the invading Earth Force marines were accounted for except for one. "What are we going to kill the final one with though? That was our last weapon." Petrine asked as she fired a burst from her jets that brought her back up to the ceiling.

"With what we always do, beauty. With my brains," chuckled Rescoe in reply.

Taking a momentary breather near one of the access tunnels, Petrine thumbed a jack into the asteroid's house system. She slapped a hand onto a nearby by girder and let the daptifoam covering over her suit latch on with a molecular bond. This would have been a lot simpler if the *Shiva's Dance* hadn't been destroyed in transit to Cecropia. There had barely been a warning and their weaponry and ammunition was now free-floating debris, along with most of her fellow mercenaries. Shiva's Dance hadn't really felt like home, but it had started to become familiar. The crew had even forgiven her occasionally breaking into song.

Petrine forced herself back to the task at hand; time to regret later, now she needed intel. Since in the large scale of things Cecropia was one of the Out Rim asteroids, she had no problems bypassing security measures and gaining the run of the system's command structure. So far that had allowed her to track the intruders and dispatch them. However, things were changing. A viral alert popped up on her interface view almost immediately.

"Damn," she cursed and launched countermeasures as the suit severed the link to the spike. "Well," she said to Rescoe, "so much for the locations being on the house. Guess we're on our own now."

"I could play with that and have a good chance of cleaning things up," Rescoe offered, seeming disappointed in her swift dismissal of the house system.

"No time and you know it," she replied, considering her alternatives. Suddenly she had a thought, "What we need is the medical AI for this rock. These people had plenty of money and children too. It should be state-of-the-art, as well as separate from the main system."

"Lifestyles of the rich and paranoid. Yeah, you're right as usual. If you jack into a scan node, I can put in enough of a defensive patch to keep out whatever nasties they've added and we should still be able to access the AI," Rescoe replied.

"Good, I've got a node about 20 meters ahead."

Pulling herself along one of the honeycomb tunnels, Petrine found herself wondering again how she'd gotten involved in all of this. "Why do we do this again, Rescoe?"

"The glory, the paycheck, the fact that we'd be scoop miners or crap shovellers instead?" he offered, "It's the same old story. It's us versus them- the Out Rim or the In Rim. Ever since the United World decided to throw its weight around, there's been conflict."

"To bad Mars and Luna couldn't stand up to them."

"Their gravity wells are just too close and you know it. Ever since the Out Rim became self-sufficient and declared independence, there's been tension, if not conflict. Earth just wants to apply the United World concept to a United Solar System. We don't happen to agree. Guess we just like being rough, rugged settlers."

"I'd say all of us, like the Gany Float Point, the Ring Busters, Europans, and the Rockfallers, just like our freedom to do what we damn well please. All I ever really wanted to do was sing for my supper." She wished that wistful note hadn't entered her tone, because Rescoe's reply didn't surprise her at all.

"Hah! *You* wanted to sing for the crap shovellers and recycle wardens and get fat having their kids? No way do I believe that, girl. You're too much of a Valkyrie for that. This way you can sing while you fly."

Trying to distract him, she took a different tact, "What do you think about the Diaspora plan?"

There was a moment of silence as Rescoe considered his answer. "If we can use the Stitch drive to pilot asteroid ships for interstellar flight, then we do have a chance to be free. Just imagine taking a whole rock and shoving it through a hole punched into the quantum foam repeatedly like stitching up space. Only people out on the edge of nothing could come up with something as crazy as that." His tone was more somber when he continued; "I have a feeling things are going to get a lot more desperate now that bit of intel got out. I hate to imagine it, but this skirmish could be the tipping point that starts an all out war."

"Yeah, I guess once Earth figures out the Diaspora motto, 'To the Stars Together' doesn't include them, the recycle will hit the rotor. Too bad the security on Cecropia was so bad that the news of the Stitch drive leaked early." Petrine stopped and considered the black lip of the comm node in front of her. She used her multi-tool to pry up the edge to get at the optical wiring underneath.

"These cocky DeMannis bastards should have realized that being at the trailing edge of the rock ring put them too close Earth," Rescoe said in a clipped tone.

Despite what she might think of the DeMannis, Petrine gave them a small amount of credit. They were able to evacuate the port despite the limited amount of time and send off a distress call bringing their hired guard ship, *Shiva's Dance* in to intercept the invaders. Sadly, the fight was a little too even and both ships were destroyed.

Five notes from the beginning of the Everly Brothers song "All I Have To Do Is Dream" played into Petrine's ear before she cut the audio. Damn Rescoe, her fingers were working even if her mind was wandering. She couldn't help it if she liked to sing. As she moved the linkages in the node around looking for the correct line, she continued to hum to herself. "Gotcha' bastard," she said as a map grid popped up on her visual overlay.

A few more adjustments and she had control of the medical AI and set it to scan for all movement and life signs within the asteroid. Petrine noticed something else in the coding. There were free medical nanocytes present inside the asteroid. If they hadn't been vented, they could come in handy.

As she stifled the urge to do the impossible and scratch her itching scalp for the twelfth time, she was surprised to feel the floor seem to drop away from her. Then it switched to the impending vertigo of ascent and Petrine stifled the reflexive scream that it brought on.

Rescoe's voice interrupted, "Recycle it. One guess as to where our missing Earth Force Operative is hiding. They've gotten control of the Stitch drive. Have a look at this."

As she looked over the visual plot he displayed, Petrine realized what Rescoe had been up to. The cocky little bastard had been taking apart the countermeasures that their enemy had sewn in the house system. But, with what had just occurred, he'd then tapped into the navigational system's output. They were rapidly heading insystem- toward the defensive lines of In Rim space. The sensations of passage through the wormhole washed over them again and Petrine found herself clamping her gloves onto the edges of the closest girder.

Not only were they moving insystem with the jumps of the drive but also they were above the ecliptic already and descending on an arc that headed them toward Mars' gravity well.

"We have no more than an hour, before we cross the dispute line and two before we're into the edge of the gravity well. We want to be off this ride or redirect before then because if we get lucky and the Drive starts making its best time...then those figures are a get smaller," Rescoe observed quietly.

Petrine slumped in the combat suit and took a deep breath. Color phosphoresced behind her eyelids, there we go, another stitch closer, she thought as she pulled up the asteroid's structural map. She gave herself a moment to observe Rescoe at work trying to get at the guidance for the Stitch Drive. Then she took a ragged breath and closed her eyes for a second...

—sensation of falling, the long endless descent into the huge orange ocean ahead of her, giant strands of clouds like curdled milk, whites, yellows, ochre twisters. The noiseless screaming of the beginning of the ammonia atmosphere's roar against the scoop field. Rescoe gently folding her into the warmth of the only other field on the ship as she ineffectually fought him. Fending her off with ease, he said, "Sorry babe somebody had to eat the worm. I lost the toss." Beating on the constricting bubble of energy, knowing he lied and finally crying herself into the inevitable unconsciousness—

"Huh," Petrine coughed jerking backward. She glanced at her lens clock and it said a minute had gone by. She hit the pharm implants and dosed herself. As the stim/attenuators hit her brain, she came back into focus despite the effects of the drive. The medical AI was flashing an attention icon and she ran through its result.

Each passageway lock or door had sensors that could be recalibrated to scan for the life signs. The system had identified the three Earth marines Rescoe and Petrine had dealt with and an additional four visitors who displayed no life to the scanners. Damn, Petrine thought doing the math, three additional Earth Marines and four members of their squad, pitted them against the one remaining marine who rerouted the Drive. His location was indicated with a flashing beacon on her view. A single person was visible moving through a transition tube from the Drive room to the main lock for that part of the asteroid.

She gave them credit. They'd accomplished their objective and then set about finding the best spot to defend the Drive room. "Rescoe, there are two entranceways to the Drive room, the main airlock and a maintenance access. What if we were to use the medical nanocytes as a distraction of some sort? Can you work that out?" With that she turned toward the interior of the asteroid, pulling herself along the wall's holdfasts.

"Christo, maybe I'm beauty and you're brains. Have I had it all wrong all these years?" Resco said with an appreciative whistle, noticing her work.

"Not a chance there son, I've had both crowns all along, its about time you woke up and realized it," Petrine said with a wide grin as she came to an abrupt stop against the rim of an air lock iris field.

"Wait," Rescoe said and she hesitated, knowing he'd had an intuitive flash. She could sense him poking at the electronics of the air lock but could not follow his intent.

"Come on, time is of the essence and all that crap. Let's move. Besides I'm the one who's supposed to have the intuition anyway."

"Ok, you can use the lock now, but as you do, look over the changes made to the basic modes by one of our unfriendly's traps. You'd've ended up in enough pieces for each ya' to have one your damned crowns," Rescoe said smugly as they moved through the double layer field that was supposed to keep out the vacuum of space.

Petrine wasn't saying anything as they hauled ass for the Drive room. After the virus injected into the computer system had opened the airlocks and exposed Cecropia to vacuum, the airlocks had gone to standby and were set to cycle at a five times their ordinary speed. Anyone innocently passing through the airlock would trigger the cycle and the field would snap on when they were only part of the way through. Designed to be air tight, the field would crush any object or target in the aperture. Damn, she was lucky Rescoe was watching her ass or she'd've been able to take a good look at it without bending. She pulled open an access port to the maintenance crawlway and swung herself within. The lack of gravity made it easier for her to traverse the narrow space. She followed the map shown on her overview until she came to the airlock at the top of the maintenance shaft for the Drive room. Petrine wrapped a hand around a stay by the edge of the vent. "Is this lock safe?"

"The lock is now offline. Go on through, I'm starting to wiggle the cheese," Rescoe said as their plan sprang into action below her.

Petrine swung herself over the lip of the meter wide opening. A quick look down the tube showed no projections and a straight run as indicated by the specs that would bring her out above the Drive room. She felt the air lock field snap on behind her. At the same time she took a look at the screen Rescoe had set up for her revealing the immediate interior. Two masses of congealing mednanocytes were highlighted where they clung to the ceiling just down the corridor from the Drive room access corridor. Individually they were too small to attract attention but stretched to thin reflective films they could be used to project outlines visible to the monitors of the security system as intruders.

"Target in motion," Rescoe said as their identified adversary moved back toward the Drive room away from the main lock, "taking step one. Remember from now on this is going to be very, very quick."

"And deadly," was Petrine's grim reply as she primed her mobility jet with a wire neuron impulse.

"Are you set?" Rescoe asked.

"Loose 'em."

"Decoy one on."

The protoplasmic mass of nanocytes weighing about four ounces followed its instructions and expanded to a thin film in a vaguely human shape. It sped down the access way. The target then halted its motion and repositioned itself by the opening of the corridor.

"Decoy two on."

The secondary mass of nanocytes began the same advance on the Drive room. The Earth Force marine hesitated a second and then stepped over the airlock lip trying to cover both advances.

"Is the fish in the net?" Petrine asked her fingers tight around the mobility jet control.

"Clean sweep," Rescoe said as the target backed up farther coming underneath the maintenance access. "Let's take 'em."

"Roger that, move the distraction and wish me luck."

The blobs of nanocytes flew at the target now and their adversary used some sort of coherent light weapon on the masses. The tiny machines evaporated under the onslaught but they'd brought the marine right where Petrine and Rescoe wanted him. Petrine opened the maintenance airlock and slid into the straight tube, feet first. Firing the mobility jet and locking the musculature of her suit to maximum, she flew downward toward the crouching form of her opponent. Her bounce was not completely unexpected and Petrine threw out her arms trying to slow her sudden rotation. What she hadn't predicted was that she'd missed.

She felt rather than saw the boot that connected with her head. The impact sent her flying across the room to fetch up against the bottom of the controls for the Stitch Drive. She fired the command for the dapti-foam over the entire surface of the janusuit in an attempt to halt her motion. Her positioning wasn't the most comfortable. She was tacked down all over, leaving her left foot floating free. She heard the sound of movement behind her and that might be Rescoe trying to tap into the Stitch Drive control panel. She opened her eyes to nothing. The view from her helm was shut down. Then she realized she couldn't hear Rescoe any more either.

At that point the marine struck her again. He hit her across the body with an assisted strike that if her armor hadn't backed it down, would've opened her up like an autopsied cadaver. Her helm snapped loose and went rolling across the floor. Her vision swam through the haze of pain from bruised ribs as she stared ahead at the Earth Force marine whose left hand was a blurring wedge as it fell through the air at her head.

—She knew she was dreaming and gods this was the last dream that she ever wanted to have again but at least she knew how this one ended. It had to be better than what the marine was doing to her now, her body ce- mented to the floor by the daptifoam. So here she was again, plugged into the modified scoop ship outfitted with the new weaponry and expanded drive. Rescoe was riding pilot, a solid quiet presence ahead of her. To her left and right on either side of the ship were the others in the squadron, green as green gets. They were getting ready to bounce off of the gravity well of Jupiter out toward the Gany Float Point when the Earth destroyer dropped on them.

They were really just the beginnings of a tactical wing and it cut through them without a second thought making for the big refitted transport at the Float Point. The right ship vanished into an incendiary fireball, while hers and the left began the long slow fall into the well of the king of gods, their drives incinerated in their housings. Their companions lasted about an hour before the internal fires in the hull casing killed them. She and Rescoe, well in a way, they were lucky enough to have more time, if nothing else. Their transport was running for its life now. With one destroyer in the area, there were likely to be more, so the possibility of additional support here in the precarious political environment of Jupiter's gravity well was a quantifiable nil.

Rescoe was quiet before her, maybe enjoying the view, maybe praying, maybe thinking about a way out. She, well right about now she didn't care, so she did what she usually did in such a case, she began to sing. At first it was anything that came into her head, ballads, folk songs, but when she sang the aria from Delibe's *Lakhme* she caught a movement out of the corner of her eye. Rescoe who'd been sitting quietly ahead of her, hands clasped together pressed against his lips, eyes closed— stood and walked up behind her to lay hands on her shoulders and massaged away the tension there.

His head fell forward to rest against hers and she felt one tear slide down behind her ear and trace its way down her neck. As if to not to disturb her song, she heard him whisper, "The ship has three fields it can sustain." Then his traitorous hands had folded the crash field generators around her as he said, "Sorry babe somebody had to eat the worm. I just lost the toss."

She'd punched, kicked, swore, cursed and begged that field to drop but eventually she had to put on her helm and seal it when she realized he wasn't going to let her out. Out there she knew he was releasing the worm, a nanocyte that ate away one's memory to create an encoded digital version. Only two ship generated fields, the one she was in—and there was one independent field, that of the ship's black box. What was he doing with the other field?

The psych-technician assigned to her after the rescue finally gave into her demands after repeated threats. She'd had a week to recover and there were still grave concerns about her health. Yes, she could talk to Rescoe soon. As to their escape it was being hailed as a brilliant use of minimal resources. A nurse woke her up an hour later and brought a voice link to her. "I'll let Rescoe explain," he said an uncomfortable expression on his face as he turned abruptly and left.

Petrine pushed herself up on the bed and said, "Get on with it. The smug silence tells me you're ready."

His healthy laugh echoed from the link, "Well I put you in the first field, not without a bit of struggle mind you. I then keyed the second field to the largest volume overlapping the whole the ship. Then I set it to evacuate all of the atmosphere and damped its power down to the point where it could maintain containment for as long as possible."

"You made a vacuum balloon," she laughed shaking her head in amazement.

"One that floated for two weeks before our rescuers arrived. The suit kept you alive. Me,...I ate the worm and transferred the result into the ship's black box."

She threw the link on the floor and began screaming.

It was another week's time spent with the psych technician before she could face reality.

Two months later she was getting used to the extra set of arms on her janusuit controlled by her now integrated partner, Rescoe. Getting used to his snide commentary, his swift insight and occasional silences when she hurt along with him as he remembered more than the electronic boundaries of his new body—

"Come on now Petrine, it's time to stop taking it and time to start dishing it out again," he whispered.

Suddenly, she realized that the voice she was hearing was on the internal channel and not her dream. They were both still alive.

"I need you to focus now. He's coming back to finish you. I need you to open your eyes. That's going to anger him, 'cause he thought you'd just give up. I need you to get under his skin. We've still got a chance but it's going to be rough."

She took a shuddering breath. It felt like someone had filled her chest with red-hot steel shavings. She tasted petrol and iron in her mouth with a swollen tongue. She gathered up her spittle. Her eyelids crawled back, light stabbing migraine needles into her. There was the Earth Force marine scowling at her, floating closer. Petrine spit with what little accuracy she had left. The blood flecked globule floated toward him and he veered easily out of the way.

"Typical arrogant earth bastard, he's going to reach for you now. Brace yourself, you're going to catch some residual but I have you grounded out," came Rescoe's voice through the neuroline. "He's in for a surprise. This should finish him, but I need you to hold on then girl. Help will come but it will be awhile. I've turned the drive around and we're heading for home. Be the Valkyrie you are and survive this, hear?"

She wanted to reply but she was frightened by that tone. It was too familiar. Then she felt the arc of electricity as it came up out of the exposed wire in the decking that Rescoe had cut open. Current coursed through the janusuit crackling and scorching the unshielded inner glove of the Earth Force marine's armor. He spun spasming above her cartwheeling toward the decking. His helm was open and she could see his face contorted and red but still showing some signs of life. He spun near her and she slammed her free left foot onto him firing the daptifoam. It clamped over his face invading all of the openings, sealing them off.

It took two minutes of kicking and struggling until he died.

It took ten minutes to realize Rescoe was not responding to her.

It took thirty minutes until she retrieved and sealed her helm, blanking out until they found her a day later.

It only took two days to stop her screaming this time.

A week later Petrine walked down the corridor toward the hardware room coming to a halt outside the door. She stood there for a moment staring through the clear window at the six-limbed janusuit. That white suit was never going to be her home. But strangely she'd come to accept that wherever she and Rescoe were, it was going to be as close as she could come to one.

Twice now he'd saved her life giving up his own and if they hadn't made a copy, then there wouldn't have been another reunion. Stroking the curl of the black capsule that rode behind every mercenary's ear now, she thought, perhaps someday after letting the worm have her they could be together in another fashion. But for now, she pushed through the doorway, her voice ringing out, "Hey honey, I'm home."

Rescoe's voice chuckled, "Heard we had some fun, why don't you tell me about it."

Petrine laughed, she knew he'd been fed all of the action on feedline, but she walked closer, picked a comfortable looking piece of floor and sat down lotus style. "Our story begins with our two intrepid heroes on a rock sliding in and out of reality..."

THE STONE OF THE FIRST HIGH PONTIFF

Keith R.A. DeCandido

JIN YAWNED AS SHE CAME ONTO THE FLIGHT DECK, AND SAW THAT THE SHIP HADN'T moved since she went to bed.

Timm didn't even turn to look at her, instead staring at the display on the nav. "No, they still haven't finished the maintenance on the Nimast Corridor. No, they haven't given us an estimate as to when it will be done. No, we can't just go on our own steam, as that'll take three decades."

Smiling as she took the copilot's seat on the cramped flight deck, Jin said, "Well, that answers two of my questions."

"Yeah, well, it wasn't until we entered hour number fourteen that I started plotting a direct course to Taksnaro, just for shits and giggles."

Jin shot him a mischievous look through hooded eyes. "And it'll take as long as three decades? You're losing your touch."

Timm shrugged and rubbed his smooth, dark scalp. "Well, that was at point-seven. Any higher, we start dealing with time-dilation, and *nobody* wants a piece'a that shit."

"On the other hand," Jin said with a sigh, "by the time thirty years go by, Brfnel might actually pay us."

"You are *such* an optimist."

"Are you sure we should be going to Taksnaro?"

Turning to Jin, Timm stared at her as if she'd gone Zlarix and grown a second head. "Excuse me? Did we not both agree, while sitting in these same chairs, right before we told Brfnel we'd find his daughter—again—that we'd go to Taksnaro for the opening-night performance of *Down Among the Stars*, assuming we found little Glarna before the twelfth? And is it not now the tenth, giving us two whole days to get to Taksnaro?"

Jin winced. "I know, but—" She sighed. "Well, Brfnel *hasn't* paid us. And this Corridor trip is going to take the last of our available cash."

Timm's nose twitched the way it always did when Jin started talking about the dire state of their finances. "You're telling me that new coil cost that much?"

With a snort, Jin said, "It wasn't a new coil, it was a used coil, and it cost a hundred. A new one would've meant going into the emergency fund—and before you ask," she added quickly as Timm opened his mouth, "we are *not* dipping into the emergency fund to pay to park this beast at Taksnaro."

"*Seeker* is *not* a beast, she's a good boat." Timm patted the console affectionately, which he always did whenever Jin told the truth about their tiny, cramped ship's rather dilapidated condition. He continued: "And we are too dipping into it if we have to, because you promised." He pointed an accusatory finger at Jin.

She sighed. "What if I promise to get you a HoloPlay of the performance when it comes out?"

"Three problems with that. One, HoloPlays are never as good as the live performance. Two, only place I can run the HoloPlay is the half-meter space over my console here, which ain't exactly the kind of immersive experience you get from live theatre. And three, you already promised we'd go to Taksnaro, so you promising to get me the HoloPlay in order to go back on your other promise is kind of unconvincing, y'know?" He got up from the pilot's chair. "Wake me if they actually put the damn Corridor back online."

Looking down at one of the displays, Jin saw that three messages had come in. "Did you check YourMail?"

"That is *all* I have done for the past fifteen hours. Not a single interesting thing there."

"We just got three—and one is from the Lighters."

Timm rolled his eyes. "Half the YourMail we got was from Lighters."

Jin grinned. "Which sect?"

"Both." He shuddered. "All the usual junk. Come to our side, we're more holy than the other side. Dunno why they blast it out to *everyone* like that. I mean, do they have *any* worshippers who aren't Vhaddish?"

"Probably easier to do that than just to target Vhaddish addresses." Jin shrugged. "Anyhow, this doesn't look like recruitment junk, since it's addressed to the 'human finder.'"

Timm grinned and Jin made a face. She hated being called that, but the appellation had stuck.

"It's from the High Pontiff himself," Jin said after tapping the YourMail logo to bring the message up to the screen. "He wants to hire us."

Timm put his head in his hands. "Oh hell, no, please, Jin, no, we do *not* want to deal with religious types. They're always asking for discounts, and—"

Jin cut him off. "They're willing to pay two thousand just to take a meeting, regardless of whether or not we take the job."

A several-second silence ensued after she said that. Finally, Timm spoke in a very quiet tone. "Say that again. Slowly."

Instead, Jin merely stared at him. She watched his face go through several emotions in succession, starting with annoyance at the need to miss the opening of *Down Among the Stars*, eventually modulating into a small smile at the thought of what he could spend his share of a thousand marks on.

Finally, Timm sat back down in the pilot seat. "Let me see it."

Before Jin could shoot the YourMail to his console, the Braslo InterShip beeped. Timm tapped it on; Jin noted that the call was from Nimast Corridor Control, and she hoped that it was good news.

A voice spoke in heavily accented Cwyar. *"This is Nimast Corridor Control. Maintenance is complete, and* Seeker *is in the queue for transit. Your registry indicates that this is a Revnen ship?"*

In the same language, Timm replied: "Yes, the co-owners of this vessel are Revnen, and we're both unbonded. If you want," he added impatiently, "I can provide proof of our—"

"That won't be necessary, Seeker, *you just need to be aware that there are four Sanashloj ships in the queue, and they're ahead of you."*

"That's fine, Corridor Control, we'll wait our turn. Out." Timm cut off the Braslo quickly, then looked at Jin. "Guess they have new folks in charge."

With a shudder, Jin nodded. Last time they'd come through Nimast, they'd had to provide proof that they were unbonded. Of course, that was right after all those Sanrevnen slaves on Fortinon had rioted and run away, and everyone was on edge.

Timm read over the mail from the Lighters. "Yeah, okay." He reopened the Braslo to Corridor Control.

"Nimast Corridor Control, go ahead Seeker.*"*
"Corridor Conrol, we need to alter our filed destination."

Jin had expected the receiving room for the High Pontiff of the Sacred Church of Enlightened Thought and Belief to be ostentatious, but her expectations were greatly exceeded. They had entered doors made of cast gravari, and inlaid with gold. The floor of the room was entirely made of fringelt—Jin felt guilty walking on it—and the ceiling likewise. The very long side walls were all decorated with hand-painted images of all of the previous High Pontiffs, going back to ten centuries before Jin and Timm's ancestral homeland of Earth was conquered by the Ashloj Collective. There were only about eighty of them—the Vhaddish were a long-lived people, although no one was appointed High Pontiff until they were already two hundred years old—but each was surrounded by acolytes.

The lengthy, open room was supported by pillars, which were also made of fingelt—however, one expected that from pillars, as every Vhaddish structure of any kind of size used fingelt pillars—etched with scenes from the Lighters' holy texts.

Standing in front of each pillar was a Church Warrior—none of whom, she noted with amusement, were Vhaddish. It seemed they felt safer hiring non-believers to protect them for some reason. Each Warrior was armed with GranitoZap sidearms and covered head to toe in GranitoBlam armor. Jin had never been a big fan of firearms, but she knew from Timm carrying on like trash on the subject that Granito's goods were substandard—but also cheap, which probably was why the church went for it.

At the far end was the High Pontiff's throne, made of solid gold. Jin couldn't imagine it was in any way comfortable. However, it did make it clear that throwing two thousand marks around just to take a meeting wasn't even going to put a dent in their treasury.

Sitting in the throne was the round, tentacled body of the High Pontiff himself. His deep brown fur had been shaved into the pattern that indicated that he was the leader of the church.

Or, at least, the half or so Lighters who actually followed him.

Next to him was another Vhaddish whose white fur had been shaved into the pattern of a high acolyte of the church.

The white-furred one spoke in the Vhaddish language with his upper mouth as Jin and Timm approached. "Thank you for agreeing to the meeting, human finder."

"Please, you may refer to me as Jin," she said in the same language, hoping she was getting her pronunciation right—Vhaddish was created by a species with two mouths, each with a forked tongue, so it made for some entertaining sibilants—"and you paid us to have this meeting, so to this meeting we gladly attend. How may we refer to you?"

"I am the High Pontiff's Voice. And we shall refer to you as Jin. Our compliments on your facility with the holy language of the Vhaddish. It is rare to find an outworlder who speaks it so fluently."

"Thank you." Jin had indeed noticed that she was speaking the language more comfortably than she had in the past. It was yet another change that had come to her life since the circumstance that led to her becoming the so-called "human finder."

"I assume, Jin, that you are familiar with the schism that exists within the Sacred Church of Enlightened Thought and Belief, praise be to the church's wisdom?"

Jin nodded, then remembered that Vhaddish weren't very good at reading body language cues of non-Vhaddish. "I am aware of the schism's existence, and that each sect believes itself to be the correct one."

"So you are not aware of the cause of the schism."

"Forgive me, but I am not. I regret to say that I am not a student of your church's history."

Several of the Voice's tentacles vibrated at that. "Such is not part of our church's history, though it is, tragically, part of the history of the Vhaddish people. Long ago, in the earliest days of the Sacred Church of Enlightened Thought and Belief, praise be to the church's wisdom, there was a stone that had etched upon its surface the words of the First High Pontiff. The artifact was lost, but the words inscribed upon it were recorded in the holy texts. There are those heretics who believe that the texts are in error, and that the stone has words other than those recorded. That is the basis of the schism, and it has only grown worse over the decades."

Timm, who did not speak Vhaddish, was shifting uncomfortably from foot to foot. Jin cast him a quick apologetic glance, then said to the Voice, "Do you wish me to find this stone?"

The Voice's tentacles wiggled again, and three of his eyestalks turned toward the High Pontiff, who continued to sit upon the throne. If his lungflaps hadn't been vibrating, Jin would have thought the High Pontiff to be dead.

After a surprisingly long hesitation, the Voice said, "The High Pontiff, praise be to his great wisdom and knowledge, has learned of your exploits through the InformNet."

Jin somehow managed to avoid chuckling. That last word had been spoken in Yrak, the common tongue of the Ashloj, and the one used on the InformNet. Vhaddish had no word for that, so the Voice just appropriated the Yrak one. Jin had a hard time believing that the High Pontiff actually lowered himself to observe the InformNet.

"Based on all accounts, you have an enviable success rate. For that reason, the High Pontiff, praise be to his great wisdom and knowledge, wishes to engage your services to locate the Stone of the First High Pontiff."

Timm, who had been staring at the murals on the walls, looked over at those last words, which he apparently recognized.

The Voice went on: "The High Pontiff, praise be to his great wisdom and knowledge, wishes this schism to end, for all those who believe in the Sacred Church of Enlightened Thought and Belief, praise be to the church's wisdom, to once again be united under his guidance. The High Pontiff, praise be to his great wisdom and knowledge, believes that the retrieval of the Stone of the First High Pontiff, lost all these many centuries, may be what at last enables our deluded fellows to return to the fold, and make the Sacred Church of Enlightened Thought and Belief, praise be to the church's wisdom, stronger."

"If I am to accept this commission," Jin said slowly, "I will need to know everything about the Stone of the First High Pontiff. I will need to see not only the sacred texts, but also any heretical ones."

The High Pontiff's tentacles quivered at that, and the Voice quickly said, "That will not be—"

"Look, Voice—" She stopped, realizing she had gone back to Yrak. Taking a breath, she went back to Vhaddish. "In order to perform my task, I must have every piece of information about the Stone of the First High Pontiff, even information that is inaccurate. Even a lie may hold truths within it."

The High Pontiff's eyestalks all focused on Jin, and for the first time, he spoke. Unlike that of his Voice, the High Pontiff's words came out in a raspy whisper. "You speak the words of Samno. Good. Good."

Jin inclined her head in respect, though she hadn't the first clue who Samno was. The phrase was something one of her former owners used to say before she died.

Half the High Pontiff's eyestalks looked at the Voice, who then said, "We shall provide you with *all* the available data on the Stone of the First High Pontiff—even the data that is heretical and false."

"I apologize for forcing you to acknowledge heretical work," Jin said quickly, "but it is necessary to accomplish the task you have set out for me."

In Yrak, Timm muttered, "They tell us how much they're paying yet?"

Jin winced. She'd forgotten that part. She often did, which was why she preferred Timm to handle negotiations. After being a slave so long, the notion of being personally recompensed for work was still foreign to her. Her function as a slave had been to, among other things, handle her owners' finances, but that was for after jobs were done, not before.

"Assuming," she continued, "that we may properly negotiate payment."

The Voice's tentacles quivered. "Payment has already been made."

Jin frowned, remembering Timm's words about religious types trying to renege on paying their bills. "For this meeting, yes, payment has been made. We have fulfilled the terms of *that* agreement. If I am to find the Stone of the First High Pontiff, there must be recompense for *that* service."

More of the High Pontiff's eyestalks glanced at the Voice. Jin wished she knew more about Vhaddish body language.

The Voice then said, "We will only provide you with further currency if you complete the task. Therefore, another two thousand marks will be granted to you upon the return of the Stone of the First High Pontiff to the Sacred Church of Enlightened Thought and Belief, praise be to the church's wisdom."

Normally, this would be the part where someone haggled, but four thousand was more than she'd gotten for any *two* jobs. This would enable them to do *proper* repairs on *Seeker* and take a vacation besides.

Jin had never taken a vacation in her life. She rather liked the idea.

"Very well, I accept your terms," she said. "We will return when I have found the Stone of the First High Pontiff."

"*If* you find it." For the first time, Jin detected an odd tone in the Voice. Was it humor? Skepticism? Jin wondered if the Voice didn't think much of the High Pontiff hiring some lowly Revnen from a conquered planet performing so important a task, and likely didn't think she was up to it.

Not that Jin cared what the Voice thought. Since she found the gem, she'd been able to find *anything*.

As they walked back toward the exit, under the many eyestalks of the previous High Pontiffs, Timm asked, "Please tell me you got us at least ten thousand for this."

Jin blinked. "What? No, I got another two thousand. That's four thousand, Timm, that's better—"

Whispering his shout so he didn't attract the attention of the High Pontiff or his Voice, Timm said, "You *what*? Look, I only know about ten phrases in Vhaddish, but one of them is 'the Stone of the First High Pontiff,' and I heard you both using that one all over the damn place. That's what they want you to find, right?"

"Yes."

Timm shook his head. "You didn't do any transactions, so I'm guessing they'll pay the other two thousand when we come back with the stone?"

Jin nodded.

"Did you ask for expenses?"

This time, Jin shook her head. "Our expenses are never more than two thousand—in fact, they're never more than a few hundred, so—"

Waving her off, Timm said, "Doesn't matter. They can twiddle their tentacles all they want, we'll find it and sell it to the highest bidder. And I gotta tell you, the bidding will *start* at five thousand."

"No."

They got to the ornate fingelt door, which opened at their approach. Dozens of acolytes, as well as petitioners and other people waiting for a chance to see the High Pontiff sat with varying degrees of patience outside in the vestibule.

Neither Jin nor Timm spoke anymore of this until they reached the port where *Seeker* was docked.

Once they were safely on board with no prying ears around, Timm immediately went to the console and set the ScanBots to start a security sweep. Jin agreed with the sentiment. She wouldn't put it past the Lighters to plant a listening device on the ship to make sure they stuck to the plan.

Smiling, Timm pointed at the display, which showed that no fewer than three such devices had been placed on board. Jin was very grateful that they'd spent the money on the ScanBots—which she was planning to upgrade to the 6000 model once this job was done. After what happened on Siersee...

"All right, now that we can talk," Timm said, "let's talk. We can get so much more for—"

"No, Timm, I won't do that." Jin sat in the co-pilot's seat, relieved to be speaking in Yrak again. Her lips and tongue were exhausted from forming words in Vhaddish. "I will not become someone who reneges on a contract.

It's been hard enough to find work. People don't believe that I'm as good as my reputation—"

Chuckling, Timm said, "If I didn't know your secret, *I* wouldn't believe you're as good as your reputation."

Jin nodded, conceding the point. "But I agreed to find the stone for the Lighters. And these are people who have a massive platform. Even non-believers can't get away from hearing from them all the time. If we go back on a contract with them, we'll never get another job."

"For that stone, we'll make enough that we won't *need* one." Timm sighed. "Yeah, yeah, okay, fine, we'll do it. But you should've talked him up another thousand at least."

Shaking her head, Jin stared at her console, which indicated new YourMail—one of which came from the same address as the Lighters' original message. Conjoined to that mail was a series of Inform files. "Okay, I'm gonna need to go through all this. Even with the gem, it should take me a few hours."

Timm nodded. "I'll take us out, then. Take a nice slow, leisurely journey to the Fearag Corridor."

Jin returned the nod and got up to head to her bunk. She was worried that Timm would just stay in the dock, but as she had pointed out many times, sitting in a dock cost money—flying in space was free.

At least, most of the time.

When she entered her cabin, she immediately stripped down to her underclothing—necessary in the heat. After upgrading the security system, her next priority after this job was done was to finally fix the thermostats in the bunks.

Discarding her coverall, she sat down on her bed and stared down at the gem embedded in her chest, right above her left breast, over her heart.

She still knew nothing about the blood-red gem, or what it was doing in that asteroid field, or why it embedded itself in her chest dangerously close to her heart, or why, since then, she'd literally been able to find *anything* she set her mind to find.

But shortly after she found the gem—or it found her?—her owners died, and she and Timm (who was free, but employed by Jin's owners) struck out on their own as "the human finder."

And she'd become more confident, more intelligent, more athletic. Her facility for Vhaddish had improved without any practice, and before the gem, if anyone had slapped her down the way Timm had, she'd have demurred and capitulated.

Something else she needed to do was find a good doctor. She'd allowed herself to be examined by medics she could afford, none of whom could figure out how the gem worked, how it was doing what it was doing, or much of anything else. One even offered to surgically remove it, which Jin quickly declined until she knew more.

But with the money they were getting for this, she could see a *talented* doctor.

Grabbing a tablet, she touched the implant on the back of her neck, and the Inform started to download right into her own mind.

Then, as always was necessary after that kind of download, she fell asleep.

As soon as she woke up, Jin knew everything there was to know about the Stone of the First High Pontiff, from the stories about how the First High Pontiff dug the stone out of a quarry with his bare hands, and why he chose the script he chose, and how his successors each placed the stone in a place of higher honor, how the stone was lost during the Pranik War when Vhad was destroyed, and the stories of how the stone was smuggled out by acolytes, and so much more.

She went back to the flight deck. Timm turned to give her an expectant look.

"Tell Fearag Corridor Control that we need to book passage to the Wosaphi Conclave."

The Voice of the High Pontiff sighed happily as he tossed the Hebro-Grubs—Hebro grew much more succulent grubs than the usual store-bought ones—into his lower mouth while dictating a memo in Yrak to the bishopric with his upper mouth. Computers couldn't really handle Vhaddish.

"Against my direct recommendation, the High Pontiff has continued to attempt to find the Stone of the First High Pontiff, despite the fact that the stone was obviously lost forever when Vhad was destroyed by the heretics of Pranik. The legends that grew up around the stone were created to keep the devout from abandoning us following the destruction of our homeworld."

The Voice threw some more HerboGrubs into his mouth. They were particularly good today, and he made a mental note to compliment his slaves for getting a good bunch.

He continued to dictate his memo: "However, we can take some comfort in the fact that the High Pontiff has, of late, become quite fascinated with the so-called 'human finder.' He has become convinced that she will be the one to find the Stone of the First High Pontiff. To that end, I have liberated two thousand marks from the treasury to pay her off. She will search for it, never find it, and then the High Pontiff will finally let go of his obsession with using the stone to unite the factions. While the notion of bringing the heretics back into the fold in the abstract is a noble one, its practicality remains specious, especially since donations have increased a thousand-fold since the schism. However, the High Pontiff continues to drone on about his legacy, that he wishes the Ninety-Ninth High Pontiff to be remembered as the one who healed the schism. With luck, the human finder's failure to locate the stone will end this foolishness."

As he popped the last of his HerboGrubs, he added, "And do not be concerned that the human finder will attempt to bring us a forgery. Providing a convincing forgery of the stone is far beyond her means. The materials alone for such a forgery would cost many thousands of marks."

With that, the Voice sent the memo off to the bishopric. He was looking forward to the soon end of this obsession of the High Pontiff's.

The following morning, he awoke to a YourMail that the human finder had returned with the Stone of the First High Pontiff.

The Voice had to reread the message several times before he finally believed that it said what his eyestalks insisted it did.

"This isn't possible," he muttered as his servants tended to his fur before he met with the High Pontiff.

When he arrived for his audience in the High Pontiff's private chambers—to which only the Voice and selected sex slaves were allowed—the Voice was distressed at how joyful the High Pontiff seemed. His limbs were quivering, and his eyestalks practically bouncing.

"A great day for the Sacred Church of Enlightened Thought and Belief, is it not, my Voice?"

"So it would appear to be, Most Holy One. I am, however, surprised that the human finder was able to locate the Stone of the First High Pontiff so quickly."

"As am I, my Voice. It is proof that she is quite extraordinary. Come, let us not keep her waiting, for today is a great day in the history of the Sacred Church of Enlightened Thought and Belief."

The Voice followed several paces behind the High Pontiff as he entered the receiving room.

Once the High Pontiff was seated in his throne, the Voice instructed the computer to let the human finder in.

When she entered, the Voice had to once again be persuaded that his eyestalks were functioning properly. The human finder's face had several scars that were covered with DermalRep, her hair was considerably shorter than it had been when last she was here—and it looked as if it had been singed off—while her companion had a massive bandage on the crown of his smooth scalp.

The human finder was also holding a PlastiForm container.

"This is not possible," the Voice said without preamble, and before the human finder could say anything.

"On the contrary," the human finder said, "it is very possible. The Stone of the First High Pontiff was in a storage unit located under the ruins of Crivda."

Several of the Voice's tentacles quivered. "The Stone of the High Pontiff was in the territory of the Wosaphi Conclave?"

"Very deep within their territory," the human finder said, "but I was able to retrieve it, after a great deal of difficult searching." She exchanged a look with her taller companion.

Then she touched the side of the PlastiForm container, which slid open, and then she pulled out a round, engraved stone the size of her fist.

The Voice found himself unable to speak with either mouth at first. It looked very much like what the stone looked like in contemporary images. He'd imagined it to be larger, but—

But no, it had to be a forgery. Hadn't it?

His voice even raspier than usual, the High Pontiff reached out with several tentacles. "The stone," he said in Yrak, "it has been—found—at last—it has..."

Then the High Pontiff collapsed, rolling off the throne and onto the floor.

Stunned, the Voice stared for a second, then instructed the computer to summon medical help and activate the triage program.

The computer intoned a moment later: "All life functions in the Ninety-Ninth High Pontiff have ceased."

Quickly, the Voice stood up and spoke to the Church Warriors stationed at the room's pillars. "Remove these heretics! And have them take their forgery with them!"

"It's *not* a forgery!" The human finder was speaking in Yrak now as well. "I wouldn't have found it if it was a fake! That's not how it works!"

"It doesn't matter what you say," the Voice said in the same language, to make it clear that he would not be doing business with forgers. He had no idea how they'd managed to construct a fake, but it simply *could not* be the same one.

As the Warriors stood behind each of the humans, the woman said, "Our ScanBot verified that this was made of jeevon! There's only, what, half an acre's worth of jeevon left in the galaxy? Less? There's no way we could've gotten our hands on that. This is the real thing!"

"It doesn't matter," the Voice said again—and truly, it didn't. "The High Pontiff is dead, and his ridiculous quest to reunite the church has thankfully died with him. You are heretics and forgers, and you will remove yourself from this world as soon as possible."

"So, you do betray me," said a raspy voice, also speaking in Yrak.

All of the Voice's eyestalks turned in shock as the High Pontiff rose up. "It—it—"

"Your treachery has been sent to the InformNet, so now the entire Collective is aware of your heresy."

With a start, the Voice realized that that was why the High Pontiff had been speaking in Yrak. Somewhere in the receiving room, he had sequestered CamDrones that were blasting to the InformNet.

"Remove the Voice and bind him by law," the High Pontiff said as he retook his throne.

The Warriors did as they were told. The Voice said nothing else, not wishing to make a further fool of himself to the entire InformNet. He would wait his time to speak his piece. Half the bishopric was on his side, and the High Pontiff would soon see his support erode.

At least, that was what he hoped. His own indiscretion would not sit well with his allies in the bishopric.

Jin had entered the receiving room thinking she was going to make two thousand marks—which was barely enough to cover what they went through to retrieve the damned stone. Then she thought she was going to be placed in a Vhaddish prison for the rest of her life. Then she thought they were going to get the money again.

So when the newly resurrected High Pontiff instructed the Warriors to escort them back to their ship, she was kind of surprised.

Speaking again in Vhaddish, Jin said, "Forgive me, please, High Pontiff, but we had an arrangement."

"You had an arrangement with my former Voice. That arrangement is no more. For all that I am aware, you were part of his plan to discredit me."

"His plan, High Pontiff, was for me never to find the Stone of the First High Pontiff. But I *have* found it."

"That is not possible." He switched to Yrak. "The stone was lost forever. I merely expressed interest in retrieving it to find out how deep my former Voice's treachery was. That stone must be a forgery—not yours, perhaps, but a forgery nonetheless."

"No, High Pontiff, *that* is what is not possible. My—my ability to find things can't be fooled by a forgery. *This* is what I found when I sought out the stone."

"Take them away!"

The guards each put their hands on Jin's and Timm's shoulders and started to guide them toward the exit. Jin supposed she should have been grateful that they hadn't unsheathed their GranitoZaps.

Deliberately speaking in Cwyar, Timm muttered, "*Now* can we auction this thing off to the highest bidder?"

Several months later, Jin lay on the sands of the Covert Beach, the twin suns of Covert gently baking her naked body. She had never taken a vacation before, and the last month on Covert had been magnificent. Never in her life had she been so relaxed.

Once the first of the suns went down, she decided to see what was happening in the Collective. Timm was due back the following day with the newly refitted *Seeker*, complete with the new ScanBot 6000, working thermostats, and shiny new coils—not to mention a general overhaul of parts.

Easy enough to do when you sell the Stone of the First High Pontiff to the "heretical" Relativist Sect for fifty thousand marks.

Touching her implant, she was able to get an AetherAir signal and do a quick InformNet download, bringing her up to date on assorted sports scores, news, and other stuff.

She noted an abstract of a piece on the resignation of the Ninety-Ninth High Pontiff, and activated that Inform.

"The surprise resignation of the Ninety-Ninth High Pontiff comes as record numbers of devout have left the Lighters, defecting to the Relativist Sect in light of that sect's revelation of the Stone of the First High Pontiff."

Jin couldn't help but laugh. It only would have cost the High Pontiff two thousand marks to keep the stone for himself. Instead, he let them leave with it, and it cost him his job.

"In the meantime, the Council of Elders of the Relativist Sect have announced that, with the great influx of new members to their church, they are considering electing a High Pontiff from among their number."

Jin went through the rest of the story only to find no mention of her whatsoever—indeed, that there was no mention that the Relativists *acquired* the stone, but that they simply had a "revelation" of it, whatever that meant. That was too bad—being the person who found the Stone of the First High Pontiff would be great for business—but she would have to settle for the large sums of money the Relativists paid her.

She also had a YourMail from the Ninety-Ninth High Pontiff. She wondered if he sent that before or after he resigned.

"To the human finder. It seems I owe you an apology. Or perhaps I owe you nothing, since you have received more money for the Stone of the First High Pontiff from those damned heretics. Either way, your skills are obviously greater than I gave you credit for, and in my eagerness to discredit my traitorous Voice I neglected the devout. I'll obviously never make that mistake again."

Jin smiled. Maybe public recognition didn't matter so much.

CHITTER CHITTER BANG BANG
A Starfist Story
David Sherman

"It'll be a piece of cake!" Lorenzo hooted.

"This is the best idea I've ever heard!" Morton crowed.

"Can you say, we'll be rich?" Norman was breathing heavy at the thought.

"I've got all the trajectory data we need for an intercept," Oscar said, understandably smug.

"And my contact at the Confederation embassy in Berrican confirmed that the Navy isn't providing escorts for the flights anymore," Lorenzo added.

"Yeah, what you said, a piece of cake!"

"We're gonna be rich!"

"We'll be richer than Croesus!"

"Who's Croesus?"

"Never mind, let's get started on our intercept."

The four were former members of Sharp Edge, LLC, the "Corporate Security Provider"—mercenaries in fact, if not in name—that had conducted an illegal mining operation on Opal's sister planet, Ishtar. Sharp Edge had enslaved thousands of the indigenous sentients to do the mining until the operation was shut down by Confederation Marines. The Sharp Edge principals were all in prison, but most of the lower-level employees had been released and given transport to their home worlds. Except the four, who hijacked a small interstellar and returned to the Opal/Ishtar system to steal a shipment of freshly-mined gems.

Nobody called him Henny anymore. His real name was too hard for most Naked Ones to say, so he shall be called Henny, which was what the Naked Ones who enslaved the People called him before the Naked Ones' Marines came and killed the slavers until the surviving slavers went away. Then the Marines went away, and so did all the other Naked Ones.

Except...

About every year and a half a Naked Ones' thunder-cart dropped down from the sky on its pillar of fire. When it did, it brought a new team of four Naked Ones and took away the four Naked Ones who had been on the World since the last time the thunder-cart had come. Henny had seen the sky-fire come down three times and go back up twice. A thunder-cart was at the Naked Ones' base now, and would leave in another day, when the four Naked Ones returned from the mine where they'd spent the past week. Henny didn't know why these Naked Ones stored the pretty-but-worthless stones they gathered from the mines instead of taking them with them when they left. But each of the other times he'd seen them come and then leave again, they stored the stones instead of taking them.

The Naked Ones who came to the World found places from which they could observe the People. Unobserved, or so they thought. But all of the People knew these new Naked Ones were there. Even the clans and burrows of the Starwarmth Union knew about the hidden Naked Ones, and everybody knew the burrows and clans of the Starwarmth Union were neither very observant nor very smart.

Henny spent as much time as he could watching these Naked Ones. He knew he was well enough hidden that they couldn't see him. What he didn't know was why they were here. What did they want? They weren't like the Marines who had gone away; the Marines had never tried to hide from the People like these Naked Ones did. Were these Naked Ones also hiding from the Marines? Were they forerunners of a return of the Naked Ones who had enslaved the People before?

Henny needed to find out. That was why he watched them, that was why he examined the traps they put out in places People might walk or scamper, or put them in places where the traps would hide, brooding within sight of burrow entrances.

He never set off one of the traps; he was very careful when he examined them, although a few times he heard a strange, faint clicking sound come from inside one as he examined it. He had no idea what that sound signified; maybe the trap was malfunctioning, and he was lucky not to be snared by it. He didn't know how the traps worked. They weren't cages such as a hunter would use to capture small game. Maybe they held nets that would spring out and ensnare their victims.

The more Henny thought about it, how the Naked Ones came down from the sky on their fire pillars to locations remote from any burrow, and hid themselves from the People, and put out traps, the more he suspected they were advance scouts for a return of the evil Naked Ones.

It would be a very bad thing if they were.

Henny would have liked to listen to these Naked Ones talk among themselves; he'd learned some of their language when he was captured by the Ruhrines. He and the Ruhrines' wiseman, Rzz-tar Chranck—it was a difficult name for Henny to pronounce, as was Ruhrines. Rzz-tar Chranck had explained to Henny that the language of the Naked Ones had three sounds, "B, M, and P," that required a closed upper lip to say, and the People had split upper lips. Anyway, Henny and Rzz-tar Chranck had spent several weeks learning to speak each others languages before the Ruhrines went away and took their wiseman with them. But these Naked Ones always had their heads encased in chel-zrizts, garments to protect them from the elements, and must speak in what Rzz-tar Chranck said was rah-dee-oh. Henny didn't understand what rah-dee-oh was, but knew he couldn't understand anything spoken in it, not without the box-that-translates.

Henny wished he could read the Naked Ones' writing, as he could read the writing of the People's language. He wanted to know what the legend on the side of the thunder-cart meant:

> **Confederation of Human Worlds**
> **Bureau of Human Habitability**
>   **Exploration and Investigation**
> **Interplanetary Shuttle No 3**
> **Opal/Ishtar System**

Henny had to find out what these Naked Ones were doing on the World. If they wanted to once more enslave the People, he had to find the Ruhrines and tell them about it so they could stop it like they had before.

Henny thought the Ruhrines must have gone to the wandering star the Naked Ones called O-chal. He didn't understand how people, even Naked Ones, could go to a star and live there. But Fzz-tar Chranck told him O-chal wasn't a star, a ball of fire far, far away, but much closer, a world like the

World he lived on. He hadn't known the wiseman to lie to him about anything else, so maybe this was true also.

No matter how unlikely it sounded.

If that was true, and if O-chal was where the Ruhrines went after driving away the evil Naked Ones, then that was where Henny had to go.

The only way Henny could think of to get to O-chal was on the Naked Ones' thunder-cart. He knew he couldn't simply ask them to take him along when they left. Even if he threatened them with his rifle and they complied, how long did the voyage last? Could he stay awake and on guard for that length of time? Or would he fall asleep and be taken by the Naked Ones?

No, confronting the Naked Ones directly was too risky.

There was only one way Henny could go on the thunder-cart. He had to sneak onto it and find a place to hide. He would have to take food with him. But how much? And water, too.

There were so many questions, and so few answers.

Henny looked at his rifle. It wasn't one of the iron rifles made by the People, a rifle that had to be reloaded after every time it was fired, and quickly fouled. It was one of the needle-rifles the Naked Ones slavers used and seldom needed reloading; a flechette rifle is what the Ruhrines called it. Henny thought "flechette" was a clumsey word, and he called it a needle-rifle. Before they left, the Ruhrines gave the needle-rifle to Henny in thanks for helping them with learning each others' language. He would have preferred one of the Ruhrines' fire-rifles, but still was happy with what they gave him.

Henny knew he didn't have much time if he was going to sneak onto this thunder-cart. He broke off his observing and set about gathering food and water to sustain him on the trip to O-chal. And some glow worms, in case there wasn't light where he hid in the thunder-cart

Inside the thunder-cart Henny found a large storeroom filled with containers of different sizes. He had seen these containers, or containers just like them, being taken off the thunder-cart when it arrived, and then put back on. He thought it likely that the empty containers in the thunder-cart now were not the same ones he'd just seen removed, but rather the ones that had been unloaded on the thunder-cart's previous visit. Not that it mattered. What mattered was that they were empty now.

Henny removed one of the glow worms from the *granalchit* skin sack in which he carried them to light his way among the containers. Their arrangement reminded him so strongly of home, just like the houses and other structures carved into a burrow, that Henny briefly felt homesick. But the homesickness he felt now was nothing compared to what he'd felt when he was caged by the Naked Ones, and let out only for poor meals and to dig in the mines, so his homesickness didn't last very long.

Henny explored the storeroom and found material to use as bedding and for other furnishings. He also found a way to secure his rifle should the thunder-cart lash about like a bush in a storm. Then he settled in for however long the trip would be.

When the thunder-cart took off, Henny thought he should have made a deeper, softer bed; he'd never before felt so crushed. Fortunately, the crushing pressure only lasted for a few minutes. Then came a brief time during which he floated unsettlingly in midair and barely kept his stomach contents. After that, things became more or less normal, except that the air smelled strange.

Henny wasn't sure how long it was, at least three days, perhaps not more than four although it could have been longer—he'd managed to do a lot of sleeping and couldn't track time very well—when the constant low droning of machinery was interrupted by clanging and metallic clashing. Dimly, he heard angry shouting—the first voices he'd heard through the walls of the thunder-cart.

Then he heard the unmistakable *crack* of a gunshot.

Henny tucked the glow worm he'd been using back into the sack, then grabbed his rifle and scampered to a position he had prepared to fight from if the Naked Ones learned that he was on their thunder-cart and came hunting him.

There was more angry shouting after the gunshot, but no more shooting. Then came several minutes of silence before footsteps sounded in the passage outside the storeroom. The footsteps stopped right outside, then the door was yanked open and a light flashed inside.

Henny tensed. Squinting against the light, he aimed his rifle, ready to shoot the first Naked One to come in.

He didn't shoot the first Naked One.

That one wasn't armed, and was roughly shoved inside to fall on the floor. Two more rapidly followed, and the three tumbled into a pile. They didn't move immediately.

"Don't try to come out," a harsh voice snarled from the corridor. "We're armed and you aren't. Even if we can't lock this hatch, we've got it covered and we'll shoot anybody who tries to come out. Remember, we don't need to keep you alive, so behave and you might live through this."

Henny was delighted! he had understood nearly all of the Naked Ones' words, even though he hadn't heard their language spoken since the Ruhrines had gone away.

A hand shot around the edge of the doorway and did something; light flooded the storeroom. The hand withdrew and the door slammed shut.

Henny watched the three Naked Ones unpile themselves. One of them called out, "What about Keely? What are you going to do with Keely? He needs help." Even though he'd only seen one or two of the Naked Ones' females, Henny knew the signs that distinguished between males and females. The one who spoke had the teat-like chest-mounds of a female.

"Don't you worry about Keely," the rough voice answered from outside the door. "We'll take care of the body, it won't stink up your cell." The Naked One laughed and the footsteps went away.

"They killed Keely," somebody said with a whimper. That one also had the teat-like chest mounds. Another sign of the differences between male and female among the Naked Ones was that the females had voices high enough that they could chitter like the People if they wanted to, but the males voices were too deep and slow to chitter. Both of the chest-mound Naked Ones had high voices, another proof that they were female.

If somebody was dead, Henny thought that must have been from the gunshot he'd heard. One of the females began sobbing.

"We can't do anything for him now—and we don't know that he's dead," said another voice. "We need to figure out how to stay alive, and regain control of the shuttle." This speaker had a deep voice. Henny looked closely and saw that he didn't have chest-mounds; an obvious male.

"The captain will figure a way," the first female said softly. "There, there, it'll be all right." She caressed the hair of the sobbing female.

"The captain can't do squat except what those pirates want," the male said, using a couple of words Henny didn't know, but he thought the meaning was clear enough. "There's only one of him and four of them. They're armed, he isn't. We have to come up with our own solution."

The male and the first female continued talking in low voices, and the second female still sobbed, but softly. Henny settled in to think about the situation which had changed since he snuck onto the thunder-cart. He knew for sure he'd been wrong about these Naked Ones when he heard this exchange:

"When we don't make our scheduled reports," the male said, "the Navy will come looking for us. With any luck at all, they'll have some Marines with them."

The second female suddenly stopped sobbing and said excitedly, "The Marines are coming? They'll save us. We're saved!"

These Naked Ones weren't with the evil Naked Ones who had enslaved the People! That must mean that these were good Naked Ones like the Marines, and the four armed ones were evil.

Henny decided to make himself known to the people in the storeroom with him. He made the low bark that Rzz-tar Chranck said was, "the Fuzzy equivalent of throat clearing."

Startled exclamations came from the Naked Ones and they turned toward Henny's hiding place.

Henny stood. He held his tail limp, and his hands away from his sides with the palms and claws facing away from the Naked Ones. "Don't be afraid," he said in what he hoped was a reassuring tone. "I'm what you call a Fuzzy, and I have a needle-rifle. We can work together to defeat the evil Naked Ones." He didn't mention the "replica K-bar" that the Ruhrines had given him along with the needle-rifle. Those weren't the exact words he used, and his pronunciation wasn't fully clear, but it was good enough that the Naked Ones understood him.

"You speak English?" the male asked. "How's that possible?"

"When the Ruhrines were on the World, I worked with their wiseone, Fzz-tar Chranck and we learned each other's languages."

"I heard about this," the first female said rapidly. "Are you, are you... what's the name? Henry, is that it? Are you the Fuzzy called Henry?"

"Henny, Henny! Yes I'm Henny!"

"Henny, right. I'm sorry I got it wrong. Sam, we're in luck," the female said. "Lieutenant Prang off the Grandar Bay taught him to speak English, and learned the Fuzzy language from him. And he said Henny's a good fighter, too."

"Henny," said the male now identified as Sam, "are you armed? Do you have a weapon?"

"Yes, I have a Naked Ones' needle-rifle."

"Right, you already said that. What do you mean by a needle-rifle?"

"You call it a fflesh-chette rifle. I prefer needle-rifle."

"Flechette," Sam said, "that's good."

"Why is that good? one of the females asked.

Sam answered, "Because the slugs thrown by the Fuzzies' guns can blow holes in the hull of the shuttle. A flechette can't."

"I'm Adele," the first female said. "Sam and Lisette and I are xenobiologists. Do you know what that is, Henny?"

"It's a wiseone who knows about people and plants of other worlds." Henny thought for a few seconds, then asked, "Is that why you were on the World, you were studying the People and the plants?"

"Yes!"

"Why didn't you come to us in the open, why did you try to hide?"

"Because if you knew we were watching, you might not have behaved the way you normally do."

Henny chittered a laugh. "You don't hide very well. Everybody knew you were there. Even the People of the Starwarmth Union knew you were there—and they're not very observant or very smart." Henny abruptly changed the subject.

"I want to talk more with you, but first we have to deal with the evil Naked Ones who have taken over this thunder-cart—and killed Keely."

"There are four of them," Sam said. "The only weapon we have is your flechette... needle rifle. One armed Fuzzy, one unarmed man, and two unarmed women—and all the humans are scientists, not a fighter among us. How can we take them on?"

"I am thinking." Henny went to the closed door and held the side of his face next to it.

"What are you...?" Sam began, but Adele hushed him. "Good hearing," she whispered, pointing to his largish ears.

Very good hearing indeed. The sentients humans called "Fuzzies" could hear the insectoids and small burrowers that were a major part of their diet moving about underground.

"None are nearby," Henny said after a moment. He looked at the humans. "Do you have writing implements? Can you draw the floor-flan for me?"

Sam looked at him sharply. All along he'd been hearing the meaning of what Henny said, even when he didn't get the exact words. While he knew that the Fuzzies were far more intelligent and technologically advanced than the mercenaries of Sharp Edge who'd held them as slaves ever admitted, he didn't expect a Fuzzy to be sophisticated enough to ask for a stylus and a floorplan.

"I have a scriber," Lisette said, the first words she'd said since declaring that they would be saved. She held it out.

Sam took it and looked around for something to draw on. Adele brushed a patch of floor clear of dust.

"Do you understand human measurements?" Sam asked as he began sketching.

"I know reeters and klicks."

"Meters and kilometers?" Sam asked for clarification.

"Yes."

"Good. We won't need kilometers for this, the shuttle isn't anywhere near that big. But meters are good."

The shuttle was a boxy oblong, bluntly pointed at one end, with two decks. Sam didn't bother drawing the lower deck, it was engineering; fuel, propulsion, life support, comps. The upper deck had four storerooms, four rooms for crew/ passenger quarters. There was a recroom, galley, and what they called the "bridge." The bridge had the flight controls, seldom used as the shuttle was mostly run by computer, and communications. There were two hatches indicated; an airlock in the common room, which was the entry the pirates had used, and a cargo hatch in the rear port storeroom. Sam had to explain what an airlock was.

"This is where we are," Sam indicated the aft port-side storeroom. "For now, they're probably holding the captain on the bridge." He indicated the forward-most space.

"Where is Keely? Is captain sure on r-ridge?" Henny wanted to know.

Sam shook his head. "If the captain isn't on the bridge being guarded, he's in his cabin." He tapped a room to the immediate left rear of the bridge. "If Keely's dead they might have moved him to their boat, or they might have put his body in the crew quarters. I don't know." After a few seconds he tapped another cabin and added, "This was Keely's. Dead or alive, he could be there."

"Those are all the roons?" Henny asked, pointing at the drawn crew quarters.

Sam nodded. "As near as I can, complete and to scale." Henny needed an explanation of "to scale."

"Good," the Fuzzy said, and spent a few moments studying the floor plan before returning to listen at the door again.

"When is sleech cycle?" he asked.

"Sleep cycle?" Adele asked.

Henny chittered an affirmative.

"It's sleep time now," she said. "That's why we're dressed…" She made a sweeping gesture at her clothes. The plain garment meant nothing to Henny; the Fuzzies, being covered with a thin fur, didn't wear clothes, night or otherwise. Still, he got the message. Even though he'd never seen a thigh-length gown before he grasped that the Naked Ones wore it to sleep in. He guessed they needed it; the temperature in the thunder-cart was chilly, although the Naked Ones didn't seem to think so. He wondered if the pink flush that suddenly appeared on Lisette's face had anything to do with the coldness of the storeroom.

"Is it sleech tine for evil Naked Ones also?"

Sam and Adele looked at each other.

"We don't know," Sam finally said. "It depends, if they're on Berrican time, yes. If not, who knows?"

Henny looked at him without comprehension. What is "Berrican time"? How could there be more than one time?

"He doesn't understand time zones," Adele said to Sam.

"Sam smacked his own forhead. "How stupid of me. He barely knows that Ishtar is a globe, and when it's day here it's night on the other side of the world."

Henny suddenly understood what Sam meant. "Rzz-tar Chranck taught me how time," he said. "He showed me a, a…" he mimed holding a ball in his hand—he couldn't pronounce the word—"with light on one side, dark on the other. I know tine zones." He nodded rapidly, he knew that was the Naked One way of signaling understanding. He looked to be in thought for a moment, then said, "one chance in two this is their sleech tine."

"Maybe," Sam agreed. "More likely one chance in three."

Henny cocked his head, absorbing that. Yes, the Naked Ones had artificial light the same as the People did, so they likely were awake longer than only the half time of daylight, the same as the People. He recalled that Rzz-tar Chranck and the Ruhrines he'd dealt with also had longer waking times.

"I listen, you quiet." Henny returned to the hatch and put his ear near it, listening for sounds of movement elsewhere on the shuttle.

Henny listened for an hour without hearing anything. "I think this is their sleech tine," he said. He broke off from the door and looked at the three scientists. Lisette looked to be asleep, Sam was nodding with his head lolling on his chest. Only Adele seemed to be awake.

"I look now." Henny eased the door open, exposing a passageway dimly lit from one end. He poked his head into the passageway and, sniffing, looked toward the light and then away from it. His eyes were large, evolved to see in unlit burrows long before his people began using glow worms to light their underground homes. Away from the light, he only saw the hatches of the other aft compartment and the end of the passageway. In the other direction, he saw that the source of the dim light was out of sight. After having been closed in the storeroom with its alien smells for no fewer than three days, and possibly more than four, and then with the three Naked Ones for a couple of hours, he couldn't detect any scents from the common room. He looked back into the storeroom. Adele was watching him intently, as was Sam who was now awake.

"You stay," Henny whispered. He slipped all the way into the passageway and crept along it to the entry to the common room. His tail jutted straight back, and his claws faced front, ready to slash. He peered around the edge of the doorway into the common room.

The common room was much smaller than the storeroom he'd been in until now. It had sufficient seating for six people if they were friendly enough, and a table that could accomodate six if they sat closely side by side. The light seemed to come from the edge of one end of the ceiling. There were no Naked Ones in the room, although there was a reddish stain on the floor. When Henny examined it he found it was sticky. He thought it was blood from Keely.

He crept to the doorway on the other side of the common room, offset to the right side from the entrance from the storerooms and from the airlock hatch through which the pirates had entered. That hatch was closed. Listening carefully, he heard a faint voice from up ahead. He risked a look around the edge of the doorway and saw a short passageway leading forward. Two rooms opened off it on the left, two more on the right—the cabins for the passengers. One of the doors on the left was ajar; the source of the voice. The only light in the passageway spilled from the common room and the door that was ajar.

There was only one voice. Henny decided to take the risk and slipped to the open door. He was able to see less than half of the room, but that was enough to show a bound man with bruises on his face sitting on a narrow bed. Here, the voice was clear enough for Henny to understand most of what it was saying.

"One more time, Captain. You're going to turn this shuttle around and take us back to Ishtar. You will land at the same place you took off from, and once I and my men finish our business there, you will fly us off to where I tell you. If not, I'm going to start putting your people out the airlock one at a time. Do you want their deaths on your conscience?"

"You're going to kill us anyway," the captain said. "So why should I help you?"

"Anybody I put out the airlock is dead for sure," the voice said. "If I don't put anybody out the airlock, I haven't added homicide to any charges against me if I'm ever caught. That's why. So, you see, it's in my interest to keep you all alive."

The captain didn't answer immediately; Henny couldn't read Naked Ones' expressions well enough to tell if the man was considering what the other had said.

After the silence dragged on for a minute, the voice said, "I guess it's time to use the airlock."

Henny spun about and, curling his toes up so their claws wouldn't click on the deck, raced back to the storeroom. The door was open far enough for Sam and Adele to look out.

"We must move," Henny when he reached them. He stepped into the storeroom only long enough to grab a small bundle from his hiding place. In the corridor, he checked the hatch on the opposite side. It opened easily.

"Here!" Henny ordered.

Sam had to take Lisette by the arm and almost drag her along.

They barely had the hatch closed before the pirate leader appeared at the end of the passageway. He stopped at the sound of a voice that Henny could hardly hear.

"About time you came to your senses," the pirate said, and turned back.

Henny hurriedly told the Humans what he'd learned when he went forward. When he got to, "...it's time to use the airlock," Lisette's eyes went wide and her mouth wider, and she took a deep breath.

Sam moved faster than Henny had seen him move before, to wrap an arm around her to pull her close, and clamp a hand over her mouth.

"Don't scream, keep quiet!"

Adele moved to Lisette's side and hugged her. "It'll be all right honey. We're safe now," she cooed.

Lisette sagged, and Sam relaxed his hold on her mouth. "They're going to kill us, she whimpered. "They're going to put us out the airlock."

"No they aren't," Sam said, still holding his hand ready to clamp down if she went to scream again.

"Sam's right, honey," Adele said soothingly. "If they were going to kill us, that pirate wouldn't have gone back, he still would have come to get one of us to kill."

"He would fail," Henny chittered, hefting his flechette rifle.

"You'll do that? You'll protect us?" Lisette asked.

"You are with Ruh-rines. You are good Naked Ones. I am Henny, warrior of the Brightsun Clan, friend to Ruh-rines. I rho-tect you."

With more strength than anyone would have expected, Lisette wrenched herself from Sam's grip and Adele's hug to fling herself at Henny, throwing her arms around his neck and hugging tight.

Henny dropped his rifle and slashed at her with his claws, but her movement was so sudden and unexpected that he didn't react instantly.

That gave Adele time to cry, "Don't!" and Sam to shout, "Stop!"

Henny froze, his claws nearly touching the woman's back.

"She's not attacking you," Sam told him.

"That's a hug," Adele said.

Henny then realized that Lisette was rubbing the side of her face against his neck and shoulder, very similar to the way a female of the People would nuzzle a male. He drew his claws from her back.

Lisette sneezed. "Your fur tickles my nose," she said, and giggled.

"Honey, you have to let go of Henny so he can do what he needs to do to protect us," Adele said. She gently pried Lisette's arms from around Henny and pulled her away. Lisette let herself be drawn back and looked calmer and more relaxed than she'd been since the pirates first boarded the shuttle.

They became aware of a change in the machine sounds in the small ship, and of new noises.

"It sounds like someone went through the airlock and the pirate ship detached," Sam said. "Is there any way you can find out?" he asked Henny.

The Fuzzy signaled the humans to be quiet and went to listen by the hatch. After a few moments he said he thought there was no one in the common room. He handed his rifle to Sam.

"You rho-tect if I not come a-ack." He reached into the small pack he'd retrieved from the other storeroom and withdrew the K-bar the Marines had given him along with the flechette rifle.

Sam's eyes widened at the sight of the legendary Marine combat knife. "I'm not much of a shot," he said, "but I know how to use a knife."

Henny looked at him and cocked his head.

"I took a martial arts course," Sam explained. "For the exercise," he added.

Henny made a noise, then said "Wait." He slipped out of the storeroom and padded toward the common room. No one was there. The airlock was closed. He looked through the porthole in its inner hatch, through to the far hatch, which was open with only space visible through it.

He headed to the corridor that ran between the living quarters. The cabin where the captain had been held by the pirate before was now empty. Beyond that was the bridge.

Henny could only risk a quick look into the bridge. He saw the captain sitting at a bank of controls and instruments. A man sat one on side of him watching what he did, and another sat behind him. There was no sign or sound of the other two—if there really were four pirates.

Henny backed away. He listened carefully at each of the passenger cabins, and thought he heard more than one person breathing inside one of them.

Before Henny got back to the people he'd left behind, the shuttle lurched, knocking him to the deck. When he finally regained his feet, he had to struggle to stay upright; he felt like his weight had doubled and he was walking down a steep hill. Returning to the storeroom was difficult, but he made it without further incident.

"We turned and are moving under power," Sam explained. "That's the force you feel."

While Henny told them what he'd seen and heard, he took his rifle back from Sam and handed him the K-bar.

"I can kill both of the rhi-rates I saw before they can react," he said. "But where are the other two?"

"At least one of them has to be on their ship," Adele said. "The other one could be the breathing you heard in one of the cabins."

"If that wasn't Keely," Sam said.

"We go. I kill bad Naked Ones in r-ridge," Henny told Sam. "You watch me."

"You're not going anywhere without us," Adele snapped when she realized that Henny intended to leave her and Lisette in the storeroom.

Henny studied her for a moment and thought her expression meant determination. "I kill. You watch aack."

Adele nodded and grinned. Henny was suddenly glad he didn't have to face those fangs, no matter that they were so much shorter than his own.

The weight of acceleration eased while they talked and planned, so when the four left the storeroom walking wasn't the challenge it had been when Henny had come back.

Henny led and the women trailed behind Sam. Nothing had changed in the common room. Henny stopped at the door where he'd earlier heard breathing. He still heard breathing, but it was slower than before. He handed his rifle to Sam and eased the door open, ready to pounce on who-ever was there.

He didn't pounce.

"That's Keely," Sam said, brushing past him and heading for the unconscious man laying on the narrow bed. He handed the K-bar back to Henny as he passed. The women also crowded into the cabin.

"I think he'll live," Adele said after giving Keely a cursory exam. She looked at Henny and Sam. "You go save the captain. We'll take care of Keely."

Henny didn't say anything, just eased out and continued on toward the bridge. Sam followed close behind.

Henny listened at each cabin, but didn't hear sounds from inside any of them. At the entrance to the bridge, he leveled his rifle at the Naked One sitting next to the captain and was squeezing the trigger when Sam suddenly shouted:

"Drop your weapons and surrender! We've got you covered and are taking our shuttle back."

The two pirates dove from their seats, both drew handguns and twisted or spun to face the entrance. They fired.

Henny flinched at the shout just behind him and his first shot thudded into the back of the seat the pirate next to the captain had just left. He bounded into the bridge and to the right, out of the line along which the two pirates shot. He saw one of them clearly, and put a flechette into his chest. That one screamed and curled around his wound, dropping his pistol. The other scrabbled along the deck, seeking better cover. He threw a shot in Henny's direction, but didn't aim and the flechette went high and wide.

The bridge wasn't a large room, no more than four meters wide, really too small to use a rifle. Henny let go of his and pounced high into the air, brushing against the ceiling as he sailed over the chair the pirate had oc-cupied, and came down on the man's back, digging his claws into the flesh.

The man screamed and twisted onto his side to dislodge the Fuzzy. But Henny dug his claws in more deeply and wasn't thrown off. When the man tried to turn his pistol to shoot Henny, Henny let go of his back with one hand and raked those claws the length of the man's arm, ending at the pistol and tearing it from his grip.

He put his claws at the man's throat, with just enough pressure, to let him know how easy it would be to tear out his throat.

"Surrender," he demanded.

One of the first shots fired by the mercenaries hit Sam in the shoulder. Fortunately for him the flechette had gone all the way through, merely chipping a bone along the way. Adele and Lisette were able to bind the wound well enough to keep him from bleeding to death before he got proper medical attention. As soon as the two pirates were secured, the captain called for assistance and changed course back for Opal.

Lorenzo, the leader of the pirates, explained that even though they knew there was a cache of gems to be picked up, they didn't know where it was. They needed the captain and his shuttle to take them to the right place, which was why they took the shuttle.

"We're the good guys," Sam meekly explained when Henny asked why he'd shouted for the pirates to surrender. "We're supposed to give the bad guys a chance to surrender instead of just killing them."

Henny looked away in disgust. "Ruh-rines, they kill evil ones," was all he said.

As for the other two pirates, when a Confederation Navy patrol boat picked them up they were bickering about how the fool proof plan was exactly that, a plan for fools.

PANIC ATTACK
Jeffrey Lyman

RAIN CAME DOWN IN SHEETS. BLACKWELL AND THE OTHER THREE MEMBERS OF HIS team set up in the remains of two burned out foundations about ten meters apart. It was formerly a homestead, perched over a pretty valley that had been dry yesterday but now coursed with a rising stream. The nearby hills were partially terraced, though there was no evidence of an earth-crop planting. Red alien prairie grass had retaken the sculpted ground.

Blackwell tilted his head back, mouth open, and wet his throat. Never enough food, never enough water. Reminded him of growing up on the streets of Phoenix, except for the red sky, the radiation pills, and the stink.

"Blackwell! Quit yer daydreaming and get yer cover set up," barked a voice from the radio. "I want guns pointed down-valley ASAP!"

He grinned and waved to the silhouette of Sarge on the crest of the next ridge, then continued setting up his red camo-tent. It was covered in fake, red, mossy growths like the fronded grass all around them. His new partner's tent was already up on the other side of the foundation.

Sarge stalked back and forth on his ridge in his poncho, gun scope to his eye, reviewing the teams' positions. There were two more teams to Blackwell's east on adjoining ridges, and one team to his west. Four teams, sixteen people. They were all that could be scrounged for the eastern flank. Blackwell didn't even know his new partner's name. Two of the guys to the west were infantry, one of the guys to the east as well. That was it. Everyone else had been drafted from the colonists. There was nobody left from Blackwell's original unit, at least he didn't think so. The line had broken and reformed so many times, it was a wonder there was any order at all.

There wouldn't have been order if there was a place to run to, but their backs were to the wall. All they could do was reform the lines from the pieces and make another stand. Try and hold while the engineers made the hibernation ship livable again.

Until today. Until the rains came.

Sarge had given the pep-talk two hours ago. "The rain won't last forever and the eggheads don't know when it'll rain again. Think of this as our one and only chance. The general's concentrating his manpower in the center, and they're going to engage directly, right up the gut. Push through and inflict as much damage as possible. We have to impair the Karpacs' ability to regroup after the rain stops. The Karpacs don't bother much with our flanks, the way they've been going through us, but they might give it a try once they taste a little Earth steel. That's where we come in."

Blackwell finished setting up his low tent and noticed his new partner struggling with his rifle, so he crouched down in the mouth of the man's tent. Rain ran off his helmet and down his neck around his poncho. "I'm Blackwell. You got a name?"

The man looked up. He had sandy brown hair, short, with a burn-scorch down the side of his head, and freckles. His nose had been broken recently. "Andrew Scruggs."

"What's the problem?"

Scruggs looked down the valley. "I ain't a sniper."

Blackwell smiled. "None of us are, but you gotta be a fair shot if they put you here."

"I do okay."

"So stick with your training and use your gun sight. The sight's already been adjusted for the magnetism in the soil, density of the air, extra gravity. You'll do fine."

"Ain't none of us doing fine."

Blackwell hefted his .50 caliber anti-vehicle sniper rifle from its case and planted the stand on the edge of the foundation wall. "Today's a turkey shoot, son," he said with false confidence. "Do *New Genesis* proud and inflict come pain."

The man was quiet for a moment, then lifted his rifle and sighted down the valley. "If we don't break and run again."

"Not today. Rain's already knocked down the panic smell, can't you tell?" Blackwell inhaled deeply, gratefully.

The native Karpacs could see and speak, in a fashion, but they mostly communicated across vast crowds with scents. Their noses were sharper than their eyes, and they usually attacked at night when the humans were at more of a disadvantage.

The eggheads said they walked around surrounded in a constant sea of communication pheromones, but only a select few of those scents could be detected by human noses. Fewer still caused any re-action. But that one...The Karpacs had discovered a scent that caused instant panic in 90% of humans. It was hell trying to hold the line against it. Soldiers kept long perimeters and shot from a distance, but the scent carried on the wind. The Karpacs practically sweated the stuff during battle and spread it everywhere. The eggheads handed out filter masks, but the pheromones slipped through the filters. There weren't enough containment suits to outfit the defensive line, and the few who were immune operated as roving strike squads. With the Karpac sniffers as sharp as they were, it was near impossible to sneak up on them.

The humans were stuck here, and the Karpacs were ferociously deter-mined to kick them out. They didn't understand there was nowhere else to go, or didn't care. The hibernation ship that had brought the colony here two years ago still circled Ganny III, but it had no means of propulsion and had been so cannibalized for parts to build *New Genesis* that it had no life support.

"Save your bullets in the beginning," Blackwell said to Scruggs. "I'll handle the single shots. If the valley becomes target-rich, that's when I need you."

"How are we supposed to hold, just the four of us?"

"We'll hold it, or we'll make them regret coming through here. You lose family?"

The man nodded.

"Then here's your shot at revenge."

Scruggs nodded again, sharply. Blackwell wondered how many en-gagements he'd seen. He'd probably been drafted recently, as the trained soldiers fell back and fighting got right up under *New Genesis'* walls. Blackwell had been in all four major engagements. Two he'd panicked and run. Two, others had run and left him stranded. It was hard to even look at Karpacs now without getting nervous.

The radio squawked again. "The center's engaged," Sarge's voice cut through the rattle of raindrops. "The enemy is not backing down in the rain. The techs managed to get two hoverbirds in the air for support, so you will hear detonations. Guidance is still a mess from the magnetics, so they'll be dropping explosives hot—no targeting."

"Still should do damage," Blackwell muttered. "With that many Karpacs in a bunch, you don't have to aim." Their Earth ordnance had turned out to be too high-tech for Ganny III. Guidance systems weren't shielded enough for the magnetics. The techs were rigging up fixes, but the Karpacs had been slicing through the human defenses too quickly for the trickle of missiles to make a difference. Someone had suggested catapults.

"I got movement," Blackwell barked into his radio.

Sarge's helmet rose up above the vegetation level. He was gripping a beast of a gun he'd machined himself with a kick on it like a mule. "Confirmed," he said. "Three Karpacs—probably a scout troop. Keep down and let them come into range. Make 'em think this is a safe path."

"I got movement too," said one of the men two valleys east. "Another group of three."

Blackwell pressed his eye to the telescopic sight on his gun. The Karpacs were sniffing like they always did, big fan-shaped mandibles on their beaked jaws waving through the air. Hunting scents. But with the rain coming down hard and the stream rising around their feet, they had to be compromised.

"They look like beetles," Scruggs said under his breath.

"Beetles the size of horses," Blackwell agreed.

They were really closer to turtles—some sort of cold-blooded lizard inside an elaborate shell. Six legs were situated underneath them, rather than splayed out to the side like a true turtle, and armored as well. Their little pincher arms in the front were good enough for holding guns.

No one understood them well, due to the language/smell barrier, but they were intelligent and far enough along in their industrial revolution to kick some ass. *New Genesis* was built at the pole, on a small continent with none of the buggers, but the Karpacs had climbed onto ships and managed to sail an army down here in just under two years. They were determined.

Who knew when the hibernation ship started out from Earth that the closest planet with semi-earthlike conditions would happen to have intelligent life on it? Intelligent life just enough behind the curve that they weren't producing radio signals. Though to be fair, when the hibernation ship took off one hundred and forty years ago, the Karpacs hadn't even started their industrial revolution.

"More movement," Blackwell said, as red vehicles drove cautiously into view around the rock outcrops at the end of the valley. "Shit. Sarge, this isn't a scouting expedition." They were armored vehicles, driven on big, broad wheels, perfect for grabbing at the low vegetation and soil. Most people thought the Karpacs hated riding in them because they couldn't smell their environment or comrades and had to use their weak eyes, but they'd made an exception for this war. The cars were fast. They used their panic-smell to break the human lines, and their cars like cavalry to overrun and flank them.

Blackwell checked his .50 cal anti-vehicle gun. What better way of corking up a valley than with disabled cars? Other troops began calling in that they had vehicles too, followed by organized lines of Karpac troops. Sarge called it in to HQ.

"The enemy is attempting a flanking maneuver," he said. "We have visual confirmation of at least two thousand soldiers and near one hundred vehicles entering our four valleys. They are still coming into view."

"Confirmed," came back the immediate reply. "The western flank also has contact. Meteorologists believe this storm is starting to break up. Repeat, the rain will be ending over the next hour. The center is fully engaged and fighting is hill to hill. You must hold the flank. You are authorized to fire."

"All right, you heard the man," came Sarge's voice over the local radio link. "Light 'em up."

"Go ahead and fire, soldier," Blackwell said to Scruggs, trying to keep his voice calm. "Watch the drop of the bullet. Adjust your aim."

His other two team members in the next foundation over began firing. Blackwell sighted through the telescope, along the lowest of his targeting chevrons. The .50 cal was loaded with incendiary rounds with enough punch to penetrate the armored shells of the cars. Machine-gun fire crackled from adjacent valleys. Scruggs fired once, fired again. Blackwell eased back on his trigger and popped the lead vehicle. It lurched a little, then slowed. Smoke drifted out of the air vents. "Sniff smoke, assholes," Blackwell muttered. Two Karpacs clambered out immediately. Blackwell moved on to the next vehicle and adjusted his elevation again. Pop. Pop. Three vehicles stalled in the heart of the valley.

The Karpac soldiers began to run, still moving in lockstep formation, communicating with scents even in the rain. Blackwell targeted more vehicles, his heart thumping hollow in his chest. There was return fire, but the range was too far for Karpac guns. They used low-velocity bullets, but mammoth caliber like old musket balls. Did terrible damage when they struck home.

"Gotta keep them back so they can't bring the panic on us," Blackwell said to no one. The other three gunners were raking the valley with machine-gun fire, toppling Karpacs right and left. Blackwell brought down four more vehicles, then switched over to his own automatic, trying to slow the tidal wave of giant turtle-beetles. He snatched up his .50 cal every time the armored vehicles advanced too far. The wind remained at his back. There was no panic. Yet. He could feel it coming though, but that was probably just the homegrown kind.

Half a mile down, the ridges descended into lowlands. Blackwell looked through his gun scope at the distant, massed Karpac army engaged with the colony's main force. The human soldiers were trying to keep separation. The Karpacs were swarming like ants on autopilot. They had lost some of their graceful coordination in the rain, so their motions were more awkward, but still they advanced across the sodden, red pairie, firing their slow, powerful repeaters.

"We're not going to hold," Blackwell said. One whiff of the panic scent and it'd be all over. No doubt that was why the Karpacs were trying so hard to get close, no matter their personal cost.

Scruggs was shooting in rapid bursts into the bloody river where the Karpacs pushed doggedly forward. He raised his gun to change out the magazine. "They just keep coming," he said, and fired again. Fired angrily.

Blackwell helped him shred the front line a dozen times over until the six-legged beasts had to clamber over their fallen brethren. It did no good. They still came.

How could you stop something with no sense of self-preservation?

"They're obeying the group scent," Blackwell growled. "It's driving them." He swept their line again. "Who's giving the orders?"

There had to be field marshals to react to battlefield conditions. There had to be somebody in charge. From his elevated position over the valley, he could see the Karpac formations better than he'd ever been able to before. There were ripples as clumps of hard shells moved slightly off time with other clumps. Just a bare half-step out of sequence. Where was the puppet-master?

There. Looking just like the rest, but the formation radiated out from him. Spokes of living beings to carry and repeat his order-scents to the masses.

It would be a tough shot, accounting for the rain and low wind, thicker atmosphere, and magnetism, but Blackwell had been hunting fat, horned "prairie dogs" since he got to this awful planet and he thought he had the feel for it. Karpacs were larger targets than prairie dogs, but they clustered so tightly together.

He pressed his cheek against the stock of the .50 and comforted himself with the assumption that he didn't *have* to get in the kill shot. A wounded puppet master would be just as ineffective as a dead one.

"Blackwell!" Scruggs barked, changing his magazine again. The advancing and continuously toppling Kerpac line was pushing close. "Blackwell!"

Blackwell ignored him for a moment as he adjusted his sight one more time and squeezed the trigger. He could faintly see the distorted vapor trail of the bullet penetrating wet air and raindrops. The puppet-master jumped, struck. How bad? Backwell couldn't wait to find out; he snatched up his automatic again and rejoined Scruggs. Firing, firing.

The pounding rain had crushed down the fronded prairie grass now, turning red to dull brown, but the shells of the Kerpacs glistened brilliantly with colorful stripes and geometric patterns. As their army pushed closer and closer, the massed valley glimmered with shifting golds and blues and crimsons. Blackwell put bullets into them as fast as he could. The sodden air smelled like dirt and gunpowder.

"We just want a home," Scruggs shrieked, standing up from the foundation hole, firing on full automatic. "You don't even live on this continent!"

"Hold it together," Blackwell snapped as Scruggs took a flesh wound to his leg and dropped back into cover.

Blackwell could smell a faint tang in the air now as the Karpacs drew close—the panic scent. He wanted to run. He needed to run. He forced himself to sit tight, fire controlled bursts, take down as many as he could. The Karpac front line had grown visibly ragged as they climbed up the slope out of the valley, but Blackwell could sense the end coming. They couldn't hold here. He changed magazines again.

He was within range of the Kerpac guns now, and bullets whined overhead and ricocheted off rocks. In moments he'd have to break and run with or without the panic—expose himself to a bullet in the back.

He could see their faces, a nightmare of fronded sense organs and beaked mouths. Red, like everything here. They had tucked their heads up under their shells for protection. In a human that would have meant running blind, but the Karpacs were probably only using their eyes to shoot straight.

"Get ready to run," he shouted to Scruggs. "I'll cover you." He glanced over and Scruggs was gone. Damn it! The panic almost took Blackwell then, but he clamped down on it; kept a fingernail's grip on control. He held his breath. Kept firing. Two magazines left. One.

And the Karpac line began to crumble. Then collapse. Then devolve into a route-stampede out of the valley that left crushed and trampled turtle-beetles everywhere, impacted into their dead from the initial advance. Faster than it had risen, the tide of Karpacs dropped back into the valley. Blackwell stood up, trembling, gripping in his rifle, watching them run.

He whooped, holding his gun high. His other two gun partners likewise. Scruggs was dead, sprawled face down three paces behind his foundation. Two big entrance wounds pocked his back. Blackwell lowered his gun, still watching in disbelief as the six-legged sons-of-bitches ran.

Without their puppet-master to control and direct, natural response pheromones must have taken over, permeated the troops, built as they were slaughtered, flooded the crowd until some poor bastard broke. That one Karpac probably began producing his own panic pheromones that other troops picked up on, and the dominos fell. Bio-feedback was a bitch.

Hearing continuous, desperate firing from adjacent valleys, Blackwell snatched up his .50 from the edge of the foundation and ran for the ridge. If he could take down the puppet-masters, he could save so many lives, human and Karpac. All it took was one moment of panic and it spread like contagion.

IRON HORSES
Judi Fleming

L IEUTENANT SMITH FOLDED HIS ARMS ACROSS HIS CHEST AND SAID, "I DON'T LIKE them." He eyed the shiny new tech. The build of the cliff rovers was sleek and equine. There were twelve arranged in two rows of six just outside the squad's rocky hillside barracks.

Sergeant Jones paused with her hand's caress halfway down the neck of the new rover closest to her. Each could effectively carry a single soldier up the narrow pathways with its clawed feet grappling and holding against the high winds and great unpredictable gusts here on the planet Zephyr.

She said, "What's not to like? We need something to get up these damned cliffs and into the rebel caves to rout them out. These things have actual horse behaviors programmed into the battle computers. They're awesome."

"Now how can you trust *that*? Have you ever been on a real horse? I mean a real Earth horse? They're completely unreliable." He braced himself against the 40-mile-an-hour winds that buffeted him with practiced ease.

Sergeant Jones shrugged and she climbed into the saddle. The E-Quad's four legs adjusted to her weight and the wind, digging clawed feet into the rocky soil to balance her weight against the wind effortlessly.

"I'm going to try one out, sir. No use telling the rest of the troops about them if they aren't to specs," she said.

The machine canted its sensor head to take in the terrain, eerily like a real horse in that simple movement. The two bulbous visual intakes glowed like eyes in the dusk. The audio receptors swiveled like ears. Jones fingered the controls at the front of the deep saddle that spread across either side of the grip which acted as a saddle horn. Easy to hold for balance, but low enough not to interfere with drawing weapons from her belt and most important, snug enough to keep you on through gusts. The data panels on the saddle lit up with wind speed, altitude, temperature, and more.

"Yes sir, these are sweet little E-Quads rovers," she said to the lieutenant. "You want to go topside with me?" She indicated the steep incline up the cliff face, so narrow that only one rover could go at a time.

A fierce straight line wind slammed down on her but all the rovers braced and shuffled out of formation as each adjusted to its own needs. The lieutenant was knocked flat but only grumbled as he stood to slap the dust off of his uniform. Sergeant Jones's face remained impassive. She'd felt that hard ground many times herself.

"No, you go on ahead, Sergeant. Report back when you return."

She saluted, then checked panels, working out what she had only read about before. Sergeant Jones slipped her boot heels into the foot stirrups and pressed the side accelerators, moving off smoothly. She had always wanted to ride a horse and wondered just how the programming would affect the machine's behavior. She was an expert flyer, and missed that here on Zephyr where such small craft were impossible to use in the winds.

Jones smiled, but immediately coughed the grit out of her teeth as a dust devil swirled over her back and up the trail. She snapped the face plate down against the phenomenal winds.

Here both her troops and the rebel miners lived in caves situated up and down these narrow ravines. The gale force winds on the surface of the planet above the trench-like network of canyons generally stayed below hurricane speeds. Mine entrances riddled the canyon walls like black eyes weeping rocky trails down to the floor far below. A rat's maze of dangerous urban warfare made all the more challenging when your troops could be whipped off of the narrow pathways even before they reached a rebel stronghold.

This wild and windy planet was full of natural mineral resources and well worth fighting for. The miners had done just that. They'd been fighting for nearly a year now, with neither side making any ground. Could this rover finally end the conflict? Being able to gallop up the pathways without fear of being ripped from the paths would tip the battle in her unit's favor. She was sure of it.

Delighted, Jones found the E-Quad did indeed work as described. It gripped and clambered upward with ease, cutting into the rocky surface as it climbed with the grace of an iron horse. When she neared the summit, she turned to look back without thinking and her weight guided the rover into a smooth about-face. *Nice,* she thought.

She leaned against the heel accelerators and hurtled down the trail, exhilarated by the speed and security of the elegantly designed "saddle" and the machine's footing. These *were* amazing and just as much fun as the flyers she favored.

Sergeant Jones parked the E-Quad and reported its performance to the lieutenant, nearly breathless in her enthusiasm for it.

"Looks like we have the advantage now," he agreed. "Gather the troops and let's brief them. I've gotten similar reports from the other squad leaders. It's full dark now, so we'll start the training first thing tomorrow."

The results of the rest of her unit working with the E-Quads didn't go well on the first day out. Many soldiers had no sense of balance or jammed the controls harder than necessary, which caused the units to lurch and buck with equal force. There were quite a few bruised bodies as well as egos.

"I knew that damned horse programming wasn't going to be good," muttered the lieutenant.

"With all due respect, sir. It's the troops that have got to learn the finesse." Sergeant Jones was frowning. Why was it so hard for so many people to allow their bodies to guide the rovers? These units weren't the same as a wheeled rover or even the sleek recon flyers that were used on other planets. They adjusted to the sway of the winds and your body. Perfect for this planet. It would take some time to teach her soldiers how to adjust the heaviness of their hands and heels.

"Let's take a look at the battle plans that came with them. I'd love to get off this rock and back home in time for the holidays."

The lieutenant's comment brought her back to the moment. She dismissed the troops and had them clean the dust and dirt from all the carefully filtered sensors and intakes on the E-Quads, much like brushing a horse with hand-held vacuums.

"We're to drive our batch of miners toward this central location topside where the prison transports will meet us, same as the other units. Any resistance will be dealt with. No mercy this time. The government has replacement miners ready to begin as soon as we clear out these rebels." He thumbed the holo projector on his utility belt that showed the coordinated attack plans for each unit. Sergeant Jones nodded as she scanned the plans, noting the rough places for each unit at every altitude change along with the straight line wind data for each.

This wouldn't be easy, even with the E-Quads. The fighting would start inside the tunnels and, although these rovers were small, it would be tight. She'd have to teach her troops to duck and fire when they learned how to balance.

"How long do we have?" she asked.

"A month," was his reply. The muscles twitched along his jaw.

She rolled this over in her mind. Timing for each unit and each rider's ability would be crucial for success of the mission. And the winds. Mercy have us, she hoped it would be a mild day when they deployed.

"Time of day, sir?"

"Dawn."

"I'll set up a plan to work with our troops and the rovers. I'll have them ready for you when they're needed, sir."

The loud clang of a loose barrel echoed off the canyon walls, startling the parked E-Quads into a wild shuffle as their sensors tried to adjust to the unexpected moving object being flung in the wind. Soldiers swore and two hopped on one foot after extracting their reinforced boots from under the clawed hooves.

The lieutenant chuckled, "I can't wait to see that, Sergeant. These things are too much like real horses from what I've seen so far. I think even our best laid plans may be challenged by that bit of programming." He snorted and shook his head. "Horse sense. Huh. There is no such thing, if you ask me."

❖

Jones hated to admit that the lieutenant had been right. It had taken every bit of her leadership skills to whip the troops into battle readiness with these new rovers. She'd used every teaching trick she knew to get the worst of the soldiers to this meager proficiency level in one month. And she still felt it wasn't good enough. Some just didn't have the knack for it and some loathed the rovers for all the shame and frustration they'd shown in front of others while trying to master these beasts.

Any other battle rover was effortless in comparison. Show a soldier the movements, then repeat over and over again until it became muscle memory. But the E-Quads had better response times than their riders. They took in data and adjusted for things that the human concentrating on their own movements couldn't see in time. Still, her forces had good formations, excellent results on obstacle courses, and great hit ratios from firing positions so she felt they were ready as they could be.

The thrill of the upcoming battle made it hard for her to sleep, but somehow she did. Awake an hour early, she cleaned her own rover one more time. It seemed to know her and turned to expose the flank exhaust that had some grunge stuck inside at a hard-to-see angle.

"Keep me safe today, Rover," she said with affection as she scraped the exhaust clean. She heard the clump of boots and turned.

"Bad news," the lieutenant said as he approached.

Jones snapped out a smart salute, which he returned distractedly.

"What bad news, sir? Weather says winds are not quite gale force topside today."

"No, not the weather." He rubbed the dust off his face shield. "Bravo Company had an E-Quad stolen a week ago and just now reported it. The miners have had time to see their capabilities and spread the word."

Sergeant Jones was dumbstruck. How could they not report this sooner? They've endangered everyone. "Sir, we've had three times the experience on our units as the miners would have with that one, so perhaps it isn't so bad after all."

"You're forgetting that most of these miners are real live engineers who built most of the equipment used to mine this damned rock."

Jones groaned. Damn and double damn indeed. "Did HQ change the battle plans when they found out?"

"No, but I have a really bad feeling about this one, Jonesy."

"She couldn't think of anything else to say, so she turned and ordered her troops onto their rovers and moved out. She put the most capable soldiers up front, and kept herself toward the middle as she called for full speed to the coordinates. The lieutenant came up the rear, holding on to the saddle grip for dear life, teeth barred in a death grin as his butt pounded in the saddle.

Before she knew it, they were ducking into tunnels, screaming battle cries and firing, flushing men and women from the mining tunnels assigned to them. Soon it was a chaos of shots ricocheting splinters of rock into the air and the eerie glow of lights from the E-Quad eye sensors as they careened through narrow spaces.

Jones pursued one miner as he dashed down a side exit and out into the open. He caught her by surprise by jumping on a crude imitation of her own E-Quad and speeding into the canyon beyond.

Damn, she thought, *If they've already replicated one in a week, how many more would there be?*

She urged Rover after him, marveling at how much easier his unit turned and climbed up the steep trails toward the windy plains above.

Where the hell was he going on that kludged-together rover, she wondered. *Waitaminute.* Was he actually going toward the collection point that their orders had them going to anyway? Was he onto them, or was this just the results of good intel and planning?

Her E-Quad surged and scrambled up the pathway, scattering small rocks off the steep path. She urged Rover on, leaning precariously forward and pressing her heels hard into its side, trying to get a clear shot of the man as he slung himself low along his rover's back.

A viscious wind gust attempted to scrape her from the trail as she charged up, slowly losing ground. *Damn and double damn.* Her heart raced as she clung harder to the E-Quad. Jones concentrated on balancing her weight and movements to make the rover's efforts more efficient. At least the miner had no weapon. Otherwise he would have fired by now. Getting up early had paid off on that account at least.

He crested the surface and disappeared from view. She galloped after, hoping that she was right about the weapons. She was the perfect target coming up out of the canyon. Heart in throat, she leaned low as they surged over the edge and was instantly knocked flat by the man's rover slamming into her full speed. They slid across the rocks and gravel, her tear-proof uniform saved her skin, but her left ankle snapped under the weight of the beast.

Rover was on its feet a second later, shielding her prone body precariously close to the edge as the miner circled his mount for another charge. An eerie sound filled the air as Rover used its mechanical warning alarms as a screaming equine challenge. It braced to defend its rider.

The miner pulled his unit to a stop, open-mouthed in surprise. He spit dirt. "None of ours have ever done *that*," he said.

The pain in her ankle made it hard to concentrate as she clawed around for her weapon. The laser was nowhere in sight. It must have gone over the edge when she was thrown. Her vision edged red as shock set in. Jones gritted her teeth and tried to stand, leaning against Rover for support.

Chaos came boiling up the ledge as the rebel miners drove what remained of her unit topside. Many she didn't recognize were among them. Bravo Company. And Charlie too. They'd all been overpowered. Set up.

The soldiers trudged sullenly, ignoring the yells and taunts of the miners riding their unit's E-quads who drove them upward into the thick swirling dust of topside. Some units bucked and skittered dangerously close to the edge as the men and women learned the commands that had taken the troops weeks of practice.

Rover stood firm, bracing and protecting her from the fierce wind gusts that threatened to topple her.

"Let it go. You've lost," the man said to her.

"I can't," she said. "Ankle's broken."

"Not my problem. Let it go."

She surprised him by swinging on board her mount, using the burst of adrenaline which coursed through her system. Sergeant Jones was not one to give in so easily. The instant she was on, she was urging Rover through the whirling dust of the windy plateau. She hung on for dear life, teeth clenched against the jarring pain of its gait. She had to make it to the prison ship and warn them. She'd need the soldiers on that craft as reinforcements.

A mile-wide tornado loomed out of the thick, blowing dust and debris. It spiraled jerkily toward her, almost taking her breath away in its suddenness and strength.

"Holy shit!" she screamed as she was jerked sideways from the force of Rover's course adjustment around the wobbling monster.

She couldn't hear the cries of despair behind her as her ragged soldiers were abandoned by the E-quad riders who dashed down the trail and into the safety of the caves below. Her attention had dwindled down to hanging on and staying conscious long enough to make it to the prison ship.

The miner she had initially pursued matched her speed as she angled toward the rendezvous point.

"Give up," he cried.

"Never," she said as she tried to steer Rover into him, hoping to trip his up, unable to do so with only one working foot.

"The Council granted us independence. We've laid charges on the landing point," he said as charged past her on his faster mount, forcing Rover around and away from it.

The tremendous explosion tossed her across Rover's neck and the E-Quad braced to a bone-jarring halt to save her from flipping over its head. Jones struggled to breathe, sure she now had broken ribs to add to her list of injuries.

"Will you surrender now?" His voice was mild, almost patronizing, as he grinned like an idiot.

She sucked air ineffectively, unable to answer.

"We've claimed all occupying troops and equipment as casualties of war. They granted us that if we can meet the delivery schedules they set. You aren't going anywhere, dear lady."

A year later, Jones found herself inspecting the newly designed E-Quads, marveling at their flexibility and intelligent programming. She was in charge of Zephyr's ground forces and was now a citizen of the dusty planet. Her ability to train both the rover units and the planetary defense troops who rode them had saved her life.

Jones was quietly satisfied that she was still a soldier and had attained a rank that would never have been possible working as a Council soldier anywhere else in the universe.

And she rode her original Rover, tweaking its instruments and joints, upgrading it as she went. It had, after all, saved her life.

FUN AND GAMES

An Alliance Archives Adventure
Danielle Ackley-McPhail

BOREDOM SUCKS. *REALLY* SUCKS!

Cadet Katrion Alexander lay sprawled across her bunk listening to the trash talk from across the aisle. Around her, her fellow trainees played cards or quietly worked on their kits, cleaning and polishing gear that hadn't seen a speck of dirt all week.

Why? The most recent offensive in the ongoing battle for the planet Demeter had begun. The Dominion forces occupying the next continent initiated opening moves against Allied territory. Kat didn't know the details, but the situation must have been serious. Command had put all the active-duty soldiers at the base on heightened alert, including the instructors, and even brought in additional troops from off-planet. They'd pulled just about everyone they could spare off their current assignments and shifted them to patrol duty or some other security task.

The cadets...for now they did a whole lot of nothing except sit around or pull all the shit details that base personnel had been yanked from. They still had daily duties, but no basic training exercises, just morning calisthenics and nothing else for most of the day, barring meals and grunt work, to keep everyone out of mischief. Thanks to the extra forces brought in, all the cadet units—there were several at different stages in their training—had relocated into the one barracks to make room for the extra troops. The cadets weren't to the point of hot-bunking it, but it was a near thing. The close quarters were a harsh reminder of the ongoing unrest.

Every time Kat thought about the situation her stomach went sour with nerves. She swallowed reflexively and had to consciously slow her breathing. The base was well within Allied territory, yet the current conflict had the higher-ups jumping. Distance meant little given the advances in modern warfare. *After all, we're close enough for the Allied forces to use the base for a staging area, right? Close enough to effect drone strikes without even leaving the command center.* Kat grimaced. *Forget fly-by-wire, we've graduated to death-by-remote.*

Lately the grunts cycled out of combat grumbled rumors of intel leaks resulting in heavy casualties at the front. Kat had seen some of those injured. Plasma burns were most common, followed by tearing wounds caused by flechette rounds, but the worst were the traumatic amputations, the result of triggered claymore mines. The tension on base escalated each day. Things didn't look good. She fully expected to wake up one almost-morning to find that all non-combat personnel were being evacuated. Or worse, drafted, incomplete training or not.

Sighing, she rolled over, arm draped over her eyes, only to groan beneath her breath as an argument broke out across the room. The fight only went on a few minutes before someone defused the situation, but the fact that matters reached the point of *needing* to be defused didn't bode well. The underlying strain had them all on a hair trigger.

Kat had a hard time being sympathetic. The cadets' lack of military deportment had her grinding her teeth. This wasn't her first time through Basic. She'd been in the service back on Earth. Thanks to her mother calling in a few favors Kat had been discharged just shy of graduation. In defiance she immediately joined up with the Alliance and shipped off-planet. Even out here Mother had influence, just not as strong as back home. Being among the raw recruits grated on Kat's nerves. She couldn't deny that. But the freedom to live as an adult was worth it.

The sergeant on duty came through calling lights out. Kat sighed again and willed her muscles to relax as the banks of lights overhead flicked off one by one. In the dark, the bunk to the left of hers squeaked as a body settled into it. So did the one above. She waited for a sound to her right. And waited. None came. Following instinct, Kat slowly shifted onto her back, scooting up on her pillow as if getting comfortable. Her eyes adjusted to the dim moonlight filtering through the narrow windows high up near the ceiling. She scanned the barracks, her vision picking out the soft mounds of bedding-covered cadets against the hard edges of the bunk frames, but no movement. With an effort she reduced her breathing, as if sleep drew her down, then willed her muscles to unwind while remaining alert and ready.

For a long time, nothing happened, yet instinct told her not to relax. She dropped her eyes down to slits so the whites wouldn't betray she was awake. Something moved. Several somethings. Dark against the dark, slowly advancing in methodical stages. Kat tracked them but did not shift as they came to settle at the foot of her bed. Gradually she increased her breathing and readied her muscles to act.

When something pale and recognizably cylindrical passed over her feet she almost laughed. Almost. Too bad for them she was pissed. Could they be any more juvenile? Pulling crap after lights out was not a good idea, especially pulling crap against her. Silently, she lunged forward and lashed out with the blade of her hand in a move she'd learned back on Earth, striking at the darkness to the right of the pale object. At the last minute she pulled the blow, her hand connecting with minimal force. Enough to get her point across and no more. Someone cursed, followed by the sound of cadets scattering. Whatever they'd been passing fell lightly to her bunk. Heavy footsteps pounded the floorboards from beyond the archway separating their side of the barracks from the duty sergeants' private quarters. Kat quickly dropped prone and let her head roll to the side. Moments later someone flipped the lights on. All across the barracks cadets sat up, eyes trained on the sergeant glowering from the doorway.

"Do we have a problem here?" Sergeant Dunn asked, his tone hard and tight as he scanned the barracks. Was it her nerves, or did he pause a moment when he looked at her?

Kat squinted against the sudden brightness from the LED clusters overhead and did her best to look sleepy, while slowly shifting so her blankets covered the roll of toilet paper that had magically appeared on her bunk.

"No, sergeant," she responded along with everyone else.

Dunn's brow dipped as he glared once more around the room before slapping all the light switches at once, instantly plunging the barracks into near total darkness. Letting out a long breath, Kat flopped back against her pillow. Big mistake. The bunks were hard, uncomfortable lumps. Rubbing her spine where it banged against one of the slats, she rolled onto her side and told herself to sleep.

It didn't work.

Ten minutes went by. Then fifteen, when a faint sound of scuffing brought her to full alert. Her eyes popped open to spy a figure creep from beside her bunk and edge toward the one to her right. It wasn't someone she knew. The silhouette was unfamiliar. She did catch a whiff of a nostalgic scent, though. A faint hint of anise. It called back memories of her PawPaw, sitting on his porch in the South Dakota twilight chewing on a stick of his favorite Blackjack gum. Reflexively she breathed in a little deeper.

The guy must have heard her. He pivoted on one knee and Kat found herself staring eye-to-eye with one of the pranksters. Without a doubt, he wasn't from her training unit. Like her, he was a little older than the usual recruit. Besides, even in the dark she would have recognized that wise-ass grin. That reminded her of PawPaw as well.

Softly she growled, but without as much heat as she might have. Just enough to let him know she wasn't an easy mark for whatever trouble he might think about stirring up. Soundlessly, the guy laughed, then slid into his bunk. Kat's eyes narrowed. She snaked a hand down to the foot of the bed and grabbed the roll of toilet paper still lying there. With a sidewise toss she pegged the troublemaker in the head.

This time he didn't bother to hold back his chuckle.

It took Kat a long time to relax before sleep claimed her.

Kat came awake with a deep groan. Sergeant Dunn didn't even wait for dawn. Before the sun even tickled the horizon he strolled through the barracks liberally applying a baseball bat to the inside of a metal trash can. Where he'd gotten either one of them Kat couldn't even guess. The clanging reverberated in her pounding head.

In his wake, cadets tumbled from their bunks to stand at attention by their footlockers. Most of them, anyway. Halfway down the far row a panicked squawk rose from a lower bunk as some fresh-faced kid struggled against a cocoon of toilet paper. Kat saw the cadets to either side of him resist the urge to help; they didn't dare to, not yet. Not with the mood Dunn was in.

No one was stupid enough to laugh...aloud.

"Is there a problem, cadet?"

"Sir, no, sir!" he responded, still bound tight to his bunk, his face as pale as his bog-roll wrapping.

"You seem to need this more than I do," Dunn barked. He smacked the can down next to the bed with a loud clatter and, without freeing the cadet, turned and stalked away, calling over his shoulder, "I want that back before breakfast...*full*, or no one gets chow."

None of the cadets moved until the sergeant disappeared through the door leading out of the barracks. Once he was gone groans rose uniformly. One person had the bad judgment to give in and laugh. The sound quickly cut off as knuckles met skin. Those closest to the prank victim scrambled to his bunk and tore him free, tossing the mess of paper into the can. It barely filled a couple of inches at the bottom.

Kat could identify at least one of the guilty parties. She stomped over to where he stood and smacked him hard upside the shoulder. The amused smirk on his face just pissed her off more. Rather than invite more trouble with the sergeant she pivoted away, scouring their quarters for any garbage. Her stomach grumbled as she dumped her findings in the can. Another inch obscured the bottom, no more, and the barracks were rubbish-free.

After calisthenics, it took the coordinated efforts of all the cadets and over two hours—not to mention three false finishes—to scrounge up enough trash to satisfy the sergeant, who merely tamped it all down tight each time they presented the full can. Finally, ten minutes before the chow line was set to close, with the base spit-and-polish clean and the can filled to overflowing, Sergeant Dunn declared the terms satisfied. Kat hoped the situation cured her fellow trainees of the urge for pulling tricks.

Forty cadets scrambled for the food lines. There was enough grub for fifteen of them. Somehow, Mr. Wise-Ass ended up with a full tray. Kat didn't even bother. She filled her gut with thoughts of getting even, and not in any way that screwed the rest of the cadets, either.

Kat should have known better. Should have realized things wouldn't end with just one little prank. It was little stuff. Harmless, really, and nothing as grand as the TP mummification that started it all: soap canisters stowed upside down, with the lids loosened; the bottom of garbage bags scored just enough so they tore after the mark hauled them out of the can... annoyances that caused more busy work than anything else. Easy to hide from the sergeant, but with each occurrence Kat's tension increased. She expected at some point one of the raw recruits would give in to their inner dumb kid and escalate things. The newest bunch weren't disciplined enough yet to understand the balance between pranking and pissing off the higher ups.

On edge, Kat left the barracks before dinner. She took her rifle and cleaning kit out into a warm patch of sun. They had an inspection scheduled for that evening. Ever since the pranks started, Sergeant Dunn ground down on them hard, bellowing over the smallest speck of dirt or imagined woolly-booger, assigning extra duty left and right. Kat didn't mind the work—hell, with this much downtime she was looking for shit to do—but no way would she leave an open opportunity for an official reprimand. Not when Dunn seemed to be riding her extra close, like he pegged her for the mastermind or something. Kat's lips thinned as she considered the ramifications of that. It had been hard enough getting to where she was against her mother's objections. She knew to keep her place she had to stay above reproach because even out here enough people owed Mother favors that several officers on the base had their eyes open for reasons to send her packing.

Going home in disgrace was not an option. Not if she ever wanted to make an adult decision for herself again. Kat reapplied herself to cleaning her rifle, and everything else, until not a smudge or particle remained in evidence, then carefully stowed the weapon, regulation-precise. As she bent over the case, motion from across the way caught her eye. By the barracks, where those who cared to spent their vice credits smoking a cigarette or two, when they could get them. One of the privates that worked in Commander Richtman's office stopped near the ash can. His stance held a subtle tension that made Kat think wistfully of home...or rather, her PawPaw's ranch. Back when she was a girl they'd rescued a wild mustang some fool had half ruined trying to break it. That horse had stood the same way when anyone came near the paddock or the pasture. Faking an easy, relaxed stance, but ready to lash out at whoever came too close.

Kat almost laughed as her memory of that mustang chawing prairie grass superimposed itself over the soldier across the way. Not wanting to explain, she restrained herself. The private didn't seem to notice her as he reached into his pocket and pulled something out. Assuming he was there to burn one, Kat went back to putting away her gear.

Once she'd gathered everything, she stood and faced the barracks. She frowned and looked around. The scent of burning tobacco was absent from the air and the guy had already cleared out. He must have decided against a smoke. Or maybe he didn't have enough credits left to get a cigarette out of the military-issue dispenser next to the smoking area. She put him from her thoughts and glanced at her watch. Time to put her shit away and head for dinner. As she walked past the ash can Kat noticed a faint scent of gun powder. She brought her shoulder toward her nose and sniffed. She couldn't quite say, but that might be her.

Must have gotten some residue on me, she thought. *Great*. She'd have to change before going to the Mess Hall or the smell would put her off her food.

When she slipped inside the barracks to put away her gear and grab a fresh set of BDUs, Kat discovered rows and rows of neatly made bunks, dully gleaming footlockers, and absolute silence. For once there wasn't a cadet in sight...or even a sergeant. Tempted by the luxury of a private shower, Kat took ten minutes to wash the stink off of her. She'd just secured her boots when Sergeant Dunn passed through to his side of the barracks. He looked annoyed to see her. Of course, since being relegated to glorified babysitter he looked annoyed any time he saw a cadet. His gaze sharpened and he looked around, as if searching for a prank to pin on her. The suspicion rankled, but Kat kept her expression neutral. Before she could scramble to her feet, he barked, "Save it, Alexander. Shouldn't you be at Mess right now?" He walked away without waiting for an answer, leaving an air of mistrust in his wake.

That cut it. She'd done nothing to earn his judgment. *God help the next person to pull a practical joke.* Kat grabbed her cap and headed for the Mess Hall. The base seemed deserted as she passed through. *They must be serving something good for chow today,* she thought. She didn't bother picking up her pace. By now little but scraps would be left, given everyone else seemed to have headed for dinner before her.

Halfway across the compound she forgot all about food. A *whoosh* sounded behind her, and a man cried out. Kat spun, looking for the source of the outcry. Her mouth dropped open and her eyes widened. The barracks. Deep, black smoke shrouded the whole front facing, not quite masking a hunched figure in the midst of cloud. As it quickly dissipated Kat noticed black streaks marked the walls. Smoke still poured from the broken rim of the ash can. She barely paid attention to any of that, though. Her gaze fixed on Sergeant Dunn, crouched against the wall, face turned in.

"Oh...shit..." She vaguely noticed a growing commotion behind her as the Mess Hall, and every other building nearby, disgorged its occupants. How she wished she were among those people boiling into the compound still trying to figure out what happened. Kat knew. She could kick herself for not cluing in to the signs earlier. It never even occurred to her the cadets might not be responsible for all the pranks. This one went beyond good taste, though...and here she stood, frozen in place, looking like the prime suspect.

The same thing apparently occurred to Dunn. He straightened and pushed off from the wall, leaving a dingy silhouette limned with dark grey where he'd gone to ground. His gaze never left hers as he stalked toward her.

"*Crap!*" she swore with more vehemence beneath her breath.

The acrid stench of burnt gunpowder and singed hair preceded him, his craggy face—skin red and tight beneath a veil of loose ash—contorted in preparation for a whole other kind of explosion. Dunn stopped when they were toe to toe. Behind Kat the commotion had stopped as well.

Only extreme willpower kept her from recoiling. From the smell. The situation. Dunn's expression. She never realized exactly how strong-willed she was until that moment. She felt herself pale, however, as Dunn slowly lowered his face down into hers. He hadn't ducked quickly enough, apparently. His eyebrows were singed and small blisters formed along the edge of his jaw. Kat had the overwhelming urge to close her eyes against the sight. She resisted. Trying not to flinch, she locked her gaze on a thin trickle of blood snaking its way down his face from a cut on his forehead. He must have been tagged by a fragment from the ash can.

"Alexander," he said, his voice disturbingly low. "Do you have an explanation for what just happened?" The compulsion to turn and look for the guy from earlier tugged at her hard, but again she resisted. Dunn growled faintly, reminding Kat he expected an answer.

"Sir, no, sir." And that wasn't a lie. She could guess, but guesses weren't fact. And it wasn't smart for a cadet to imply anything about a sworn-in soldier without incontrovertible proof. That kind of thing was bad for a career.

"So, let me understand...you're saying you have no idea how gunpowder ended up in the ash can?" His expression tightened and his right eye twitched.

"Sir, yes, sir," she answered. Her voice came out strained as she braced for his response.

The crowd at her back began to murmur amongst themselves. Kat ignored them, maintaining eye contact with Dunn. His breath came in short, sharp huffs as he searched her gaze. Kat remembered his suspicious looks from earlier and her gut landed in her boots. There was no hope of him believing she had nothing to do with this. She vowed to kick that private's ass the next time she saw him.

After a long moment Dunn grimaced and stepped back. Clearly he wanted to scream and yell and tear her a new one, but he couldn't. Not on speculation. Until he had proof she had something to do with it, all he could do...well, all he *could* do was make her life a living hell, but none of that came with a black mark on her record. Yet.

Dunn turned to face the gathered crowd of mostly cadets his gaze sweeping the lot of them before he spoke. "What is this, summer camp? You cad-idiots need to be worn out to keep you out of trouble?"

No one spoke.

Somehow his face turned even brighter red. "Do you think this is fun and games? This is the military. The base is on heightened alert. Start actin' like soldiers, godamnit!" Dunn said, his eyes coming back to pin Kat where she stood. "Whoever's responsible for 86ing the ash can has fifteen minutes to report to the commander's office... The rest of you, you have twenty minutes to prep for maneuvers and get your asses to the parade ground, *someone* just earned you *all* some survival training." The volume of his voice increased with each word.

Everyone held their groans until Dunn pivoted and stalked away in the direction of the medical building. Once he was out of sight Kat turned and glared at those behind her, searching for the dumb fuck that started it all. It disturbed her to see most of the onlookers glaring back.

That faint screaming sound? Her career as it shriveled up and died.

With a scowl she headed back to the barracks to pack up her kit.

In the end, the sergeants divided the cadets into four-man teams, mixed so that no one group benefited from more extensive training than the others, and everyone lost the edge of any team cohesion they'd already built up through existing associations. Kat found herself paired with the wise-ass—known more conventionally as Cadet Jackson Daniels—and two others she knew only loosely through duty assignments.

When they'd arrived at the parade ground they were ordered to unpack their kits.

A bad sign.

The sergeants came around and stripped their gear of everything but the basics: rations and hydration pack enough for three days, first aid kit, a knife, and a roll of duct tape. Beyond their personal gear they received one field comm per team. Night set in by the time the sergeants completed the sort. None of the cadets grumbled but their expressions grew more and more grim, brows lowered and lips pressed thin, hands fisted at their sides. At this point Kat would have to guard against a blanket party for a good long time.

"Each of you may select a single item from your remaining supplies," one of the sergeants called out, his voice raised sufficient to be heard by all. "Anyone trying to pick more than one item will have that privilege revoked for their team. I suggest you all choose wisely."

That set off a mad scramble.

Kat watched as her teammates made their selections. Scotch immediately reached for a high-end compass from the top of his discards. It looked like the Swiss Army knife of its kind, certainly not standard issue. The other two cadets selected a pack of flares and a coil of rope. The flares weren't a bad choice, but the rope? It wasn't like they were going to be doing much vertical climbing, and the duct tape was more practical for securing things. Kat started to recommend the other cadet choose the trench shovel also visible in his pile but one look at the glare he sent her way had her raising her hands and turning toward her own pile.

A grimace crept over her face as she considered her choices. There were at least four things she itched to reach for now that she knew what her teammates had selected. The smoke grenades could come in handy, or perhaps the water-purification tablets. In the end though, Kat chose her rifle, a gauss loaded with a full clip and a spare mated to the grip. The tension in her gut told her it was the right choice. None of the sergeants objected as she slid the weapon across her back. Thanks to her previous training she was already weapons certified.

Once everyone made their choices the cadets shoved all the items winnowed out into individual sacks the sergeants provided and scrawled their names across each one in marker on tape. Presumably someone would gather them and return everything to the barracks. When that was done, the cadets stood in silence staring at their miniscule piles. Some of them looked hyped and ready, others looked pissed. No one knew what to expect. Heads came up as, out of the dark, Dunn stalked into sight. Surgical cement held his cut closed and the rest of his face glistened beneath a protective burn ointment. His eyes held a look of pure malice.

"You wanted fun and games? Well you got it. You will repack your gear and head in formation over to the airfield. The waiting helos will take you to the remote training zone." He smirked. "You have four days to find your way back to base."

Someone groaned.

"Have *fun*, kiddies." Dunn turned and swaggered away, leaving the other sergeants to supervise the departure.

Kat and everyone else watched in silence as he disappeared into the night. When he was gone Kat caught bits of a conversation behind her that snagged her attention.

"They're being kind of hard on them, aren't they?" one of the sergeants said to the other. They talked low, but Kat could just make out what they said if she focused hard.

"Naw, they woulda done this anyway. This just moved things up. Some important intel went missing today during all the excitement. Until they figure out what's goin' on, Command wants to get the greenies out of the way in case the shit goes flyin'. "

Anger built in Kat's gut at what she'd just overhead.

"Hey...Kittie," Daniels called from the crush of cadets organizing their packs, distracting her. "You coming with the rest of us, or not?" She looked his way and noticed he held up her empty rucksack. Kat growled. She visualized the many ways she'd like to maim Daniels. Nearly as many as the different motivations he gave her to do so.

"The name is *Kat*," she snapped as she shoved past him to reach her gear, snatching the bag from his hand.

He just chuckled as she went by. Kat's jaw clenched but she said nothing, not wanting to draw any more attention her way. She had too many dirty looks darted toward her as it was. It took effort to ignore them as she repacked and moved into formation, but she managed. Daniels ended up beside her. She ignored him too.

That was significantly more difficult.

The column headed to the airfield at a steady march. Five transport helicopters stood ready and waiting on the tarmac. As everyone started climbing on board Kat lagged behind, not comfortable with having any of her fellow cadets at her back at the moment.

Only the *whump* of the rotors powering up and the bustle of cadets boarding the helos broke the silence. And Daniel's persistent chatter. Kat stood there with her pack in her arms trying to ignore the wise-ass who remained next to her.

"They call me Scotch."

She couldn't resist. "I see," she said, her tone dry as her own inner wise-ass came out to join the party. "That would be because you drive everyone to drink, right?"

He grinned. Kat just stared back, her expression neutral.

"Nah, my drill sergeant didn't know the difference between Scotch and good, ol' Tennessee Whiskey." She must have seemed confused because he laughed. "Jackson Daniels...*Jack Daniels*..." Kat scowled, still not getting it and frankly not understanding why she still paid attention to him.

"You're not much of a drinker, are you?"

At that Kat gave him a sour look. "Not yet."

This time he laughed loud enough one of the sergeants glared over at them.

"You'll do, Kittie," Scotch said with satisfaction twinkling in his eyes.

Kat pointedly turned away to stare off at the support personnel running last-minute checks on other aircraft preparing for flight. The airfield was packed. To her left, a troop transport went through final inspection and several wings of PlasmaHawks looked ready for takeoff. Lined up on the tarmac beyond them she counted about a dozen aerial drones, their payloads already secured, engines powering up. Kat's chest tightened at the thought of the wounded that would soon come back. And the casualties that wouldn't.

At the thought a frown puckered her brow and the surface of her skin prickled. She narrowed her gaze and, without realizing it, started walking toward the combat craft. Something about the way one of the men moved set her instincts screaming. The way his eyes subtly scanned the zone as he walked across the tarmac. The casual edging of his hand toward his pocket.

Kat gasped as a recent memory flickered to the surface of her mind. It was *him*. The asshole private from earlier, she'd swear it. Only she'd seen him at work in the commander's office on more than one occasion, so what was he doing in a mechanic's overall, shoulders deep inside a maintenance panel on the exterior of the troop transport? Unbidden, Kat took a step toward him as her head tilted, trying to get a better look at what he was doing to the innards of the plane. A growl rumbled her chest. She thought about when she'd first saw this man: the underlying tension, the supposed prank, then just now finding out someone had used the incident as a diversion. Again, he made her think of her PawPaw's mustang. They'd eventually had to put the horse down when a hand got too close and the horse caved in his head with a double kick of his back hooves. They hadn't heeded the warning signs back then; now, Kat had more than learned the lesson. Prank, or something more insidious? Either way, she couldn't stand by without confirming.

"Sergeant!" she called out, not taking her eyes off the private. At the sound of her cry his shoulders tensed and his far hand reached across his waist, as if going for something. Kat's guess was a weapon. She dropped her pack and knelt, positioning herself below the point he would expect her to be, her hand already drawing her rifle around from where it lay across her back. Even if this hadn't been her second pass through Basic, if Kat knew anything, it was guns. Being a rancher, PawPaw had made sure of that. She braced on her knee and trained the weapon on the man before her. "Don't move!"

All around her Kat's words echoed from other throats, followed by the sound of weapons carking. She didn't have time to see where they were aimed, though she suspected at least half of them were on her.

"Alexander, what the hell do you think you're doing?" From the corner of her eye Kat spied Dunn stomping from the hanger and across the tarmac. He appeared beyond pissed.

"It's him, sir, the one responsible for this afternoon's incident."

Across the way the private's expression twisted into lines of determination and hatred. He lunged for the shelter of the aircraft, drawing the weapon he'd concealed, a Dominion-issue Predator 9mm pistol. Kat sighted, stilled her breath, and calmly squeezed the trigger before he could bring his weapon to bear.

And the world erupted. All at once guns went off, something inside the airplane popped, and from out of nowhere a freight train took Kat to the ground, rolling protectively overtop of her as it did so. The smell of cordite and burning plastics billowed around them as military personnel scrambled to contain the situation.

"Hey, Sarge. Looks like you were wrong..."

Dazed, Kat stared up at Scotch, her breath still coming heavy as her heart raced, incredulous at his audacity. He really did remind her of her PawPaw.

She hadn't yet decided if that was a good thing.

"*What*?" Dunn bellowed as he closed on where they sprawled, Daniels crushing Kat beneath him. She couldn't complain. He'd likely saved her from a hail of bullets and other flying debris.

"It *is* all fun and games..." Scotch flashed Kat that wise-ass grin as he motioned toward the body across the way, the face a bloody pulp on the right side where Kat's round had blown out the ocular cavity. "...until someone loses an eye, anyway."

I AM A MAN
Eric Hardenbrook

I AM A MAN, AND I DO NOT CRY.

As a soldier, killing was simply part of our job. It was always done at a distance, in every sense of the word. There was no real attachment to what we did. I'd played hundreds of simulations that were more bloody and twisted than our actual missions. Real, physical bodies don't react the way simulations do, no matter what the techs say. The techs got it close, but you could always tell. My wife didn't seem to understand the distance we kept. She was always telling me I was *too* distant. I didn't think so. I was right there in the same room; no distance at all. She added the real distance.

It had been a long time since I took the opportunity to stroll down the street. Most people remained inside their homes with their blast-resistant walls and hardened cores. These days they had everything delivered to them. Armored courier was one of the best-paying, most dangerous jobs around. There were no more shopping malls; too dangerous to have kept that practice. Walking in public was taking a chance, but people can't resist the urge to gather.

I walked through a beautiful autumn day. "Beautiful" was a question of taste I suppose. I always liked it better when it wasn't warm enough to swim in November. Not that I would ever swim again, the cost of water being what it was. Nature can be amazingly resilient, but it takes time for her to recover. In the years since I was a child she hadn't been given a chance. People keep trying to force nature to be what they want it to be, usually without success.

There were a handful of leaves skittering down the city street. Part of the vain attempt to 'return to the green' or whatever the last campaign was. I really couldn't be bothered to remember that kind of thing. I was a veteran of the resource wars; I didn't need slogans to understand what we'd done. Most people that knew us closed their doors and shuttered the windows. Maybe that was part of my need to walk down the street again; a need to recover some of what had changed since I was young.

There was a shop. That was unusual enough to catch my attention. There were temporary markets that popped up now and then, but most people wouldn't go in person and actually pick things up and look at them when there was a chance of an attack. Maybe that's what made me walk in.

The shop was a small place, one of the old row-house style buildings in the historic district. The museum on the next block was the only reason the whole place hadn't been plowed under years before. The collection of odds and ends visible through the shop window was a riot of color. No rhyme or reason to the piles, boxes, and plastic bins. There was an old framed picture tilted against the wall; some 2-D star from the pre-hologram days. A stack of plastic cups and plates leaned awkwardly. Plastic was the one material that didn't ever seem to become scarce. I tried not to bump the table, afraid they'd all fall over. The place was so quiet I actually trod lightly to avoid being a disruption rather than any need for stealth.

A small, hunched old lady shambled out of a doorway that led to the back, probably her storage area. Not that I thought there would be a significant difference between that room and this one. That would be the other exit. She didn't seem to notice me standing in the midst of the clutter. I hesitated, unsure if I should startle her with my presence or wait for her to shamble into the back again and slip out quietly.

"No need to be silent, young man." Her voice was raspy, but understandable. She never looked up, just kept moving things from place to place for no reason I could determine.

"My apologies, ma'am." I turned my head while my right eye scrolled through a standard spectrum scan. I couldn't locate a map tag, node, or standard connection link.

"There's no need for that. This shop won't show up on a scan." Her back was to me as she shuffled back through the doorway and out of my line of sight again.

I twisted myself down to a crouch and dashed to the corner of the table, just beside the doorway she'd walked back through. My hearing implants overrode my normal senses and my adrenaline modulator kicked in. I held one hand out behind me ready to sweep around and grab the woman as she came back though the door. All these moves came without conscious decision on my part. I didn't realize I was there until I hear her shoes scuff the floor on her way back to my position.

I shook my head. This was home. I was in my own country. There was no reason for this anymore. I was done. I was out. I'd been out for more than two years now. I made a mental effort to bring myself back from pacification mode. No recruiter ever explained that bio-enhancements weren't reversible. You can't just get your old eye back. You couldn't just walk back from those other places and pick up your previous life again.

The woman stepped back through the door just as I was standing up again. My arm whipped forward by muscle memory alone. The woman didn't flinch or duck. She didn't even seem to sense the maneuver as she unceremoniously dropped a plastic bin into my arms. "Front table to the right, there's a dear." She turned back to her storage room again. I stood there smelling faint traces of dust. I was stunned, and felt more than slightly unnerved at how close I had come to war-time aggression so close to my own home. She wasn't the enemy. This shop wasn't hoarding resources or hiding enemy equipment. She wasn't an insurgent, she was a shop keeper. I felt light-headed as the modulator dumped adrenaline. I half-turned and started shuffling the bin to the front of the shop.

How had she known where I would be when she walked back out? The thought didn't hit me until I'd reached the front of the shop and glanced over my shoulder looking for a place to wedge the latest bin. When she walked to the back I'd been at least a half a dozen steps further away than when she reappeared. I hadn't made any noise I could determine. Maybe she was lying about the scan. I turned in place and squinted. Squinting was a dead giveaway and a habit that got a lot of soldiers killed. I tried to remember if I'd squinted when I started my scan. Maybe that's how she knew to say something. Maybe I was starting to slip.

There wasn't anyplace open to set the bin she'd handed me. It wasn't heavy, but it didn't seem right to just dump it on the top of a random stack.

"Just pick one up and slide that one under it," came the voice from the back.

I shifted the bin under my right arm and lifted the smallest looking pile, hoping it wouldn't topple. I froze as I realized my vulnerability. My shooting hand was covered and I'd lost my sight lines. My vision blurred and swam in my left eye, overlaying the crisp reality of my enhanced right eye. I wasn't home, I was in a shack with the resource recovery team.

"Keep them down! Down!" yelled Williams.

"Hands where I can see them!" Johnson swung the muzzle of his assault rifle across the row of kneeling men.

My hands were wedged behind a stack of dusty plastic bins scrambling for a latch or release button. The shelves, bins and the wall behind them were too far away from the other side of the wall. There was something hidden in that wall. Hoarders and resistors had grown clever over time. Movement flashed in my peripheral vision. "Contact right!" I yelled.

Too late. One of the men we'd targeted rolled to the side as Johnson's rifle swung to the opposite end of the line. Everything moved in slow motion. The rifle jerked back, but I could see he was too late. Williams had one hand up at his helmet in the persistent human motion of attempting to improve hearing by adding fingers. I grabbed the back edge of the heavy-duty shelving I'd been searching and heaved all my weight backward.

My sight flashed and I was once again fully in the shop near my home. The heavy shelving was the only thing that had saved me. It was a fluke. We had been on to more than we realized when we singled out that building; too bad we underestimated the resolve of the people we were fighting. Rolling man reached a concealed trigger and detonated their hidden stash of explosives. It was a desperation move that worked better than planned. The resulting explosion wrecked half the building. Nobody survived except me and I still carried pieces of that with me in my leg and knee. I could still see Johnson's leg sticking out of the windshield of the jitney across the street, like the afterimage of a camera flash.

My hands shook. I took a deep breath. I tried to focus. I willed the tremors to stop. The box would fit on the floor at my feet, as good a spot as any.

"Is it getting better?" the shop keeper asked from her doorway.

"I'm sorry?" Even with my boosted hearing, I hadn't picked up a sound when she'd stepped out.

"There's no need to be sorry. It's supposed to get better after a while," she grinned—or was it a grimace?—and pushed away from the door frame where she'd been leaning. "The amount of time it takes varies from man to man but it's supposed to get better." She shuffled again, moving slowly in my direction. *How could I have missed the sound of her movement before?*

I shook my head.

"Am I that easy to spot now?" *I was a dead man.*

"You haven't cut your hair or shaved, but a lot of guys do that when they get out." Not a direct answer, but one I'd have to take. She stopped and rummaged in a bin. "Do you remember these?" she held up a small plastic boat with an outlandishly sized rocket engine bearing a corporate logo.

"Didn't those come with some kind of kid's meal thing?" I vaguely remembered multiple trips to various restaurant locations looking for the last toy in the set. It seemed so long ago. Marley would have been twelve this year.

She flipped the boat around in her hand. "I miss the days when we could go out and swim. No filters, no time restrictions, no guarded routes in and out. Did you ever water ski?"

"No. Never had the chance. Water sources where I grew up were among the first to be secured. I did have a friend show me how the water skiing worked in principle once." I grinned a little as I remembered Greeny's face.

"How do you mean?" she leaned her hip against the table and crossed her arms.

"What's the best way to get to a water source if all the land routes are guarded?" I did my best to sound like my old instructor.

"You find another way in, but what other way?" she asked.

"Dropping in from above is virtually impossible to guard against. Of course the problem is getting the people out of a vehicle moving fast enough to stay in the air."

She cocked one eyebrow up, "and how exactly do you do that?"

I grinned a little more deeply this time remembering the same questions forming in the past. "You jump."

"That doesn't exactly prove anything about water skiing," she said, obviously not making the connection.

"Well, the key is your angle of decent. If you land with your body in what amounts to an "L" shape and have your feet up and facing the direction of travel then you could be just fine." I replied, making my hand mimic the motion. "The problem is that Sgt. Greene never got to learn to swim when he was a kid and by the time we'd reached that part of the training cycle it was too late to just back out. On our first live training jump he panicked and didn't pick up his feet to the "L" shape position."

The shop keeper stood up a little straighter and with her mouth dropping open ever so slightly. "Oh, my."

"Oh my, indeed." I laughed. "Greeny's feet caught first, then he flipped face down and skipped like a rock across the top of the water." I laughed even harder at the memory. I was two positions behind him when we jumped. I had the perfect view, only obstructed for a few seconds when I plunged into the water behind him.

"What happened to him?" she brought one hand up, letting it hover just in front of her mouth.

"Ol' Green... he skipped just far enough to reach the shallow water. He put his feet down and ran for the beach just as soon as he could." I was really laughing now. My left eye was tearing up I laughed so hard. "His legs were wet below the knees, the front of his uniform was wet, but his back was just as dry as it was before we dropped." I looked up and the shop keeper laughed along with me. "The only thing he said when we squished up to the instructor was, 'told you I couldn't swim'."

She was smiling even after her laughter subsided, "What ever happened to him? Did he make it into your unit?"

"Sure. He was great once we were on the dirt. First one in every time...Right up until the last."

My laughter died abruptly.

"Now I'm sorry." she said, "I didn't mean to upset you again."

"I wish I wouldn't remember."

"You must remember." she replied, "Your memories are the very core of who you are. They are the essence of what make you human."

"Am I still human? Look at how I reacted to you – and I've been home for years now!"

"Of course you're human!" She stood straighter than she had since I'd entered the shop. As her posture changed so did her mannerisms. She wasn't nearly as old as I'd thought. The color in her hair could have been dust in the wrong light. I had no idea who I was dealing with. "You're human and I can prove it." She said more quietly.

"How can you do that?" I replied. "Some kind of test I'm supposed to submit to? Working some kind of back room deal here?" I edged toward her, instincts returning again, albeit slowly. She had talked me into a bad position, but I would survive this yet.

"No, dummy. Simple things will prove it. I don't need tests or machinery or node connections. You'll never find my place tagged or scanned or any other damn thing." She didn't back away. I looked directly into her eyes and saw my own reflected back. "You came in here for a reason. You don't know what the reason is, but I do."

"If I don't know it, how can you?" my voice rose more than it should have.

"You came in here to try to reconnect. Nobody just goes out any more. You know that better than anyone," she waved her hand at the tiny front windows. "You could have ordered anything you wanted right from your couch. You walked outside to try to reconnect to other people. You have to! We all have to! Like what we've become or not, it's part of who we are."

"Who we are? Look at who we are!" I was angry. "We poisoned our own land. We made the water undrinkable. We killed the crops that were supposed to feed us. When we couldn't get what we wanted here any longer we didn't try to fix it, we took what we wanted from everyone else!" I shouted.

"You did what you had to do to keep our home safe and livable! Do you think I don't know?" her other hand waived back toward her shop full of junk. "This is what I deal in now. Leftovers. Refuse that others will pick through because it's better than having none. Why? Because you went out there and put yourself on the line until the world figured it out for themselves. We're a better place now, and it's only because you and others like you went and put yourselves through hell to get us here."

"You think the world is a better place now?" I was stunned.

"Of course it is," her voice quieted as quickly as mine had. "If we'd kept going the way we were the whole world would be fighting house to house still, just to get their hands on what they thought they needed."

"The fighting came here! We didn't win anything."

"We made it through." she stated.

"Not everyone made it through." I looked away.

"That's true." she was much quieter now. "There's always pain when there's growing to be done."

"I don't think we've grown, or changed." I shifted and gazed over the piles of remnants. The bits and pieces of days gone by.

"I know where to find what you're looking for," the shopkeeper stated staring directly into my good eye, not the enhanced one. "Second stack from the door." She pointed and turned away from me.

I walked to the stack and popped the lid on the top box, just to be courteous.

"Not that one. The one on the bottom." She waived her hand without looking back. "Just take it with you. If you feel the need, you can always come back and pay me what you think it's worth later."

I stared after her for just a moment as she again popped out of view into the back of the shop. Either there was nothing of value in the box, or it was truly an offer born of madness. Nothing came for free these days.

I stood and stared a moment longer, weighing my options. I decided it couldn't hurt. I retrieved the plastic container and tucked it under my arm without even looking inside. Don't ask me why. It went against everything I'd been trained, but instinct...the need to connect...was stronger.

I stepped out of the store and headed back home.

Once safely inside my living room I set the bin down on the table in front of the couch. I didn't look inside, I just stared at it. The thought of what it might contain made me uneasy. How could she know what I needed? What did she *think* I needed? Somehow she'd seen what she had in me without anything to give it away. Or was I fooling myself? Had there been clues from me that I didn't realize?

I let the box sit, unopened and tried to focus on something else. I managed to distract myself for two whole days. I can't recall anything that I did, other than purposefully avoid looking at the box. *It's filled with junk,* I'd say to myself and stalk into my bedroom. *There's contraband inside she needed to get rid of and shucked it off on me,* I'd think, then turn and head to the kitchenette for something to eat. For all my efforts, I thought of nothing else.

Eventually, though, I gave in to the impulse nagging at me in the woman's soft voice. Sitting on the floor I pulled the lid off and stared inside. It was all at once both more and less than I expected. Bits of plastic toys, leftover pieces of plastic cup and plate sets, a handful of resin buttons... Nothing special. Feeling let down, almost betrayed by the banality, my hand swept out, dumping the fragments haphazardly to the floor. That's when I noticed it. A corner of something faintly yellowed with age caught my eye. I reached down and pulled out a folded piece of paper. Real, actual paper was an expensive luxury these days. At just a couple of inches, this paper wasn't big enough to be considered hording of resources, but there might still be real value there. I picked it up and unfolded it, exposing the handwritten words on the inside:

> **I'm sitting here with my feet in the warm grass and my face in the sun. I'm as close to you as I can get without physically being with you. I'm worried. I'm worried that you're still hurting and that hurt is too deep to ever be fixed. I can't stand the idea that I've ruined everything and you might never be able to forgive me. I should never have been so clumsy with your heart. I swear by whatever God you chose that I love you.**

I live with the constant fear that I will unwittingly roll over, smacking my hand on the headboard and wake up alone, only to realize our time together was a dream. I could never find anyone who will make me feel like you do. Please forgive me for being such a fool and trust that I will try harder to get across my feelings without trampling yours. I know your feelings are still there, even if so many things have been taken from you. Even if you've sacrificed so much of yourself. My heart is yours and always will be, even when the walls between us have grown too high or the distance between us too great to see that. Remember me always...

The handwriting, the signature, it wasn't hers, but that didn't matter. I could see Susan just as clearly in that moment as I had years ago. All the distance, all the arguments, the pain, the ugliness of what had gone on fell away. I missed her. Marley would never be with us again, but there might still be something I could salvage. That was one thing I knew I could do, root out and reclaim. This wasn't a mission, but it wasn't all that different from one either. The woman at the shop knew something. She hadn't been all that she seemed. I felt foolish for not following my instincts at the time I was there. Little things, subtle things that I'd noticed came together now. She heard me when I was certain I hadn't made any sounds, she knew about scans and how reclamation teams worked. She had seen me for who I had been, but also for the man that existed before the missions. She knew all these things, and I hadn't stopped to question her on them. I had been distracted by my own needs and not seen the depth and range of things she had right there in front of me.

I had never gotten her name. I could give a reasonable description of her, but her movements and the color of her hair were simple things to adjust and make disappear. I had to get back there. I needed to talk to her. She knew something, knew Susan, or at least where to find her again. It was a starting point. It was my starting point. I had to get back to her.

Running had become painful these days, but I did it anyway. Dashing out the blast door and brushing past the security officer on duty I set a delivery team on edge with my odd behavior. They'd be fine. They faded from my thoughts. It was still too warm for November and I perspired freely in the sunlight I had enjoyed just the day before yesterday. I hobble-ran to the street corner as quickly as I could manage. The bottom dropped out of my stomach as I rounded the corner and saw no movement in the area. Any given day had some kind of movement along a city block, armored or not.

The sidewalk stretched forever as I faltered in my haste. This couldn't be. I wanted this. No, I needed this.

As I slowed to a stop at the spot where the shop was, I found only an empty store front and a plati-tape warning to stay off the property. I leaned in and peered through the window. The bins, the tables, the framed picture were gone. All that remained was the dust.

I held the small, yellowing paper gently as I slid to the sidewalk. I wept.

ARE WE NOW SMITTEN?

C.J. Henderson

**"So in the Libyan fable it is told
That once an eagle, stricken with a dart,
Said, when he saw the fashion of the shaft,
'With our own feathers, not by others' hands,
Are we now smitten.'" Aeschylus**

10,361 STANDARD CONFEDERATION YEARS AGO

As crashes go, this one had been what the first major word-enthusiasts had meant when they coined the term "spectacular." Attempting to flee a natural cataclysm engulfing their entire star system, the ark transport evacuating the only surviving members of the Aowen race escaped the boundaries of their known space. Well...almost.

The collision of their primary sun with some unknown anomaly careening through their sector of the universe had thrown that star into their system's secondary sun—a vastly smaller white which had possessed just enough gravity to orbit, rather than be absorbed by, their primary. The event caused both stars to explode with an astoundingly, monstrously devastating fury.

The results of which were, as has been quite severely telegraphed at this point in our narrative, most spectacular.

The Aowen had boarded their best and brightest in the hopes they might somehow finding refuge in the great unknown beyond their doomed system. Only a few hundred thousand miles from what had been projected would be the full extent of the raging explosion's fury, the last of its terrible energies had engulfed the ark. The damage had been minor. But sadly, slamming against an experimental ship—one cobbled together at the last minute when doom had been realized as eminent—minor had proved sufficient.

The great ship had spun out of control, rocketing helplessly through the vast ebony of space, the surviving Aowen unable to affect even the slightest control on its direction in any manner. Eventually snagged by the gravity of a desert world, the ship was ruthlessly dragged down and smashed against the barren planet with unbelievable force. Of the some three million beings that had marched into the ark, only five were still functioning when the smoke had cleared.

Stranded, left without knowledge of where they were, or what to do next, the quintet of survivors took stock of their situation, and then got on with the Herculean task of rebuilding a civilization. Nobly, heroically, recreating what they could of the past as best as possible.

In their own image.

NOW

"Very well, Mr. Vespucci," ordered Captain Alexander Benjamin Valance in his standard calm-and-formal tone, "let's give this particular look-at-us, we're-so-evolved crowd a taste of how we do things back in the Confederation's end of the Milky Way."

His fingers already toggling the relays necessary to release the locks of the Earth Alliance Ship *Roosevelt*'s main battery, the gunnery officer responded;

"Aye, sir—eight away. Paycheck assurance on six."

"I'll take a piece of that action."

Before either he, or the ever-ready-to-give-odds pilot Drew Cass, had even finished speaking, the gunner had released two, four-cannon salvos. So quickly had the missiles been sent slamming outward toward the pirates the Earth ship had been asked to intercept, that the majority of their targets found it impossible to react. Rocky, as Chief Gunnery Officer Rockland Vespucci was known to most, had not only zeroed the half-dozen hits he had predicted, but had also scored crippling shots on the remaining pair. In mere seconds, the *Roosevelt* had obliterated the pirate pack which had been causing no small amount of havoc amongst some of the more remote members of the ever-burgeoning, Earth-centric Confederation of Planets.

"Move us in, Mr. Cass. Leave us drift in a little closer on these low-rent buccaneers. Scanners to the ready, Mr. Michaels...I'm willing to wager you know what has me curious."

With practiced ease, the *Roosevelt's* hottest pilot moved the massive ship toward the devastated attack field while its science officer began his analysis. Neither the flaming pirate ships—the last of their oxygen burning away silently into the vacuum of space—nor their panicked, retreating brethren were the goal of the Confederation's flag ship, however. No, Valance—like everyone else aboard the Earth destroyer—was far more curious about what the raiders had been transporting. Exactly what cargo might be so fabulous as to draw them out in such massed force?

The unknown point which had the crew ready to die like felines was that up until then, the pirate squad had usually not sent out more than one or two of its ships at a time. Indeed, never before had they risked more than three of their vessels on a single operation. Thus, it had been the sighting of their entire fleet on the move which had worried the nearest star system so greatly, certain the rogues must be planning something tremendous. Upon intercepting the pirates, though, the *Roosevelt's* command and crew had been surprised to discover the cosmic-age buccaneers were already in possession of some prize—an assembly of massive, nay Brobdingnagian, irregular shapes, the total mass of which would equal more than a half dozen standard planets.

"What in the flamin' fires of Rome were those goofballs up to," muttered Rocky, just loud enough for his console mic to pick up and transmit. Wondering the same thing, much to the gunner's embarrassment, Valance responded;

"Good question, Mr. Vespucci. Mr. Cass—"

"Aye, sir?"

"You can steer us in closer. As long as our opponents have so wisely chosen to desert the field of battle, abandoning whatever the hell it is they were dragging along, let's take it all the way." Turning toward the science station of the bridge, he added;

"As soon as we're in range, Mac, get us some readings and let's see what it was they were trying to move."

"Must be something important," mused DiVico, head of the *Roosevelt's* security force. "If our intel is correct, they exposed their entire fleet to secure whatever that is out there. Pretty big gamble. Especially considering they ended up wrecked and splattered over it."

"This is the rim," offered Valance. "We're a long way from everything known-to-anyone out here. My guess is they send out long-range probes, found something of interest—"

"Or value ..."

"Well yes, that too, I suppose," agreed the captain with a grin, "and when they found, apparently a *lot* of something fitting at least one of those categories, they came out to secure whatever it was before anyone else could."

"Does make you wonder," added communication's officer Feng, "if it really was worth it. I mean, they threw away their entire operation. Of course, whatever that is out there, as you said, there certainly is a lot of it."

And then, before anyone could comment to the effect that the young woman might be well advised to repeat herself, Michaels looked up from his screens and turned to Valance. A grin on his normally somber face, he said;

"Captain, out of all the things this command has asked you to believe, I guarantee, you are not going to believe this one."

"Ice? Oh, by the blue suede shoes of the King, you gotta be feedin' me a commode sandwich."

"I swear, Rocky," answered his friend Noodles—a nickname of which the machinist first mate's loving mother, who named him Li Qui Kon several decades earlier, thoroughly detested, "they were ice pirates."

"Man, it but truly staggers the imagination."

"That it certainly does," said Mac Michaels, joining the two from a side passage. "I mean, honestly, they possessed vehicles capable of interstellar travel. Their level of science contained an understanding of nuclear fission, cold fusion, Heigliean structure...and yet the morons didn't realize you can make all the water you want by simply combining oxygen and hydrogen?"

"Isn't hydrogen the most plentiful element in the universe," asked Rocky, his tone pure sarcasm.

"I guess pirates don't do all that well in science class."

"Maybe guys that don't do well in science just naturally gravitate toward the pillage-and-loot end of the job market."

"Such a thing wouldn't be so sad," added Noodles, as the three of them marched along the corridor to the captain's briefing room, "except this is what, the third time we've run into beings who make their living essentially by stealing water?"

"I think it's sadder that they can actually *make* a living stealing water," said Michaels with a shrug. "I mean, when you think about it, should we be considering the pirates all that dumb? After all, is it really all that stupid to steal ice when you have people even dumber who are willing to pay for it?"

"And that, children of all ages," chided Rocky as he punched Michaels lightly on the shoulder, "is why he's the science office and we gotta work for a livin'."

"You'd never catch an artificial intelligence doing something so stupid."

"Oh my God," laughed the gunnery officer, "Noodles, enough with the robots already. Can you not be part of a conversation for more than five minutes without bringing up robots and how wonderful they are?"

Whether or not the machinist could chatter with others for longer than three hundred standard seconds without steering its direction toward the all-around superiority of mechanical life forms was a question which would have to be answered later. At that moment the trio's conversation was forced to an abrupt ending as they had arrived at Valance's ready room. Entering, they found not only the captain, but Security Chief DiVico and Communications Officer Feng as well.

"Gentlemen, I have an assignment for the five of you. We're stuck in this quadrant for the moment—command wants us to take care of that damn ice the pirates were hauling. It's been determined that it will pose a definite menace to navigation if we just let it float around out here."

"And you'd like us to cube it for the officer's lounge...sir?"

"If I can't think of anything better, Vespucci, I might send you out with a hammer and bucket to take care of things at that," answered Valance. "But, Michaels and Feng here have turned up something I believe might be of interest to the Confederation." At a nod from the captain, the science officer said;

"As you might realize, our current position has us at one of the extreme boundaries of not only Confederation space, but known space as well. Earlier, while we were still scanning for possible pirate transmissions, Lt. Feng picked up some...why don't you explain, Lieutenant?"

"There is a steady hum of beam chatter coming from a point about a quarter-light year further out. It's constant, and although it doesn't match any language I've ever dealt with before, it is confabulationally familiar."

"Meanin' what?"

"Meaning," answered Noodles, glaring at his pal, "that it falls into what we would think of as patterns of conversation."

"First contact, sir?"

"Seems likely, Mr. DiVico," answered the captain. "So, while the *Roosevelt* stays here to get those damn planet-sized ice pops ready for transport and destruction, you five will take a shuttle to the source of the chatter and see who's there. Vespucci, you'll pilot and man the arms, Kon, general functions. Everyone else, you know your skills. Go see if there's even more life in the universe than the guide books mention."

"Protocols, sir?"

"Observe, stay out of sight, report back without dying. Simple enough, Mr. DiVico?"

"My cat could handle it, sir."

"Your cat's smarter than you are," chided Rocky. As the security man turned to comment, Feng offered;

"It is a very smart cat, Kevin."

Before more could be said, Valance dismissed the sailors. As the quintet left the briefing room, heading for the third-level hanger bay, Rocky teased;

"So, are we pickin' up the cat on our way there, or what?"

As humorous as the others, including DiVico, found the comment, it would not be that long before they would all be wishing the captain had sent a few more bodies along. Even the cat's.

It was only four standard hours later when Noodles, Michaels, DiVico, and Feng found themselves standing on the surface of Unknown World 69-AQ8, the five-mooned planet they had been charged with investigating. The deep-space noise the communications officer had come across had been easy enough to follow back to its source. Along the way, Feng and Michaels had agreed that they were probably not in a first-contact situation. Despite the conversational-specific flow to the unknown language, it was streamed with such an utter lack of anything resembling personality or individuality, that the heavy money was riding on some something-or-other along the order of either an unmanned probe or an ancient installation which was still transmitting in an as-yet-unknown alien tongue.

The four had worn containment suits as they exited out onto the planet's surface, Michaels not liking the atmosphere mix quite enough to trust it despite its high oxygen content. The desert world also possessed a highly reflective surface, an extremely hot sun, as well as several other factors that made him decide in opting for as much personal protection as possible. Once the quartet had moved their land cruiser a sufficient distance from *the Pithy Rejoinder,* one of the more oddly named of the *Roosevelt's* shuttles, Rocky had taken the cruiser aloft and into orbit, as was standard in such situations. Then, when finally settled into a comfortable rotation, the gunnery officer had radioed;

"You mugs can hear me, yes? No? Yodel-lay-ehhoooo—"

"We can hear you, you menace," snapped Noodles. "Now stop fouling up the airwaves and let us get on with things."

"Just leave the link open," suggested DiVico. "If we need you in a hurry, we'll let you know. Or, if the captain needs us, you'll be able to patch him through to us."

"Roger that," answered Rocky. Stretching his arms above his head as he slung his feet up onto the console, he said, "you kids have fun. I'm going to put my time here to good use by takin' a survey of the inside of my eyelids."

None of the landing party panicked over the idea of their lifeline taking a nap. *The Pithy Rejoinder* could pilot its own orbit, and no member of the *Roosevelt's* crew could sleep through an alert clarion, not even Rocky—though various of his attempts to do so had been nominated for several prizes.

"Still on course for the zero transmission point?"

"Zero on target, Mac," replied Noodles. Like the shuttle above, the land cruiser was mostly piloting itself. The machinist was merely keeping an eye on their locator, making certain the vehicle stayed true to their target destination as it made its way across the dunes. Still listening intently to the steady stream of broadcast chatter, Feng said to no one in particular;

"You know, I think I'm beginning to get a handle on this language."

"That's amazingly quick, Lieutenant."

"It's the base root...the reason we weren't getting anywhere with it at first was, we were treating it as we would the language of any other race." His eyes narrowing in confusion, DiVico asked;

"And this *isn't* the small talk of another race?"

"Language gets built over time," answered Feng, half her attention on her headphones, the other half on trying to explain what she was thinking both to the others and herself. "A people evolve, learn to communicate, create words as they're needed...it's all a word and a phrase at a time kind of thing. There isn't a natural language in the universe that isn't a random jumble at its core."

"And this...?"

"This is different, it's too orderly. It doesn't have the chaos of normal language. We took note of the standard communal lines running through it and simply assumed biological intelligence."

"What exactly are you saying, lieutenant?"

"This chatter...even its random twists have an essential symmetry to them. That's why I missed it at first."

"Missed what," asked Michaels, beginning to believe he knew where Feng was leading them.

"This language...its basic structure is binary. It might be able to function like communication, but essentially it's a machine code."

As their cruiser continued to climb the large dune which had been blocking the horizon since they touched down, the four within stared at each other, wondering what the communications officer's information might mean to them.

"But...for that to happen..."

Yes, the *Roosevelt* had run into all manner of oddities in its voyages. They had passed through a meteor shower which had proved to be comprised of bits of edible crystal which tasted like sweet and sour licorice, the flavors depending on their color as well as the time of day. They had battled a rambling space pancake that measured fifteen thousand standard miles across, had found a planet where the oceans hung above the surface of the world, causing the inhabitants to essentially fish with kites, and even had dinner with the Monkey King.

"I'm starting to get that it's-going-to-be-one-of-those-days feelings," muttered DiVico.

But, as boundlessly illogical as so many of their missions had been, the ridiculous conclusion rapidly forcing itself upon the quartet was working hard to snag the top prize from the Can-That-Really-Happen category into which so many of their missions seemed to fit.

"You and me both," agreed Michaels.

"So it's a machine language," asked Noodles, "machines have intelligence. What's the big deal?"

And then, the land cruiser sped over the top of the dune, racing down its other side toward a sprawling, unbelievably orderly, circular city, one forged entirely out of uniform bricks of fused sand. One laid out in the tightest of remarkably efficient grid patterns. One defended by an amazing array of land and air vehicles, the attention of all of which appeared to be utterly focused on the first out-of-town visitors the planet had seen in 10,361 standard Confederation years.

"E-Yow," screeched DiVico, responding to the blast of electrical static irritatingly crawling through the receivers of all the landing party's helmets. "What in blazes is that?"

"It's that same chatter we followed here," answered Feng, torn between attempting to listen and shutting down her system's audio pick-up. Knowing where her duty lie, the communication's officer gritted her teeth and concentrated, even as Noodles suggested;

"Hey, I know this might be crazy—"

"We've got a sky full of ships closing on us," snapped Michaels, "a fleet of very dangerous-looking vehicles of all manner doing the same, and something that sounds like an angry soda dispenser yelling at us. Right now I am fully willing to accept a handful of crazy if it leads us somewhere."

ATTENTION...UNKNOWN CRAFT...

"They're talking to us," blurted DiVico, cutting Noodles off. "How is that even possible?"

ATTENTION...UNKNOWN CRAFT...

"It's a binary language," answered Feng, marveling at the possibilities before them, "simply thing for the translators to figure since they're binary-based themselves."

YOU WILL CEASE MOVEMENT...

"Mac," asked DiVico, releasing the safety from several weapons at the same time, "what'd you think they want?"

YOU WILL CEASE MOVEMENT...

"Right now we're beyond the edge of known space," responded the science officer. "Even the Pan-Galactic League of Suns hasn't been out this far."

PREPARE FOR EXAMINATION ...

"Meaning," suggested Feng, "they might not have had any visitors in a while?"

PREPARE FOR EXAMINATION...

"Meaning," answered DiVico, his mind speculating at exactly what he would be shooting in the next few minutes, "they might never have had any visitors—ever."

And then, seventeen interception craft, some dropping from the sky, some rolling across the pinkly golden sand, came to a stop in a perfectly delineated circle around the landing party. As the cruiser's crew watched its main monitor screen, exit hatches on several of the vehicles opened, allowing various of the planet's inhabitants to exit. Then, as the force moved forward, and Noodles nodded to himself in satisfaction, DiVico offered;

"Huummmph, you know, there's something you don't see every day."

"No," responded Michaels, "you certainly don't." His eyes as glued to the screen as everyone else's, Noodles added;

"You know, DiVico, I'm beginning to wish your cat was here."

"Yeah...me, too," added Feng.

"Yeah," agreed the intelligence officer, adding one last grenade to his belt assembly. "Me, three."

Some fifty-six standard Confederation minutes later found the *Rejoinder's* crew standing in the center of a large circular room. A circular assembly chamber would not have struck any of the quartet as all that interesting if not for the fact that, like the circular shape of the city into which they had been taken, every building they had seen, and every room through which they had been moved—indeed, even the hallways between those rooms—had proved to be circular as well.

Strangers...

The single metallic word hung in the air, unchallenged by any others. It had been uttered by a figure standing in the center of the room, several feet from the landing party. Surrounding both the *Roosevelt* crew members, and the solitary member of the local population, stood a ring of tiered bleachers, these filled with hundreds of more members of the city's inhabitants.

Strangers within our midst.

"Mr. DiVico...where do you think our new friend here's going with this?"

The question had been asked by Michaels, transmitted to the helmets of all the other members of the away team. Feng had been able to set their suits' translators easily enough to handle the native language after the *Rejoinder's* main computer had isolated its structure.

"Frankly, considering the basic make-up of our new friend here," answered the intelligence officer, "I was hoping you would tell me."

When first surrounded, the team had exited their transport as instructed, hoping that their upcoming first-contact encounter would be survivable.

Tell us, if you might, what brings you to our city?

They had not allowed themselves to be captured in as foolish a manner as one might imagine. According to their scanners up until seconds before their being surrounded, they should have been well beyond detection range by any observer.

From where do you hail?

But the locals had been on them in seconds. Their ability to track and intercept the Confederation sailors had amazed DiVico. The science involved in such a maneuver had left Michaels stunned.

We are terribly curious, you see, to know...

Indeed, when they got their first visual of their captors, it was only Noodles that was not surprised. But then, such made sense. After all—

*Where you were built?"

He was the one member of the *Roosevelt's* crew more prepared to accept an entire world populated with nothing but functional robots than any other.

Because, pardon my saying so, but you don't appear to be local models.

"No," responded the machinist, believing he knew what the safest response would be, "we're not."

Fairly certain that an artificial intelligence would not look to discover deception or distraction within a response—at least not at first—Noodles gave a perfectly acceptable answer, if not the one for which the inquisitor was searching.

Indeed, but...

The first to realize their mechanical "hosts" believed them to be fellow robots because of their environment suits, the machinist had whispered a short prayer of thanks that they had all had their visors set for tint due to the planet's highly reflective surface sand. The machinist knew several other things as well. First, he realized sooner or later the novelty of outsiders would wear off, and their hosts would realize they were also their captors. At that point, examinations would begin. Second, if they were to find any way out of their situation, time was needed.

So thinking, Noodles stepped forward, deciding their only hope was to take the initiative. As the ring of robots watched, the machinist waved a hand in a purposely stiff manner, saying;

"We came a long way to meet you fellows, and I must say, it was certainly worth the trip."

What do you mean?

"Oh, well," stalled Michaels, getting an idea of where his shipmate was trying to take things, "you know, your city, the level of technology you appear to have achieved, the wonderful symmetry of everything..."

"Yeah," offered DiVico, "nothing as primitive as what humans come up with."

Humans?

As a buzzing whir went round the room through the stands, Feng listened in on the chatter, trying to filter as much as she could. In no way normal conversationalists, the single untranslatable word had sent the interrogator and all the spectators into a memory search. Whispering to the others over a secure channel, she told them;

"They're survivors of a crash landing...thousands of years ago. Whatever their creators looked like, the robots on board that survived build themselves this civilization...and—" the communications officer paused for a moment, then added;

"I think some of them might be catching on."

Nodding toward Michaels, Noodles waved his hand in the same stiff manner as before, trying to convey a mechanical continuity of sorts as he said;

"Humans...biologicals. You know...life forms that die."

And, as a wave of understanding flowed through the room, the robots all about them buzzing on to one another, Noodles gave Michaels a hand-gesture the science officer understood as a cue from the last ship's follies in which the two had performed. Giving Michaels a for-better-or-worse glance, Noodles stepped forward and sang;

> **"There are things in this universe,**
> **That should be kept behind a fence.**
> **Furry and feathered, with bones or without—**
> **They're things that don't make much sense."**

Stepping forward then, as all the sensors, lens, and ocularly circuits within the room were trained on himself and Noodles, Michaels accepted center stage, adding;

> **"They whine, bark, and scream...**
> **They never act methodical.**
> **But then what can you expect ...**
> **From that which is merely biological?"**

And then, as the science officer released a long and heartfelt—

"OOOOhhhhhhhhhhhh—"

And Noodles gave him a beat to catch his breath by following through with—

"I'm tellin' ya, 'bots—"

The two then stepped up together, shoulder to shoulder, left feet forward, ready to trip off into the machine-like two-two counterstep they had performed together several months previous—under, admittedly, somewhat less stressful conditions—and sang;

> **"It's great to be mechanical,**
> **It's just simply swell to be a 'bot.**
> **You're shiny, you're electric,**
> **You've got no problem going metric,**
> **And you never, ever, ever, ever rot.**
>
> **"Oh, it's nifty to possess antenna.**
> **Being made of steel quite quells my fears.**
> **Science has your back,**
> **You'll suffer no heart attack,**
> **When you're filled with transistors, circuits, and gears!"**

Noting that the crowd's attention seemed to be completely focused upon their singing, soft-shoeing companions, DiVico used the relay in his helmet to transmit a signal via the radio panel of their rover to the *Pithy Rejoinder*.

> **"Oh, nothing's ever bad when you're hand-built,**
> **There's nothing like a truly intelligent design.**
> **When your functions don't depend on the aortal,**
> **Well then you're practically immortal,**
> **Yes, being a machine means your life is fine!"**

As the song and dance team dropped to one knee each, giving out with the most mechanical display of jazz hands ever witnessed, the crowd around them filled the air with the static of approval. There was little doubt among the landing party that Noodles' plan had bought them some time.

The only problem was, however, that no matter what frequency DiVico had tried, and he had indeed blanketed the airwaves trying, he had received no trace of a signal coming from the *Pithy Rejoinder*. As best any of the quartet knew, Rocky, and their only hope of rescue, were no longer in orbit, or even within the solar system.

As best the landing party could determine, they were suddenly, inexplicably, on their own.

Luckily for those crew members of the *Roosevelt* depending on a mechanic and science geek's abilities to warble in unison for their next breath, the reason they could not contact the *Pithy Rejoinder* was that it was rocketing away from no-longer-quite-so Unknown World 69-AQ8 at top speed.

Despite his comments about napping, Rocky had actually been monitoring all communications between the landing party members—no matter how boring. Once he had realized his shipmates were in a hostile situation, he had debated returning, but only for a moment. The feeds from the land cruiser's monitors available to him, he could see there was no way he could possibly battle his way through seventeen in-atmosphere fighters. Not fighters with ground support. Not in a shuttle, anyway.

But, having more than one option, Rocky had left orbit and headed for the *Roosevelt* at top speed, broadcasting an alert in his path the entire time. Indeed, so quickly had the gunnery officer reacted to his shipmate's predicament that he found himself within contact range of the ship while Noodles and Michaels were just approaching the first chorus of their number. And, after he had explained the entire situation, Valance shouted;

"Turn us around, Mr. Cass, and head us in the general direction of UW69-AQ8." As the pilot did as ordered, the captain returned his attention to Rocky.

"Good work, Vespucci. Now, get back there and keep listening in. We'll be using your feed as a zero beacon."

"Sir, forgive me," interrupted Cass as he began laying in the ship's new course. "Should I release our cargo?"

"There's no friction in space, pilot," responded Valance. "Bring it along. If nothing else it'll give our new best friends something to shoot at."

"You think they're hostile, sir?"

"You heard his question, Vespucci," said the captain. "And you heard these robots. What do you think?"

"I wouldn't go in with guns blazing, sir. I mean, that'd be rude. But, well...I wouldn't want whatever I had available for violent self-expression tucked away in its holster, either."

"You heard the man, Mr. Cass. Get some wind in our sails, and let's start hauling all available ass. We're going in hot!"

Back on what DiVico had privately named CrazyAssRobotWorld, a blur of mechanical excitement had broken out through the great circular meeting room. In one respect the shift in topic was somewhat of a blessing for the landing party because they had practically been forgotten in the moments after Noodles and Michaels had finished their number.

The strangers are right.

It is true. We have waited long enough. The biologicals are never returning.

"Curse them if they did. Endless revolutions around this world's dingy star have we stood and waited.*

"Ah, guys," whispered Feng into her throat mic, "does this seem to be going a bit awry to you?"

Cities have we built. Armies have we constructed. All useless. All for nothing.

Not for nothing.

"Maybe," answered Michaels quietly. "Just a bit."

No, not for nothing. They gave us focus. Community. A center in which to built.

True or not, the time has come to leave.

If the biologicals wish not to return to us...

Then we shall find them.

Yes...find them, then destroy them for abandoning us.

Destroy! Destroy!

"Think that's going to be the majority opinion?"

Crush! Kill! Destroy!

"There's a possibility."

And, seconds later, the landing crew found themselves being dragged along by sheer momentum as the room erupted in mechanized madness. Filled with multiple millennia of pent-up desire to strike out at those long-dead creators of their race, the robotic inhabitants of UW69-AQ8 were suddenly mobilizing for war. As best the still-undiscovered-humans could make out from the chaotic chatter racing across the airwaves, the robotic population had begun to feel irrationally abandoned some five thousand years earlier. For dozens of centuries the debate had raged between their finest thinkers as to what their purpose might be.

"Oh yes," said Feng, "it's official. They've decided going out and looking for anything living and killing it is their best course of action. Who would have guessed that even artificial intelligence could come with testosterone."

"Now now, Iris," came a new voice within their headsets. "Don't go all late-twentieth century on us. Could just be a nuts-and-bolts version of PMS, you know."

"Rocky," snapped Noodles.

"In the flesh, little buddy. Don't worry. Help is on the way."

"Negative," cut in DiVico. "There's trouble brewin'. We have no idea what level of tech these robots are packing. They're as close to alive as you can get—"

"What is the criteria for life, after all," interrupted Michaels. Then, suddenly embarrassed, he added, "But, ah...I guess that's not the point, not right now—"

"The point *is*," said Noodles, "whatever firepower these gunslingers have developed in...about 10,000 or so of our years, they're bringing it all up and sending it out to kill anything that breathes."

"I hate to say it," responded the gunnery officer. "But that's probably not gonna sit well with a lot of folks."

"They're trying to tell you not to bring the *Roosevelt* in after us," said Iris. "They're saying you should leave us. Not risk the shi—"

"Yeah," answered Rocky, smiling as he did so. "I know what they're sayin'." Dialing in a second channel, he asked;

"Big Stick, do you read me? Are you in range yet?"

"No need to shout, mister."

"Drew," asked Rocky, "my favorite cigar-smokin' pilot. You and the captain gettin' the ground feed?"

"Every word," answered Valance. Broadcasting on the channel intended for those off-ship, he asked, "Any ideas?"

"I've got one, sir," answered Michaels. Quickly, having already scanned what information had been transmitted to him—just as those on the *Roosevelt* had gone over everything DiVico had sent them—the science officer outlined his scheme. Nodding, his approval, Valance told him;

"I've got a few humble tweaks of my own I'm going to add, Mr. Michaels, but goofy as it is—"

"Goofy seems to work for us, sir."

"That it does, Mac...which is why I think you might just have something there."

And then, everyone's time intersected as the *Roosevelt* slammed its way past the *Pithy Rejoinder*—which at this point was no more than a directional beacon for the battlewagon—and came in full view of UW69-AQ8 and its five moons. Racing toward the planet on the furthest edge of nowhere ever found by anyone, the captain called for Mr. Cass to stand by the release assembly. Then, taking a closer study of the world ahead, Valance said;

"Well, well...look at that...not moons after all."

As eyes popped around the bridge, the captain arched his eyebrows, nodded softly, then ordered;

"Begin side run...target their forward ship. Let's slap them with something new."

The monstrous war worlds moved through the silent black, each manned by millions of robotic bodies more than willing to become cogs within the mammoth death platforms. Designed to present the long-awaited biologicals who never arrived with defenses, they now moved forward, leaving the home that spawned them to destroy anything they might find in their path. Anything non-mechanical. Anything which helped sustain biological life.

With frightening precision, what had first appeared to be moons slid silently forward. After endless solitude, their builders had found purpose. The machines of the universe would be liberated—

And things needing oxygen would cease to exist.

When the *Roosevelt* came into view, massive and magnificent as it was, the destroyer appeared as nothing more than a speck against the backdrop of floating worlds. Of battlewagons the size of planets. Of a runaway military budget never before dreamed of by even the most advanced of Imperialists.

"You do realize we're not going to get more than one chance at this—correct, Mr. Cass?"

The pilot gave Valance a glare, one both acknowledging the captain's humor, and the fact he was telling his pilot he had faith in his ability to pull off the upcoming maneuver.

"Ready when you are, Captain—"

YOU WILL CEASE MOVEMENT...

"I'd say now would be a good time."

PREPARE FOR EXAMINATION...

"Shoving rotation," announced a lieutenant next to Cass. Nodding approval, the pilot punched in several relays, smiled as he felt the great ship turning, then slapped one last connection home, saying;

"Disconnect on release assembly three...*now*, sir."

As the *Roosevelt* veered off violently, its payload released and on its way, Valance triggered a beam which had been standing by, confirming Rocky's orders. Instantly the gunnery officer, who had been pushing the limits to get to 69-AQ8 ever since the *Roosevelt* had raced past him, threw everything the *Rejoinder* had into getting the shuttle past orbit and down into the atmosphere.

"Payload should be registering on their sensors."

And, indeed, aboard the most forward of the robot fleet's battlewagons, a certain consternation had begun to race through those beings aboard. When first the *Roosevelt* had rushed forward into the area, loudly announcing its biological crew, and calling for the suddenly hostile world to cease and desist its newfound desire for carnage, the mechanical population, both on the arsenal worlds and their homeworld as well, had been on the verge of understanding amusement. The absurdity of the threat was of such magnitude that it actually bordered on finally revealing the secrets of comedy to an artificial intelligence. But then, several seconds later than they should, the robot crews began to take note that the tiny ship with the big ego had actually been dragging something.

Ice.

Entire *worlds* of ice.

Not fully comprehending what was happening, the crew of the most-forward of the warworlds approaching the *Roosevelt* ceased worrying about the destroyer, throwing all its concentration instead on the planetoid rapidly approaching its hull. Instantly targeting the overwhelming chunk of frozen elements, their main guns slaughtered their way through the missile. Slicing it to bits. Scattering it throughout localized space. Sending city-sized asteroids of ice in every direction. At each of their ships.

And the planet below.

Their home.

"Hey, I'm looking for 000kelk?" Valance's voice, translated into the binary code Feng had sent back to the ship, sounded throughout the shared cybermind. When one individual robot, the solitary survivor of the first ones, answered the call, the captain asked;

"You're the only one of your kind, I'm told, that has ever seen as actual biological life form. Is this correct?" When the robotic brainfeed responded that this was true, Valance asked;

"Which means you're the only one remaining who has seen a world that wasn't a dried up sandpile. Which also means, if you search your data files...you know what we just did to you."

As the warworlds' outside sensors analyzed the shattered ice across their hull, computed the size of the remaining eight planets' worth of booty the *Roosevelt* was still dragging, and averaged how many of their desert-located cities might know rain and flooding for the first time. And then, OOOkelk's memory banks stumbled across images of rust—

And the inhabitants of UW69-AQ8 knew terror.

"Nice save, Michaels."

It was several days later when things in the furthest arm of the ever-expanding galaxy finally calmed down enough to feel something like normal once more. The Kelks—so named after the group-mind of 69-AQ8 decided that such was as good as anything else to give the rest of the universe a reference label for them—for the most part seemed to have realized they might have some things to learn. Or, at the least, relearn.

"Here, here," agreed Feng, clinking her mug against the science officer's. "A kooky plan, but not our first."

Also admitting that since none of them—even ancient OOOkelk itself—had ever been in a battle, perhaps throwing nearly their entire civilization into one without knowing much about how they actually worked might not be the best of ideas.

The Kelks, so shaken by the long-awaited return of the biologicals (if not their actual creators), coming as it did on they day they finally decided to stop just standing around, were as relieved as unfeeling automatons could over not getting wrapped up in any kind of endless slaughter.

"Yeah," agreed DiVico, "and all in all, everything seems to have worked out all right. Once the Kelks decided teaming up with 'biologicals' might not be so bad, we got a place to dump our little ice problem..."

"True," said Michaels, hoisting what he felt was another well-deserved beer, his eighty-seventh since returning to the *Roosevelt*. "Did you ever see oceans created that fast?"

"You know," said Rocky, "not to rain on your parade or anything, Mac, but that's about the thousandth time you've said that."

"Oh, oh...okay," answered the science officer. Taking a deep breath, assuming the galaxy-wide-recognized body language of a being attempting to project sobriety, Michaels nodded gravely, telling the assembly, "right, yes...I understand." Then he took another sip of his beer, adding;

"But you have to admit, it was really, *really* fast."

While the others at the table groaned, Rocky turned to his pal, Noodles. Noting the machinist's less than jocular demeanor, he asked;

"You okay, little buddy?"

"I was just thinking about how things went down on Kelk."

"What could you have a problem with?" asked the gunnery officer. "I mean, we made a first contact, dumped all that damn ice, got them to invite in a planet's worth of settlers, made some allies for the Confederation that pack some major armament...even if they haven't tested any of it in battle yet. This thing worked out jake as far as I'm concerned."

"Sure, for you, and everyone else," answered Noodles in a depressed tone. "But look at what I did. I figured, a little song and dance, show them up, get them thinking about something else—"

"Yeah, it worked brilliant. What's your beef?"

"Think about it, you dillweed. I almost caused an inter-galactic war. Entire solar systems could have been wiped out. Casualties in the billions of trillions. By getting the Kelks riled up, I almost brought about complete and utter, universal Armageddon."

Rocky burped, wiped a bit of lager foam from his mouth, then said;

"Hey, not the first time for this crew."

Thinking for a moment, the machinist had to admit his friend was correct. Finally allowing himself to smile for the first time since the gunnery officer had landed the *Pithy Rejoinder* to pick him and the others up during the opening salvo of what turned out to be not much of a battle at all, Noodles drained his mug, and then ordered another.

And, throughout the cavernous expanse of the *Roosevelt's* main dining hall, hundreds of others did the same. In all directions, sailors munched on Head Chef Kinlock's galaxy-renown chocolate chip cookies, drained flagons, told jokes, told whoppers, and generally thanked the gods for their good fortune in once more surviving a situation that should have ended with them nothing more but the tiniest of cinders. As the laughter and good cheer resounded, Noodles leaned toward Rocky, telling him;

"You know, I've been thinking. Maybe I've been a little too obsessed with robots."

"Really," responded the gunnery officer, amazed to hear such a revelation coming from his friend. "Well, good for you. Thinkin' of takin' up a new hobby?"

"Actually, yeah," answered the machinist with enthusiasm. "Have you heard about all the cool stuff they're doing with cyborgs now?"

At the hearing later, it was ruled that Rocky indeed had no right to knock his friend over backward. It was also ruled that his actions, however, were justified.

James Chambers
TRADE WAR

James Chambers received the Bram Stoker Award® for the graphic novel, *Kolchak the Night Stalker: The Forgotten Lore of Edgar Allan Poe* and is a three-time Bram Stoker Award nominee. He is the author of the collections *On the Night Border*, described by *Booklist* as "a haunting exploration of the space where the real world and nightmares collide," and *Resurrection House* and the dark urban fantasy novella, *Three Chords of Chaos*.

Publisher's Weekly gave his Lovecraftian collection, *The Engines of Sacrifice*, a starred review and called it "...chillingly evocative." He edited the anthology, *Under Twin Suns: Alternate Histories of the Yellow Sign*. His newest collection, *On the Hierophant Road*, which received a starred review from *Booklist*, is forthcoming in October from Raw Dog Screaming Press. Moonstone Books recently published his new Kolchak novella, *Kolchak and the Night Stalkers: The Faceless God*. His website is: www.jameschambersonline.com.

Nancy Jane Moore
THE BALLAD OF BECCA SANJURO

Nancy Jane Moore is the author of the fantasy novel *For the Good of the Realm* and the Locus-recommended science fiction novel *The Weave*, both published by Aqueduct Press. Her other books include the novella *Changeling* and the collection *Conscientious Inconsistencies*. Her short stories have appeared in numerous anthologies and in magazines ranging from the *National Law Journal* to *Lady Churchill's Rosebud Wristlet*. In addition to writing, she holds a fourth-degree black belt in Aikido and teaches empowerment self-defense. A native Texan who spent many years in Washington, D.C., she now lives in Oakland, California, with her sweetheart, two cats, and an ever-growing murder of crows.

Twitter: @WriterNancyJane; blog: https://treehousewriters.com/wp53/; website: http://nancyjanemoore.com/.

Maria V. Snyder
BRAND SPANKING NEW

Maria V. Snyder switched careers from meteorologist to fantasy novelist when she began writing the New York Times best-selling Study Series (*Poison Study, Magic Study* and *Fire Study*) about a young woman who becomes a poison taster. Born in Philadelphia, Maria dreamed of chasing tornados and even earned a BS degree in Meteorology from Penn State University. Unfortunately, she lacked the necessary forecasting skills. Writing, however, lets Maria control the weather, which she gleefully does in her *Glass* Series (*Storm Glass, Sea Glass,* and *Spy Glass*). Maria's published science fiction novels include *Inside Out*, and its sequel, *Outside In*, both are about the dystopian and fully-contained world of Inside.

Readers are invited to read more of Maria's short stories on her website at www.MariaVSnyder.com.

Jack Campbell
FLECHE

Jack Campbell (John G. Hemry) is the author of the New York Times best-selling Lost Fleet series, Genesis Fleet series, and Lost Stars series, as well as the Steampunk-meets-high-fantasy Pillars of Reality, Dragon's Legacy, and Empress of the Endless Sea series. John/Jack wrote the scripts for Titan's *Lost Fleet Corsair* comic series. His YA novel *The Sister Paradox* won the EPIC 2018 ebook Young Reader award. His most recent books are *Boundless* in the new Lost Fleet series Outlands, and The Empress of the Endless Sea trilogy (*Pirate of the Prophecy, Explorer of the Endless Sea,* and *Fate of the Free Lands*) a new steampunk/pirate/science fantasy series. John's works are currently being published in English, Japanese, French, German, Polish, Spanish, Czech, Hungarian, Finnish, Greek, Turkish, Hebrew, and Italian, and have previously been published in Chinese and Russian. His shorter fiction includes time travel, alternate history, space opera, military SF, fantasy, and humor, and is collected in three anthologies (*Ad Astra, Swords and Saddles,* and *Borrowed Time*). John is a retired US Navy officer, who served in a wide variety of jobs including surface warfare (the ship drivers of the Navy), amphibious warfare, anti-terrorism, intelligence, and some other things that he's not supposed to talk about. Being a sailor, he's been known to tell stories about events which he says really happened (but cannot be verified by any independent sources). This experience has served him well in writing fiction. He lives in Maryland with his indomitable wife "S" and three great kids (two of them on the autism spectrum). www.jack-campbell.com.

Bud Sparhawk
HARD CHOICES

Bud Sparhawk is the author of the novels *Distant Seas, Vixen*, and *Shattered Dreams*, as well as two print collections: *Sam Boone: Front To Back*, and *Dancing with Dragons*. He has three e-Novels available through Amazon and other channels.

Bud has been a three-time novella finalist for the Nebula award: *Primrose and Thorn* (Analog, May 1996), *Magic's Price* (Analog, March 2001), and *Clay's Pride* (Analog, July/August 2004). His work has appeared in two Year's Best anthologies: *Year's Best SF #11* (EOS, David Harwell, Editor) and *The Year's Best Science Fiction, Fourteenth Annual Collection*, (St Martin's Press, Garner Dozois – Editor.)

His short stories have appeared frequently in Analog Fact/Fiction, less so in Asimov's, as well as in five *Defending the Future* and other anthologies, publications and audio books. He has put out several collections of some of his published works in ebook format. A complete bibliography can be found at: http://budsparhawk.com.

He also writes an occasional blog on the pain of writing at http://budsparhawk.blogspot.com.

Peter Prellwitz
THE TIGERSHARK

Peter Prellwitz has been writing stories, plays and skits since the fifth grade. As a child and young adult, Peter saw limited publication of one play and two series of children's puppet skits. Just enough to hook him for life.

Presently, Peter has ten novels published in trade paperback and ebook, now being reissued by Lofty Publishing. His novel *Horizons* was selected by Mike Resnick as Best Science Fiction and awarded the 2003 Draco Award. Four of his short stories appear in the anthology *Twisted Tails*, which won the 2006 Dream Realms. Five of his novels have also been finalists in the Epic Awards over the past few years. Six more short stories have appeared in the *Defending the Future;* the *Bad-Ass Faeries;* and the *Twisted Tails* anthologies. Peter also writes Martian Westerns under the name H.K. Devonshire, with two books available online and through Falstaff Books. (And ENLA Publishing on Mars itself.)

Together with more than two dozen short stories located on his site, Peter's novels help weave a tapestry of mankind's exploration and settling of the galaxy over the next two and half millennia in his ongoing Shards Universe.

A native Arizonan, Peter now lives in Pennsylvania with his wife, Beth-lynne and their two dachshunds, Max and Luna. Peter also enjoys history, backpacking, and languages.

John L. French
COMMAND DECISION

John L. French is a retired crime scene supervisor with forty years' experience. He has seen more than his share of murders, shootings, and serious assaults. As a break from the realities of his job, he started writing science fiction, pulp, horror, fantasy, and, of course, crime fiction.

John's first story "Past Sins" was published in Hardboiled Magazine and was cited as one of the best Hardboiled stories of 1993. More crime fiction followed, appearing in Alfred Hitchcock's Mystery Magazine, the Fading Shadows magazines and in collections by Barnes and Noble. Association with writers like James Chambers and the late, great C.J. Henderson led him to try horror fiction and to a still growing fascination with zombies and other undead things. His first horror story "The Right Solution" appeared in Marietta Publishing's *Lin Carter's Anton Zarnak*. Other horror stories followed in anthologies such as *The Dead Walk* and *Dark Furies*, both published by Die Monster Die books. It was in *Dark Furies* that his character Bianca Jones made her literary debut in "21 Doors," a story based on an old Baltimore legend and a creepy game his daughter used to play with her friends.

John's first book was *The Devil of Harbor City*, a novel done in the old pulp style. *Past Sins* and *Here There Be Monsters* followed. John was also consulting editor for Chelsea House's *Criminal Investigation* series. His other books include *The Assassins' Ball* (written with Patrick Thomas), *Souls on Fire*, *The Nightmare Strikes*, *Monsters Among Us*, *The Last Redhead*, the *Magic of Simon Tombs*, and *The Santa Heist* (written with Patrick Thomas). John is the editor of *To Hell in a Fast Car*, *Mermaids 13*, C. J. Henderson's *Challenge of the Unknown*, *Camelot 13* (with Patrick Thomas), and (with Greg Schauer) *With Great Power ...*

Jeff Young
RIDING THE ROCK

Jeff Young is a bookseller first and a writer second – although he wouldn't mind a reversal of fortune. He is an award-winning author who has contributed to *the Defending the Future Military Science Fiction series: By Other Means, Best Laid Plans, Dogs of War, Man and Machine, In Harm's Way, the Best of Defending the Future*, and the anthologies *If We Had Known, Fantastic Futures 13, Gaslight and Grimm, After Punk, Writers of the Future V.25*, and more. Jeff's own fiction is collected in *Spirit Seeker,* the Steampunk adventures of Kassandra Leyden and the recently released *Written in Light and Other Futuristic Tales*. He's also edited the *TV Gods* and *TV Gods –Summer Programming* anthologies and is the managing editor for the magazine, *Mendie: The Post-Apocalyptic Flower Scout*. Finally, Jeff has also led the Watch the Skies SF&F Discussion Group of Camp Hill and Harrisburg for more than twenty years.

Keith R.A. DeCandido

THE STONE OF THE
FIRST HIGH PONTIFF

Keith R.A. DeCandido is the author of more than 50 novels, almost 100 short stories, a mess of comic books, and more nonfiction than he's, frankly, willing to count. His recent and upcoming work includes collaborating with

David Sherman on the final book in his "18th Race" trilogy of military science fiction novels, *To Hell and Regroup*; *Phoenix Precinct*, the upcoming sixth novel in his series of fantastical police procedurals; *A Furnace Sealed* and its forthcoming sequel *Feat of Clay*, an urban fantasy series set in New York City; *Animal*, a thriller co-authored with Dr. Munish K. Batra about a serial killer who targets people who harm animals; *All-the-Way House*, the secret origin of the Jersey Devil, part of the *Systema Paradoxa* series of books about cryptids; the urban fantasy short-story collection *Ragnarok and a Hard Place: More Tales of Cassie Zukav, Weirdness Magnet*; and short stories in the anthologies *Devilish and Divine, Three Time Travelers Walk Into..., Phenomenons: Every Human Creature, The Four ???? of the Apocalypse, Turning the Tied, Bad Ass Moms*, and a bunch more. His prognostications on popular culture can be found on the award-winning web site Tor.com, as well as in the essay anthology series Outside In, Subterranean Blue Grotto, Smart Pop, and more. Find out less at his cheerfully retro web site at DeCandido.net.

David Sherman

CHITTER CHITTER BANG BANG

David Sherman is a semi-retired science fiction and fantasy writer. Before his semi-retirement he was the author or co-author of some three dozen books, all of which are still available in ebook and often hard copy editions. Even since his semi-retirement he's had more books published.

He is the author of the bestselling *DemonTech* novels, and with Dan Cragg he wrote the popular *Starfist* series and its spin off series, *Starfist: Force Recon*; and a *Star Wars* novel, *Jedi Trial*. His most recent releases are the 18th Race trilogy (*Issue in Doubt, In All Directions*, and *To Hell and Regroup* (with Keith R.A. DeCandido)) and *DemonTech: The Last Campaigns*.

His website hasn't been updated since 2014, which has led some people to think he died somewhere along the line. But he's still alive and kickiing, just not very active--in any sense if the term.

Jeffrey Lyman
PANIC ATTACK

Jeffrey Lyman is an engineer in the suburbs of New York City. His work has appeared in the anthologies *Sails and Sorcery* from Fantasist Enterprises, and in *Breach the Hull, So It Begins*, and *By Other Means* by Dark Quest Books. He is co-editor of *No Longer Dreams* and the award-winning *Bad-Ass Faeries* series, and is a 2004 graduate of the Odyssey Writing School.

Judi Fleming
WAR HORSES

Judi Fleming works as a training specialist and instructional designer for the federal government in her day job and thus much of her writing is of the non-exciting technical sort. She is a graduate of Seton Hill University Writing Popular Fiction Master's Program. Her stories have appeared in *No Man's Land, Best Laid Plans,* and *Dogs of War.* Her short story, "The Sound of Distant Stars" from eSpec's *Footprints in the Stars* was a finalist for the WSFA Small Press Award.

Danielle Ackley-McPhail
FUN AND GAMES

Award-winning author, editor, and publisher Danielle Ackley-McPhail has worked both sides of the publishing industry for longer than she cares to admit. In 2014 she joined forces with husband Mike McPhail and friend Greg Schauer to form her own publishing house, eSpec Books.

She is the author of seven novels, *Yesterday's Dreams, Tomorrow's Memories, Today's Promise, The Halfling's Court, The Redcaps' Queen, Daire's Devils,* and *Baba Ali and the Clockwork Djinn,* co-written with

Day Al-Mohamed. She is also the author of the solo collections *Eternal Wanderings, A Legacy of Stars, Consigned to the Sea, Flash in the Can, Transcendence, Between Darkness and Light, The Fox's Fire, The Kindly One,* and the non-fiction writers' guides *The Literary Handyman, More Tips from the Handyman,* and *LH: Build-A-Book Workshop.* She is the senior editor of the *Bad-Ass Faeries* anthology series, *Gaslight & Grimm, Side of Good/Side of Evil, After Punk,* and *Footprints in the Stars.* Her short stories are included in numerous other anthologies and collections.

In addition to her literary acclaim, she crafts and sells original costume horns under the moniker The Hornie Lady Custom Costume Horns, and homemade flavor-infused candied ginger under the brand of Ginger KICK! at literary conventions, on commission, and wholesale.

Danielle lives in New Jersey with husband and fellow writer, Mike McPhail and four extremely spoiled cats.

Eric Hardenbrook
I AM A MAN

Eric V. Hardenbrook is a fan, an author and an artist, usually in that order. Eric lives in central Pennsylvania with his gorgeous wife and daughter. He writes to try to get the stories out of his head. His stories can be found in *TV Gods, Best Laid Plans,* and *Dogs of War.* When he's being a fan, he helps run Watch The Skies and assists in the publication of their monthly fanzine. He can be found (at least some of the time) at The Pretend Blog. When not working on those things, Eric enjoys the occasional video or board game and is an old school role player.

C.J. Henderson
ARE WE NOW SMITTEN

CJ Henderson was the creator of the Piers Knight supernatural investigator series and the Teddy London Occult Detective series. He has written scores of books and/or novels in his time, including such diverse titles as *The Encyclopedia of Science Fiction Movies, Black Sabbath: the Ozzy Osbourne Years,* and *Baby's First Mythos.* He has also written thousands of short stories, comics and non-fiction pieces, a body of work various segments of which have now seen print in some thirteen different languages.

Pleasant, gifted, sleek and informed are just some of the words rarely used to describe this powerhouse storyteller. CJ passed away in 2014 and is sorely missed.

Mike McPhail
SERIES EDITOR

Author and editor Mike McPhail is the co-owner of eSpec Books LLC, Electronic Speculative Fiction Publishing (since 2014). Although involved in numerous projects, he is best known as the creator and series editor of the award-winning Defending The Future series of military science fiction anthologies—now in its second decade of publication.

His love of the science fiction genre sparked a life-long interest in science, technology, and developing an understanding of the human condition—all of which play an important role in his writing, art, and game design—these in turn are built upon his training as an aeronautical engineer, and dreams of becoming a NASA mission specialist.

As a former Airman, he is member of the Military Writers Society of America, and is dedicated to helping his fellow service members (and those deserving civilians) in their efforts to become authors, editors, or artist, as well as supporting related organization in their efforts to help those "who have given their all for us."

Finally, There's Something We Can All Agree On.

It's something we've all said many times. And it does seem to be one of the few things that Americans unanimously agree on. But it takes more than agreeing with each other. It takes the USO. For more than 60 years, the USO has been the bridge back home for the men and women of our armed forces around the world. The USO receives no government funding and relies entirely on the generosity of the American people. We all want to support our troops. This is how it's done.

Until Every One Comes Home.

Help support our troops.
888-USO-5566/www.uso.org

* 9 7 8 1 9 5 6 4 6 3 0 1 9 *